THE LAST WATCHMAKER

SURVIVAL

SHIRLEY DAY

PUBLISHED WITH
PASSION

PUBLISHED BY PASSION PRODUCTIONS

CHAPTER 1
MARCO'S FIRST MEMORY

IT'S DARK. Dark night. And maybe he is only seven, but Marco knows for sure there is something badly wrong.

'Get up! Get up! Get out. Get out!' Mum shouts, hustling him out of the apartment. Even in the hallway, nothing is normal. Marco feels like he's been drafted into a disaster movie. It's all dressing gowns flapping and Mrs Kent still has her rollers in.

Even the air is wrong – salty and damp, carried high on an ice-cold blast from a broken window. Why is the window broken? Why is there water all over the floor? Marco reckons he's on twenty things wrong already and he's still counting.

The people, including Mr Hancock who's barely stepped off his sofa in a year, every one of the people is running. They're going left. They're going right. In short, they're going nowhere fast. All the people from all the apartments, are spilling out into the hallway dazed as rabbits when you shine a light in their eyes.

Marco's flat is four storeys up. A council building. Corridors narrow, ceilings low. They bought it themselves. Well, his parents did. Marco's not sure he contributed. The lifts are broken, and the lights in the hallway are permanently 'on the blink.' Only now they're permanently *off* the blink, not even pretending they can be bothered to do their job. All the panic, the shapes and the bodies and the shadows, it's all caught in sharp random flares lasering out from hand-held torches.

Through the windows, Marco can see an oil-slick night-time waiting outside. He has no idea what's going on out there. Is it the same? Panic? Can't be. But how are they going to get out?

His parents don't have a clue. He can tell because their eyes keep snapping around wild as pinballs; flicked side-to-side till it's making him dizzy. They're looking for answers but getting nowhere fast. He reckons he's past forty things badly wrong now and the count is no way finished. But he figures if he just holds on to the maths, skips the emotion, maybe it will all equal out to be something just about okay?

They choose a direction and go for it, sprinting down the corridor quicker than a pack of greyhounds on a track. Dad in front carrying their papers and his music; he'd actually gone back into the apartment to get it! Did it lose them time? Probably. Does it matter? It does to Dad. Between Dad's fingers, he's clutching rare vinyl, and passports. Though Marco's none the wiser about the record choice because they're all running: Obademi. Fourth-generation British Nigerian. Up and running for their lives.

They round the corridor, and quick-smart Mum rams Marco flat up against a doorway. He tries to catch a breath, but it's difficult with his heart in the way. Only he knows he should. He's got to fill those lungs. He's going to need it. That's when it happens. The roar and then the wave sending out its first wet punch, catching Dad at the knees, bowling him over easy as a skittle. Off Dad goes, disappearing down the corridor double-quick time. Gone. But Mum's not giving up. She's holding Marco tighter, eyes all a panic. She's holding him so fast, and he's holding her right back. So tight he thinks his bones will pop through his skin. he's not letting go. No way is he letting go. Especially not when he hears that snake-like hiss of the wave as it pulls back in on itself. Mum's face turns to his, and time goes slow, slow, slow. And her eyes are… not so much scared as sorry. He's only five, and they had so much planned. Her eyes are saying it all. He never knew eyes could talk that much. But they can, and they say every bit of it real quick because she knows time's running out. The roar fills his ears like dragon breath, and he knows deep down you can't argue with a body of water that big. You just have to let it do its stuff.

And that's what it does. When it smashes up against them for that final round it's cold like death and just as determined. Marco feels it wrap around his body firm as a tentacle, squeezing the air right up through his lungs in one last, final gasp. Then he lets go. Mum's hand gets pulled from his, scuttled off and away, and the air that he'd been holding on to so tight comes out in a scream. A cry so filled with pain the noise kills a bit of him as it leaves his body, and Marco feels his organs collapse; as though they're being packed away, stored up neat for something, somewhere, safer.

———

Tick-tock, tick-tock. Tick-tock, tick-tock. Tick-tock, tick-tock.

———

'Because that is exactly what happens,' the girl is saying. The girl sitting on Marco's slim, white hospital bed. Marco guesses she's the same kind of age as him, but darker and stringier and, from the way she's hammering on without barely stopping for a breath, mouthier. This girl is just itching to fill him in on her oh-so-newly-acquired medical knowledge about the human respiratory system. 'Kids' lungs' she's saying, 'they kind of go into storage. You and me, and all these others,' she indicates the room with a quick flick of her hand, as if the *others* are hardly worth her attention, 'that's what's behind the survival story. Now if you're an adult and you drown,' her forehead creases into a series of crisscross knots. 'No two ways about it, you are going to be deader than dead.'

Marco isn't sure this is even possible. But the girl doesn't look like the kind of kid you can pick up on stuff like this. Besides, he's wondering about his mum and dad. They're adults, so surely that means …? He can feel the cold wave wrapping around him again.

'Molly, back to your bed,' a pretty, but so thin it's as if she's only half there. Her blue-washed eyes are empty, too tired to smile. She's checking the readings on the monitor above Marco's head. So many lights blinking and winking it's like one of Dad's Disco gigs.

'Bum,' Molly sighs, looking at Marco with a touch of irritation. 'None of this is going to plan. I had hoped he was dead.'

'You mean *thought*,' Nurse Curtis corrects, as Molly pulls herself from the sheets and cocks her head for a moment, mulling it over.

'No. I meant hoped. Hoped, was it? I do really like his gran,' she says, working on some kind of logic which went sailing merrily over Marco's head.

'Gran?' His gran had been to see him! Because of course, Gran wasn't in the flood, and that meant Gran didn't have to be dead.

'She's been in.' Nurse Curtis gives a swift, sharp nod. 'You were out for a couple of days. Still got some nasty bruising. Your gran claimed you.'

'She comes back in, you tell me.' Molly throws the line out with all the sass of an adult trapped inside the body of a munchkin.

Nurse Curtis simply raises one long, thin warning-eyebrow. 'Oh, and when did I become your messaging service?'

'Hey, I'm an orphan,' Molly comes back, sharp as a blade, 'Need all the help I can get. Tell her. Macko.'

Marco isn't happy about the way the girl called Molly drops the 'R,' like it's something she can't be bothered to hold. He's lost way too much already. Whatever is left, he needs to keep it all together.

'You can tell your gran I'm okay with you bunking in with me if it's space that's the problem,' Molly says, as she walks towards the door. 'S'not ideal. But seeing as you're alive, it's just going to have to do.'

'And this time, Miss Molly, no leaving your ward,' Nurse Curtis calls after her.

'Yeah, like that's gonna happen,' Molly mumbles back, helping herself to an apple from a kid's tray, before disappearing out of the room.

So, Mum and Dad?' He feels a sense of dread wrap around him. 'They're…'

'Looks like they didn't make it.' Nurse Curtis says, her voice as soft as cotton wool, but the softness doesn't help. Not really. There are no kind words or medicine for this. Marco lets the thought slip down, deep into his soul, which feels so empty of everything it's not so difficult to fit a large wedge of sorrow in.

So, it's just him and Gran now. He isn't sure how that'll work because Gran is tough as old boots. Not like Mum, who is soft and kind and good at listening, or dad who is all music and dancing and joy of life. Is? Does that even work anymore? Can they still be all the things that they were if they're… He can't go there. Not now. He can't do this.

He glances around the room, at a ward filled to bursting with kids, every one of them under eighteen; some spluttering, some broken, some whimpering, one fidgeting. Marco isn't spluttering anymore. He never did fidget. He has one eye puffy and bruised, but nothing's broken. He's not crying because his soul is so numb; he's sure the icy wave's got in there permanently. They're going to have to drain him out before he can feel again – like Mum does at the swimming pool when his ears get water in.

But then, maybe he doesn't want to *feel*. Not yet anyway.

'Marco?' Nurse Curtis is talking, bringing him back. Because back is where he has to be. And he decides then and there that he won't tell them about the ice in his soul. He won't ask them to drain it. Because ice might work better than sadness.

'Your gran says you're a bright spark.' Nurse Curtis' eyes are shining sad like they're trying to create a bridge for him to just walk right on over, come back to the world of the living. She hitches her starched, white skirt up at one side and half-perches on the edge of his bed, taking hold of Marco's wrist between her middle finger and thumb as she glances at her watch. It seems an odd move, and Marco wonders if she's been allocated set times for affection; every kid on the ward has to have a one-minute wrist-hold along with clean sheets and an apple.

But then he sees something curious, shining and open on her pale blue dress, and his jaw almost hits the floor as his fingers reach out to touch.

'What?'

Nurse Curtis smiles. 'It's a watch. The old kind.'

He can't keep his eyes from it, all the moving hands, each one getting on with a different job. And it's pulsing under his fingers. Pulsing like the thing is actually alive. Tick-tock, tick-tock. Tick-tock, tick-tock. Tick-tock, tick-tock. He can remember the water pulling away from him and the sound of the man with the large spaghetti arms. Because the man ticked like a clock. Not like the new ones. Everyone he knows wears the smart type now. His mum's watch wakes her up, puts her to sleep, and tells her when she's eaten too much.

The timekeeping bit, well that's kind of an afterthought. Tick-tock – like a heartbeat. Like Nurse Curtis' watch, which only has the one thing going on. He doesn't know why, but he finds that satisfying in some way. Just doing one thing, but doing it spot on perfect, and that sound!

'Present,' she says, not looking up. 'The guy who found you washed up gave it me. Sanderling. Colourful kind of a chap. Know what he called himself?' But she's not asking a serious question. She's heading right on full-steam to give him the answer. 'The Last Watchmaker,' she sighs. 'Kind of poetic.' Then she snaps closed the casing of the watch and drops Marco's wrist neatly back onto the starched sheet. He just stares at the casing. There's some kind of insignia engraved into the silver. He can just make out a circle a hammer, some kind of map and what looks like a pen twisted inside.

'Tired?' She changes the feed on the drip, lacing it neatly into a spout which is sticking out of his hand. His actual hand!!!

How can he be tired? He's been asleep for days! He's had enough sleep for a lifetime.

'So a lot of us kids…' he says, glancing around the room, 'we survived?' His voice seems quieter than normal. Like it's not really his own.

Curtis gives a half nod. 'There's ten wards full. Molly's right, kids have the advantage as far as drowning goes.' She pulls up his notes from the bottom of the bed. They read Marco WU in bold, black letters.

'Obademi,' Marco corrects. 'It's not WU. Marco Obademi.'

'Not now. Now you're all WU: Wash-Ups. All of you that survived. Unless you get claimed.'

'But Gran…'

'Gran can take you, but for a name change, it needs to be a parent. Now… you need to get some rest. They'll be testing you soon.'

Testing? Marco is good at exams, passed his SATS with flying colours, but he isn't so sure this is a good time for school exams. His hands are bruised as blackberries, not to mention the water in his soul or his left eye that's screaming purple and lost behind a good half-inch of swelling.

'They're going to stream you. All the bright kids,' and she gives Marco a look that says *that little label has your name on it,* 'they'll be going to the academy. The others.'

She glances around the room, resting her gaze on an olive-skinned kid around the same age as Marco, the guy who was fidgeting earlier, and has now taken to bed bouncing.

'Well, they'll be up for adoption. Tee!' She shouts at the kid who, while bouncing, has managed to tie his sheets from the bed and is attempting to hook up a hammock. 'No!'

'But?'

She doesn't even bother replying. Just shoots him a crippling gaze.

'If we're going to sort this problem,' she says kindly, 'and believe me, it is way bigger than a few thousand lives lost in a flood. If we are going to get to grips with it, stop it from pushing us around, we need all the bright sparks we can get. Oh, and of course, there's the lung thing.'

He looks blank at this one.

'They want to know if the WU's…' She stops in her tracks, giving him a long, hard, *your turn* look.

'Wash-Ups?' he suggests, and she nods, satisfied that her words aren't being wasted.

'They want to know if Wash-Ups continue to develop advanced lung capacity.'

CHAPTER 2
NOW

TICK-TOCK, tick-tock. Tick-tock, tick-tock. Ten years on and once again Marco's got gallons of water crushing down over his head. Frightened? Confused? Not this time. This time he's bored. Bored out of his mind. He's tried focusing on the sound of the clock, the one that he carries ingrained in his head, but it didn't help. So he ditched it for the news feed, which is blaring away on the screen in front of the tank. Finbow, the CEO of Texicom, is smiling that thin-lipped, middle-aged smile that got just about everywhere these days. His – *we're the good guys* smile. Then images of the desalination plants, monstrous things. Taking up so much room in the underbelly of the city that there was barely enough room for the people. Drown in seawater, drown in fresh water. Was there that much difference? It's the same old story, a planet in crisis. But Marco's supposed to be part of the solution. He got into the academy with flying colours. It's just the lung capacity bit he has problems with. So, he's practising; sitting in a tank filled with water, twenty-five metres long, two and a half metres wide, and ten metres deep. He's in what they call the tank room. There are ten of these giant vats; four chlorine the rest salt water. Each one has a wide, standing platform at one end, accessed by an open lift. There's very little artificial light in the room. The screen shouldn't be on. The intention is to keep the environment as *natural* as possible, so too much artificial light's a no-no. But today someone's forgotten. Not that it's easy to see. The colours are all bleached out because directly above the tanks, strung all along the walls, there's this long line of massive, industrial windows. They're shaped like the segments of an orange, modelled on the windows from Grand Central Station. Marco knows this from his lessons in architecture: Pre-Civil Collapse. He's seen the faded black-and-white images of people in dark overcoats, standing in a vast atrium, showered by mote-filled beams of light. The shadowy figures have, by now, been bedded deep in silt, hidden under the sea. But, captured in that moment, in the photograph, they're about to step out on their journeys, never realising how fortunate they are to have a tangled network of villages and towns at the end of each and every metal track.

When the sun shines in through the tank room windows, it's just like the original station, those beams of light flooding down. Only this time, instead of the station concourse, the light pours like liquid sunshine into vast water tanks, where it fractures and plays in mutating, neon-white elastic bands, as if liberated.

He's sitting on his backside at the bottom of one of the practice tanks, his hands gripping two weights that are fixed to the floor. It's not just the weights that are fixed; his hands are trapped inside the weights. The guy on the outside, the operator, releases you when you've had enough. Or maybe, more to the point, when he thinks you've had enough. Today it's Tee on the other side of the glass. Which is a good thing. Maybe? Some of the trainers have an element of sadism built into their 'motivational' strategies. They're happy enough to let you fall unconscious if they think they can squeeze another fifty seconds out of you or get a good story for the locker room. But Tee's alright. Tee, the kid at the hospital, the fidgety, bouncy one, with the bed sheet hammock design. Another WU. But no one claimed Tee. After the hospital, he went straight to the dorms at the academy.

Academy? Yup, and no one was more surprised than Tee and Nurse Curtis when he got in. He was hardly the brightest button in the box. You have to put information in to be bright and Tee, Marco knows, has the attention span of a newt. Marco can see Tee fidgeting now on the other side of the glass. He's the one who left the screen on, but he's not even looking. He's flicking through social websites. His finger on the *like* button, not even bothering to read the comments. Tee got into the academy solely because he had advanced lung capacity and could stay under the water, happy as a fish, for three minutes. He could do that right from the get-go. Now after twelve years of training, three minutes is nothing. Tee can rack up ten minutes easy as pie. Marco is still only on four. That's why he's practising. But there's a fundamental flaw; Marco doesn't like getting wet.

Maybe in a normal world, if the world had been left to be normal, to travel along on its own sweet way; if the meteorites hadn't come, or if some superpower had done some nifty fancy-pants side-step about the terrestrial bodies before they hit, then probably, maybe, actually… Tee and Marco would not be friends. Marco is still head-down serious, and Tee still can't see a bed without bouncing on it, or a pillow without throwing it. But somehow, over the years, they've kind of got attached.

On Tee's documents, it says he's the same age as Marco – seventeen, European, fourth generation. This is good. Europe is good. Fourth generation is okay. Anyone sixth generation or more has long since been shipped out. But Marco knows the full story. Maybe Tee is seventeen, maybe he's not. But origin? Marco knows Tee is fourth generation, Hyderabad extraction. That was India. His papers were lost, so Nurse Curtis 'placed' him. She figured dark eyes, olive skin, pestering her 24/7 for spaghetti carbonara: got to be Italian. And he got through because Marco, Tee, Molly were all in the first wave. The DNA tests weren't set up. Tee wouldn't stand a chance in hell of getting away with it now. All that 'origin' malarkey counted so much more these days now that space was proving to be more valuable than diamonds.

But Marco's safe, Marco's okay. He's doing well on his tests, straight A's all the way. His lung count, his LC rating, well it's hardly anything to write home about, even if he did have a home. It just needs a little work. All Tee has to do is press a button to release Marco, then the weights fall off and up Marco pops. Tee's trying the weight thing out because it overrides the *fight-or-flight* instinct. You can't flee far if your fingers are ram-jam-stuck into two 50 KG weights, resting on the tank floor.

'Nobody's died from it yet,' Tee had said earlier, as Marco lowered himself into the tank. Marco wasn't so sure he liked the sound of that *yet*. Especially not now his lungs were getting a warm achy feeling.

He tries to think of something else. He needs to slow his heart rate down. So, he runs through a couple of differential equations he's been mulling over. The news on the screen is hardly helpful on the meditation front, but neither is bore-dom. He's at two minutes forty-eight seconds on the clock. Suddenly the news feed switches to the leaderboard – the board they post up that says who's going to be repatriated. For a moment, Marco's confused. He has to rack his brain, looking for the day. Was it Saturday? No, no, it was definitely Thursday. Leaderboards only ever went up on a Saturday. Straight off, this is getting him worried.

Sure, there has been more flooding, but... and suddenly he doesn't care about his LC score. The red names flick up and down the board, jostling, pushing each other off as their scores get calculated. Was a person good at exams? Were they second generation, third generation, fourth generation,

British? But he knows what he's seen. He's sure of it. And he keeps catching it, catching a red line of letters, a name, as it flicks like a pinball over the grid. Molly. Molly is on the board.

Panic hits. He has to get out. Only problem is, Tee is sitting with his back to the tank. He's got no intention of pulling Marco up before Marco gets to four minutes, but Marco's let go of that last bit of oxygen he had tucked away, and now he's really in trouble. You're not supposed to panic when you're under. You're supposed to slow everything down. That's the only way to preserve oxygen. But Marco can't help it. Molly is on the list and he's beyond panicking now; he's on the road to a quick burial at sea. He brings his legs out from underneath him and starts forcing them forward along the bottom of the tank, aiming for the wall. His limbs feel heavy as lead and drained of all fight. The oxygen's gone, every last bit. There's nothing but determination holding his movement together. He can only just reach the edge of the tank with his toes, and now the burn in his chest is so bad, he's sure he'll vomit. And if he vomits, he'll choke, and if he chokes, he'll drown. He'll vomit and choke and drown, and the flaming half-wit on the control panel - Tee, his best bloody friend – won't even…

There's a click. The weights release. Marco draws his legs in quick, bounces down on his knees and propels his body fast, up through the water.

One loud, thankful gulp. He hangs from his arms over the side of the tank, hearing the lift whir, as Tee reaches the viewing platform.

'Rubbish,' Tee says, as Marco fills his lungs again, drinking it all in. Air… nothing is more delicious.

'That's not even up to your last score,' Tee continues, oblivious. 'You'll have to go down again.'

'Leader…' Marco manages to splutter out, though the

words have no breath behind them, so Tee won't hear, especially since Tee's not really listening.

'I told you about the meditation thing and the heart rate. Man, you ever listen to me?'

To be honest, Marco tries not to listen much to Tee. Tee talks more than most people Marco knows all put together.

'Leaderboard,' he manages.

And even as he says it, Tee's face drains.

'But it's…'

'Thursday.' Marco's look says so much more than his words: this is all wrong.

Tee grabs a remote, shooting the news display against the wall, so it's larger than life and just as ugly. Fifteen feet by fifteen feet. Red demonic lettering on black. Neon crimson names crawling over the board, flick flicking around, busy as flies, moving up, moving down, barely stopping to rest.

There's a chance it won't settle on Molly. Maybe she'll get away with it. Maybe. Maybe.

'Jeez, you see that, man? Three hundred.'

Normally there's fifty, maybe seventy-five names on the board. Today there are three hundred, and it's not even Saturday.

London, Marco thinks. London must be going under, and the northern territories are keen to poach the best brains. They're clearing out the deadweight.

'Oh, man!' Tee shouts, as Molly's name comes up on the screen again and the square red light in the top corner flickers on, indicating that the calculations are done. The file is locked.

Molly WU. That's it. She's been marked – repatriation.

'You seriously heading over to the terraces, this time of night?' Tee's asking, as Marco throws his clothes on over wet skin, not even bothering to shower.

'I'm more afraid of Gran than I am of running into Off Grids.'

Tee nods. He knows Marco's gran, a woman you do not want to be on the wrong side of. 'She's gonna be mad.'

But *mad* does not even begin to describe what Gran is going to be. It was true, she'd taken Marco home after the hospital. But when he got there, Molly was already installed in the guest bedroom. He'd had to make do with the box-room at the back.

Turned out the Molly / Gran relationship was deeper than a quick chat over a comatose grandson. Gran had pulled Molly from the water. So, there was this big *saved-your-life-eternally-in-your-debt* deal going on. Which was kind of understandable. He had a bit of that with Sanderling. But in Molly and Gran's case, it kind of worked both ways. After the death of Marco's dad, Gran's one and only child, well maybe Molly kind of saved Gran's life too, gave Gran something to live for. So yeah, Gran was going to be mad.

Marco grabs his backpack and heads for the door, double-quick time.

'Don't forget,' he shouts back at Tee, 'tests tomorrow.' Unless swimming is involved, Tee can oh-so-easily miss the beginning part of the day, catching up with the rest of the world around noon.

'Man, I knew that. I had that.'

But where exams were concerned, truth be told, Tee never did.

Marco dashes through the door, vaults over the exit barriers, and jaunts up the stairs two at a time.

Tee was right about the terraces; they weren't safe at night. But at least most people would be off the streets. It's the crowds more than the criminals that Marco finds hard to stomach. He knows he's living in a bubble. He used to be able to exist on both sides of the divide, but the more time he spends on the inside, the harder it gets to revert. As he crosses the smart, white stone plaza in front of the academy, with its half-empty street cafes piping out soft music, he glances through the long glass windows at the washed and well-dressed tucking into candlelit, real protein. It's a good life.

He turns the corner onto Central. It's a mile to the end, but this time of night the pods have stopped running anywhere but the inner-city, so he'll have to walk. He takes his academy tie off, pushes it deep in his pocket, and slides his green wristband up his sleeve. As soon as he gets out of the 'bubble' all those extra details are going to be screaming *mug me,* and that's the last thing he needs on top of everything else, because he has to get to Molly, fast. Normally you get five days to say your goodbyes, but according to the last newsflash, they're making an exception: this time the ships will be leaving in the morning. He breaks into a light jog, passing well-dressed people unaffected by the leaderboard. They saunter and smile in the bright city lights. He wishes it was him. Wishes none of this had happened, still can't quite believe it has.

As he draws close to the end of the road, he can see the darkness standing there, solid as a brick wall. They don't have streetlights in the Glaire. *The Glaire* - Gran had explained it all when they were kids. She'd cracked an egg in a pan, with Marco and Molly's full attention peering at the hob, rapt as if waiting for some magic show.

'See, the city's divided, just like this here egg. There's the yolk, and there's the white: the glaire. And in the yolk, it's all golden and creamy; the best of everything, making you fat and slow. And in the white, it's all skinny and basic and crammed to bursting with absolutely nothing but ways of figuring out how to make itself attractive enough to get on your plate. Yolk wants to keep hold of everything, white just wants to survive. Problem is, none of that's a good way to live.' Then she'd take the fork and smash the yolk into the

white. *'Mixing it all up …'* she'd say, *'it's healthy.'* *'When there's barriers and differences, there'll always be a shedload of trouble brewing.'*

He puts his hood up over his short, cropped, tidier-than-tidy hair and crosses out of the light into the darkness. His hidden wristband gives a gentle buzz, not a shock. The shocks are saved for anyone yellow and below trying to come the other way, not that many people do. Once is enough.

The streets should be empty. The Guard don't come down here at night, at least not on anyone else's business. You get into trouble down here at lights out, and you're on your own. But there's a group of no-hopers clustered around the entrance. Off Grids by the look of them, their clothes so thick with grime they could stand up without the aid of a body.

'Angel.'

'LSD'

'Monkey Dust.'

They mumble out their *specials*, their menu of drugs, like shifty promoters outside a restaurant.

Marco shakes his head and keeps right on walking.

The Bacchus district is next. The air is so thick with smells it's hard to breathe; food, sweat, body waste, live chicken. Chaotic light spills out in pools from neon signs. Music blares from bars. The streets here are crowded: people, a few live animals, even kids. They have their own kind of 'protection' here. If you're partying or buying, you're safe. He's hoping he'll be okay just passing through. Trick is to walk with purpose and lay off the eye contact.

'A few of your points?'

He looks down. There's a young girl, his kind of age, huddled in blankets, shadowed in the doorway. Damn, what did he just say to himself? *No eye contact.* But now he can't look away. It tears at his soul. How can anyone get that thin and still be alive?

He can't bring out his wristband; it'll only attract attention, so *points* are a no-no. He reaches into his pocket and pulls out a protein bar.

'You're a hero, sir.' The girl says, ripping it open before it's out of his hands.

'Any more of that, sunshine?' There's another woman beside him now, blocking his way. She's older. Her red lipstick smeared over her face, barely hitting her lips. She's all made up in gaudy colours, so bright he can see them all despite the shadows.

'Sorry,' he says, pulling the lining out of his pocket. 'Another time.'

She grabs hold of him, pulling him towards her. Her hair is all in dreads, wiry against his skin. She smells of the terraces, of primitive sanitation, of washing in sea water.

The woman sniffs, inhaling him like he's some kind of meal she's about to devour.

'Chlorine?'

Her skin glistens with a silver, salt crust in the dim light. She pushes up his sleeve, laying one long bony finger on his green wristband.

'Long way from home?'

'My gran lives on the terraces. I only moved out of the Glaire last year,' he says.

'Leave him, Flo.' The skinny girl says between mouthfuls. 'Look, you can have a bit.'

But Flo's not interested. 'Only part posh then?'

Marco shrugs. He shouldn't have come. Should have waited till morning. 'Just my toenail.'

She nods and smiles.

'Flo, just leave him.' The skinny girl holds a tiny piece of protein bar out, the only piece that's not eaten.

Flo doesn't even look at it.

'My sister, Molly WU, she's been repatriated.'

'Molly!' The skinny girl says. 'I know her. Mate, I'm sorry.'

The skinny girl appears to be gaining strength. Solidarity is seeping into her marrow, giving her one last burst at life.

'You leave him, Flo.'

Flo sneers at them. Then, seeing an opportunity, grabs the last bit of bar, sticking it in her mouth and sucking hard, her eyes closing over in ecstasy.

'Hey!' The skinny girl shouts.

'You offered it.'

The women start to bicker.

Marco doesn't need a written invitation, he's off.

There, but for the grace of God. That's what Gran always said.

CHAPTER 3
MOLLY

'SO, how's it going then, saving the planet?'

Gran's apron is tied, dark slap-you-if-you-mess-with-me hands, fingers stretched over wide hips. She's greeted Marco the self-same way ever since he moved out twelve months ago. At first, Marco thought Gran wanted an answer. Then he thought she was being sarcastic. Now he thinks that although she's being sarcastic, she genuinely would like an answer.

'Working on it, Gran.' Well, what more can you say? Besides, he is. He really is working on that very thing, day in day out, at the academy. He'd even won a prize for his research. The Clause Herbit award. Not many kids could say that.

But none of that impresses Gran. She's standing larger than life in the hallway of her home on the terraces, the low-rise Victorian villas that should have been condemned years ago. Somewhere behind her in the house, the curious analogue radio station she listens to blares out sounds from her past. Same kind of thing as Marco's dad used to play at his mobile disco, retro stuff. Sounds to cook by, that's what Gran always says, and tonight she's cooking chicken.

It's real chicken, the type without legs, but all the rest of it's there: body, breast and short stubby wings. In a world short on space, food without legs is the only way to go. Marco feels the amputated legs are a small sacrifice. Fair enough, it's not his sacrifice, and if he were a chicken, then maybe he'd feel differently about the whole thing. But tolerance for anything beyond survival is not really entertained anymore, at least not for those living in the Glaire. The terraces were the last place clinging hard to some kind of respectability. Regular work, occasional real food, an inside drinking tap. As many morals as could be afforded. Besides, the kind of chicken Gran's cooking is the kind that smells like home when you open the front door. And Gran's is the closest thing Marco's got to a real home.

'Smells like I arrived just in time.' Marco takes a deep breath, inhaling the mouthwatering aroma of bird, hot oil and herbs.

'Not sure there's enough for you,' Gran shoots back, a sharp edge to her voice. He's neglected her since he moved out. With all the work, training and exams, sometimes it's difficult to fit life in.

''S'okay' Marco shrugs, trying hard to backtrack on the salivating. 'I've already eaten,' he lies.

He should be back in the hamster cage – his ten by fifteen, fully functional, uber grey personal pad – going through past papers. He has exams in the morning, and exams are important. They're the only thing keeping Marco off the leaderboard. So far, professionals and students at the academy have not been entered. But then, Molly was council operations.

'Thought all you council operatives were safe?' He asks, and Gran just shrugs. No doubt Gran and Molly have been over this a million times since the board went up.

'They introduced some new criteria. Molly's got no next of kin,' Gran scoffs bitterly. She's taking it personally.

'Plus, she's got a…' Gran struggles for the word. 'What do you call it?'

'Attitude problem?'

Gran nods her head slowly like she's got the wisdom of Solomon. 'Attitude problem? Boy, hasn't she?' And despite herself, Gran gives a small, proud smile. Like *attitude problem* is a character trait Gran's been nurturing all these years.

'Well, if it's <u>just</u> company you're after, I suppose you better come in. Though I can't say as we'll be much fun.' Gran steps back into the dark, narrow hallway and Marco hangs his coat on a hook that's already way too cluttered. His sleeve slips and Gran glances down at the green wristband. He should have made sure it was out of view. He's taken off his academy tie, that always gets her goat, but … he sees her fingering her own band. She's yellow. It's always been a bone of contention. He slides his band neatly under his jumper.

'I saw the leaderboard,' he says, stepping into the hallway, staring up the stairs to see if there's any sign of Moll.

Gran nods, disappearing back into the kitchen. There's chicken to baste, but Marco knows it's not just that; she doesn't want to catch his eye.

'You'd have to be deaf, dumb and blind to have missed it.'

Gran had a point.

'How's she taking it?'

'Molly?'

He doesn't bother answering. It's not as if there's anyone else for Gran.

'How d'ya think?'

'Dork.'

Marco turns to see Molly standing tall and proud on the stairs above, her make-up perfectly pitched. If she has been crying, there's not a sign of it.

'Goliath,' he shoots back. It's not just the stairs. She'd been taller than him for most of his life. He'd only just caught up with her last year, even overtaken by a couple of centimetres when he stood straight. Not that she'll be around for him to gloat much longer.

'What an honour.' She's ladling on the sarcasm with a trowel. 'See you found time to tear yourself away from your busy schedule, squeeze in a visit to the condemned woman.'

'Woman!' Marco scoffs. She's the exact same age as him.

'She's about to get flung to the other side of the world,' Gran shouts from the kitchen. 'Think she's earned the upgrade.'

'Sorry,' Marco says. Because he can't think of anything else to say, and besides, he is.

'About not coming around before? Or about challenging my *womanhood*? Or about the fact that I'm heading off on the next boat?'

'Everything.'

'Great,' shouts Gran from the kitchen, 'I can pop a few things in the mix.'

In truth, Marco has always been the perfect kid, no tantrums, no going off the rails, no drugs, no alcohol, no breakdowns. But Gran doesn't need an excuse, and he does not want to get her started. He tries for a quick realignment on the conversation front.

'You packed?

Molly shakes her head.

'See you found time to hit the straighteners, though?'

Gran laughs, not a belly laugh, but at least there's a shred of humour. 'Let's hope they've got plugs where she's going.'

Molly's long hair is straightened and dyed to within an inch of its life; a trellis of pink, black, and blond, run through with braids, extensions, and clips. It sounds a mess, but actually, it kind of works. Gran had to put a special desalination tap in just for the hair.

'Yeah well,' Molly mumbles, 'got to make an effort. Not that they'll have the cameras on us for long. They're going to want to forget us quick. You coming up?' She turns and climbs back up the stairs, pulling herself along with the handrail like her feet are extra heavy. Gran buries her head in the hot oven as if she's so busy she can't tear herself away, and Marco follows Molly up to her room. The room that used to be his dad's and is, by rights, his. But he has never, not once in all his life, regretted giving it up.

Marco stares at the small backpack laid out on the bed.

'Seriously?'

Molly shrugs. 'What can I say? I travel light.'

She's got more hair kit than clothes laid out on the covers.

'You need a jumper, a rain mac.' He's sounding like his gran.

'Dah. It's Africa. Besides. I'm going to wear the mac.'

'Can they get you to Ghana?' Ghana was where Molly's great-great-grandparents were from.

Molly shrugs. 'They just do continents now. Countries can be difficult to find. Shouldn't you be home, studying? Tests tomorrow.'

Marco doesn't need reminding.

'I'm always ninety percent,' he says, trying to sound like none of that's a problem. But deep down, test scores are the kind of thing he worries about.

'All that swotting paid off.' Molly nods sadly.

'You could have done it, Moll. You should have tried harder.'

'Maybe.'

Molly was bright, had always been bright, but she was stubborn. She wasn't going to fit herself into anyone else's box, thank you very much.

'You keep it up, boy. Wear that wristband no matter what Gran says and keep that head down.'

'I don't just keep my head down.' But Marco kind of knows he does. He's part of the academy, part of the solution. Even when people used to protest about the repatriations, he'd never go. Kept his head in a book, trying to speculate for a brighter future, rather than getting out on the coal face and tackling the problems of today. She's got him sussed. She hugs him anyway. Hugs him tight. She hasn't hugged him since they were kids. Not since bodies became not so much something that carried you around, but more something that strutted you forward.

'I'm gonna miss you.'

'You could refuse to go.'

'They just arrest you, drug you, carry you out through the back door. You know all this.'

He nods. He'd seen people carried out. Once your name goes up on that board, as far as life in the city was concerned, you were on borrowed time.

'You'll be okay. You're always okay, Moll.'

But for once, she's not looking so sure.

'One last visit to the garden?'

He glances anxiously back down the stairs. 'You think we've got time?'

She shrugs. 'If we can't make time now, we can't make time never. Come on.' She pushes the sash window up, takes his hand in hers and, high stepping over the sill, leads him gently out of the window onto the flat roof of the kitchen. He hasn't been out here since he left, but it's just the same as always. That damp smell hits him like a freight train as soon as he steps out onto the rolled black felt. All the odd bits of life that get salvaged, the Glaire and the terraces are where it ends up. And up on gran's flat kitchen roof, you can get yourself a ring-side seat. A sharp westerly wind and those nostrils are in for a treat. It's all damp mattresses, rusting metal and somehow, somewhere, someone is always barbecuing something feral, often still with the fur on!

There's the old swing chair looking out over the terraces towards the city. Just like it always did. Only now the terraces seem even darker than they did when Marco and Molly were kids. There are pockets of liquid blackness rippling far below

– dark, stagnant water. Where old foundations that have filled up over time, and no one has bothered to drain them out. In contrast, the city has its halo on. It's shining so brightly it's a wonder anyone in the Glaire ever gets any sleep.

'Careful of the moss.' Molly says, just as his foot goes sliding out from under him, and she laughs. 'Should have let you go over on your backside.'

'And you guys wonder why I'm not banging on the door 24/7.'

'If you can't stand the heat… Wimpoid.'

'That's not even a word.'

'You know what it means?'

'Yeah but…'

But she just looks at him, hands on hips, big bold eyes staring steady, and this time Marco just laughs. She's got him.

They used to spend hours out here growing up, even when it was raining. It was their special place. He could just about remember parks and gardens from when he was a kid, acres of space with football pitches all marked out in straight, white lines. Flowers and trees wafting sweet perfume into the air. As a garden then, this roof-top terrace was on the small side. There were a few pots of herbs, some geraniums shining blood-red through the summer and scenting the air, which was a good thing since Gran kept her pigeons here too. He'd asked her once, why pigeons? Why not chickens?

'Cus I'd eat the blessed chicken. Never could hold on for the eggs.'

So, pigeons it was. Just three now, all caged up and cooing.

'We were lucky, you know,' Moll says, staring out into the night. 'Lucky to be in that first wave.'

Marco knows she's right. It was because they had got caught up in the disaster right from the start that Marco and Molly did okay. After the first floods, it was broadcast over the public stations, the thing about the lungs and how kids could survive. A lot of people went out looking. They'd step over the adults. There was no hope for them. But they'd pull kids out of the water, drag them on shore. Pump their lungs: place their hands on the bodies and press. When the floods continued for the next twelve months, people just left the kids floating like they didn't even see them.

Molly shivers and pulls at her yellow band. 'Be glad to get rid of this. My wrists'll look a damn sight prettier without it.' She holds her slim arms up in the half-light.

'Shan't take this off, though.' She fingers the tin watch Marco made her, crafted from battered metal and leftovers picked up from Sanderling's floor.

'Why don't you wear yours?'

'You know this, Moll – no jewellery at the academy.'

'Stamp out all personality.'

He wasn't in the mood to disagree.

'It still works, you know.' She twists the watch around on her wrist. 'Well, sometimes. Sometimes it gives the odd signal.'

He looks at it carefully, at the clumsy insignia that he'd etched on the back: a circle, a hammer, a map and a pen.

'What does it mean?'

But Marco just shrugs. It was just a pattern, something he'd tried to copy.

'Makes Sanderling laugh, that logo thing,' she says. 'He told me it's all there, but you kind of have to know what you're looking for. Going to see the old guy early tomorrow. You know, like, say goodbye.' She sighs, tilting her body back. Giving the seat a bit of momentum. 'You think you'll be able to fix it?' She asks.

'The watch?' And for a moment, he's lost.

Molly laughs, 'No, knucklehead. The planet?'

It was a tall order, and no way would it get fixed before Molly got shipped out.

'Reckon you're part of the team that can. Soil sciences. The good guys. I mean ocean sciences… they've got the biggest market share,' he smiled ironically.

'All well and good if you're a fish. And those space sciences, head so far up in the…'

'Clouds?' he offered. 'That's what they say, all the kids at the academy.'

'All the ones that aren't space scientists. So, soil sciences, my vote's on you. Can see you now in that Museum of Human History.'

Marco snorts. 'Now that would take a miracle.'

One miracle that Marco's more than happy to land is - that night, he sleeps like a baby. He thought he was in for nightmares. So, he put his old alarm clock on; wound it up and fell into dreamland just listening to that tick. It's the sound of Sanderling - the man who pulled him from the waves. Marco can't remember anything much after the wave hit. Only the sensation of being lifted from the water and circled in a pair of wiry arms, strong and twisted as metal cables, and the sound of the man. Tick-tock, tick-tock. Tick-tock, tick-tock. Just like Nurse Curtis' watch.

In Marco's dream, he's back in Sanderling's workshop. It was a place that he loved, felt safe in, for the first twelve months or so after the wave hit, with its smells of polished wood, hot drinks, and freshly baked biscuits. As always, the ticking is so loud. It's like every clock wants to get in on the action: Tick-tock, tick-tock. Tick… He's about eight, Sanderling's given him free run of the workshop, and he's having a ball. Scooting around on Sanderling's chair, searching through all the drawers. He's looking for just the right cog, just the right wheel. Sanderling's there, spindly as a spider with his warm face beaming its full-on ironic smile – like he's got all the answers, but he's saying nothing. He's tending his plants, which are growing like a jungle, trailing down the oak-lined walls over the clocks, the workbenches, snaking over the floor.

'Five more minutes, then I look.' Sanderling says. 'Five minutes, not one second more.'

Marco lines all the bits up. He's got a back plate polished and ready, and some of the largest cogs he could find. We're talking millimetres here, but they're beauties, all copper and brass and shining like they're just oh-so-chuffed to get taken out of that drawer.

'Three minutes and counting.' Sanderling says, and those clocks, they just keep right on ticking. Tick-tock – hurry-up – Tick-tock – arrange that stuff – Tick-tock.

'One minute, boy.'

Wow! Time is going so much faster than it normally does!

'I'm hoping for something special.'

Tick-tock, tick-tock. Tick…

Then, suddenly, all the clocks stop. Every single one, and it's like the whole world is holding its breath. 'Time.' Sanderling says as he peers over Marco's shoulder. And Marco knows, he knows deep down in his eight-year-old soul, that somehow, somewhere, he has done something wrong. One of those rookie heart-sink mistakes that he'll end up kicking himself over.

'It's pretty,' Sanderling says, and Marco wants to hold on to the compliment. They can just stop there. Pretty will do. But Sanderling's not that kind of a guy. Sanderling's all truth or nothing.

'But you see what you did?'

Marco gazes down at the small pile of copper and brass.

'You picked all the biggest bits you could find.'

Sanderling places one of those large, soft hands-on Marco's shoulder. 'Watches don't work like that. Machines don't work like that. People don't even work like that.'

Sanderling opens a drawer and takes out a series of smaller cogs, different shapes, different sizes.

'It's the combination that does the trick. Never just the one thing on its own.'

He slips on his eyeglass. The large one, like a telescope that fits over one eye and makes it bulge-big out of its socket.

'Every mechanism is a world unto itself. It's never just *the big*, just *the impressive*. Everything has to work altogether.'

Sanderling gives the largest cog on the plate a flick with his nail, and instantly the others click into action. Then he smiles, that warm, kind smile, and Marco knows that the ice inside his soul, the one the wave put there, has melted. Everything's going to be alright.

But then the music? He can hear music: the bright sound of birds filling the workshop, drowning out the clocks, and the smile, and the soft sparkle of Sanderling's eyes. Marco's alarm. Morning glory setting: a range of birds that you would never hear in the city. Not now. Maybe you would never hear them anywhere anymore, apart from Marco's alarm. And suddenly he remembers. It all comes crashing back. Marco remembers that today he's losing an essential part of his world, his mechanism – Molly.

CHAPTER 4

NO SHOW

HE'D WORN his running shoes, the ones that cost him two months' wages. The ones he'd had to hide from Gran, on account of the very *two-months-wages* fact. His smart academy slip-ons were in his backpack with his shirt and academy tie. He'd have to change at the test centre. He'd checked out the quickest route when he got home late last night. Running around the inner city was easy. You had to be a green band or above to get in, but the Glaire, the terraces, any place outside green zoning and it was a different story. There were a hell of a lot of people crammed in, and not all of them were happy campers. From the map it looked like, if he cut out under the pod track and headed down through the marketplace, there was a short cut, a small alleyway between the customs building and the detention centre. That should bring him out near the exam centre. It was tight, but he could make it.

The plaza had been shrouded in sea-mist when he arrived. Even so, straight off he noticed some kind of movement in the far, right corner, an area with limited CCTV. Protestors? He didn't watch the repatriation ceremonies anymore, hardly had time, but he'd thought the protests had stopped. These people were probably lefty-liberal academics: they'd need green access and above to get into the plaza at this time in the morning.

At first, Marco thinks there's a constant stream of people wheeling in shopping trolleys stuffed to bursting with placards. But he soon realises it's just one woman on the trollies. She's wrapped tight in a grey headscarf and coat, and keeps dipping in and out of the plaza, pulling those bone-shaker silver trollies behind her. No wonder there's no news coverage on the protests, Marco thinks to himself as he stares down at the woman's steady, dogged determination. It's not exactly a riveting watch.

But he doesn't have time to mull it over, because suddenly it dawns on him that it's not just lefty-liberals down there. Bulking up the headcount are three Off Grids. OGs are lawless. They've escaped repatriation or detention centres. Their wristbands are off. So, in theory, they could travel anywhere, but it doesn't quite work like that. If the authorities see them, there is a strong chance of *shoot first, catch up for a chat morgue-side.* Why in the hell would an Off Grid be bothering to help set up a protest? If the protestors cut a sad sight, the Off Grids are in a whole different league. They're the kind of beings that nightmares are made of. Their faces dirty, and scabbed. Their feet bound in rags. Marco pulls his trainers underneath him, not wanting the flashy white latex to draw attention.

At seven thirty, the largest OG, a man who towers above the others, puts the last placard in place. It reads *'Rights For All, Not Some.'* Then he taps the shoulders of the other two who, without a moment's hesitation, disappear. They just melt into the mist. Marco stares hard at the plaza. How is this even possible? There must be a drainage system under the plaza. They've got some kind of quick access route, some plague-ridden tunnel that the guards won't go down.

It's just the tall OG and the three regular protestors left.

'You need to get out, mate,' Marco mutters under his

breath. Even with their secret tunnel, one clear shot through that plaza could fell the OG in a second.

The zone limiters that operate the wristband system must have been taken off because a few stragglers are shuffling into the square. Marco glances at their wristbands. There's a lot of yellow. The newly condemned are assembling. The poor, sad souls who got picked out of the hat with Molly. He feels his mouth run dry. If people are beginning to arrive, the guard won't be far behind. But still that last OG stays, as if his feet are rooted to the ground. The woman in grey, who appears to be in charge of the protestors, has stopped working, as if some inner-warning system has started to ring loudly in her brain. She glances up at the OG.

'Now, mate, you need to go now.' Marco can hear the high whir of a free-pod pulling to a halt somewhere just beyond the plaza. The only people who have free-pods are the guard and the Committee. Everyone else has to travel on the regular pods, the ones bound by tracks. It can't just be Marco that heard the whir. The others must be aware of it too. But for the OG and the woman, it's like they're part of a whole different time spectrum. The OG slowly, slowly, walks towards the woman, takes her face roughly into his large, dirty hands and reels her in like a fish, locking her in a kiss. Marco can't help it. He feels his nose wrinkle in disgust. He chews his gum a little harder, as if the OG might benefit some from Marco's own personal dental hygiene.

A kiss? Really? Now?

Reluctantly, as if his body is laced with weights, the OG pulls away, then turns back into the square and stares straight in Marco's direction. Marco looks behind him, expecting to see an even larger OG standing over his shoulder, about to break Marco's neck or steal his shoes. But the steps behind Marco are empty. He glances back quickly into the plaza. The giant OG is still standing there, proud as sin. His legs planted firmly on the ground. His ragged, dirty face held high.

Slowly, purposefully, he brings up one sack-clad arm and, to Marco's absolute horror, the OG gives Marco one long, deliberate, salute.

Marco feels his stomach lurch before tying itself into a large uncomfortable knot, and without thinking, he dives down behind the wall. He cannot believe this is happening! If anyone saw! He must have been mistaken. Why? Why would the OG salute Marco? The gesture must have been aimed at someone else.

When Marco raises his head again, the OG has gone. People are starting to arrive. Going by their dress, these are families from the Glaire. Some are hugging each other, some are weeping, most are pulling out strings of those well-trodden phrases from self-help manuals. 'New adventure.' 'Say hi to your Aunty.' 'Don't forget to take your vitamins.'

Marco hears it all, an odd jumble of reassurances and regret. What will he say, he wonders, when it gets to be his turn? Molly? He thinks. Where the hell is Molly? He glances back at the protestors. There's only one left now; the woman with the headscarf, the one that the OG had kissed so tenderly. She's standing there alone, solid and silent as an oak, as the plaza begins to fill. Marco scans the faces in the crowd. All shapes and sizes, but no Molly. He steps back, trying to get higher onto the wide stone staircase. He's never seen so many people crowded into such a small space. It's not just those being processed. The guards have also arrived, dressed in their homogenous black shell-suits and hard helmets. The visors blacked out. He's not used to so many people, not anymore. The guards take up position on all exits, guns held at the ready. They might as well be robots for all the emotion that leaks out of those hard shells. Marco keeps scanning, scanning the sea of faces. They're all lumped together- Europeans, Asians, Africans. But no Molly. Suddenly he catches sight of an old guy from the terraces, a friend of Gran's, Mr Benson. Benson's standing near the steps.

But he's standing bang smack in what has become an impromptu thoroughfare; people continually shoving and pushing past. He's on his own. A small suitcase, the sum of all his worth, clutched tightly in his dark, walnut hands as people smash up against him, knocking his shoulder hard like he doesn't exist.

'Hey!' Marco calls out to a large woman, who has just launched her bag with a WTF attitude into Mr Benson's legs. 'Watch it.'

But the woman isn't interested. She doesn't even bother to glance in Marco's direction. It's a free-for-all. Manners are no longer relevant.

'Marco,' Benson says, a sad smile flickering across his face.

'Here…' Marco pushes down the steps and through the crowd, holding his hand out to Benson, as much to anchor the old guy as to offer any form of greeting. 'I'm sorry, I didn't realise you were going.'

'Not a problem, son. I've had a good innings.' Mr Benson glances around him nervously at the teeming sea of people. 'Nice to see a friendly face.'

A large man with quarter-back shoulders pushes past, knocking Mr Benson's elbow. Benson says nothing, just lifts the elbow up and, without even bothering to give it a look, he rubs it gently.

'Here, stand on the steps.' Marco takes the old man's arm and leads him back to the stone staircase. It's filling up, but not as bad as the plaza.

'Goodness,' Mr Benson says, looking down into the fray. 'That's a lot of people.'

'Have you seen Molly?'

Benson shakes his head.

'I saw her name was on the list, but… I'm sorry, Marco. Your gran's going to take it hard.'

There's no need to answer. They both know this is one hell of an understatement.

'But I can't see her,' Marco continues searching the crowd.

'It's quarter to. She must be here by now.' Benson also begins to scan. 'My eyes, they're not so good these days. She'll be here somewhere.'

Marco looks down at the frail old man at his side.

'We should try to get you in early, avoid the crush.'

'Oh no, please don't you trouble yourself. I'm fine.'

But Mr Benson is not looking *fine*, and Marco wonders when the old guy got so frail, so withered. When did he get the life sucked out of him?

'No one's down by the protestors,' Marco says gently.

Mr Benson laughs. 'No surprise there. I used to do it too, protest. We all did. Fat lot of good it did us.'

Marco looks down again; the crowd appears to have become an entity all in-itself, pushing and shoving and reeling like a many-headed serpent. Mr Benson won't stand a chance. Marco scans one last time. Molly's not there.

'Okay. Follow me.' Marco takes Mr Benson's bag, grasping the old man by the hand. 'We'll have to push back a little if we want to get through.'

'Excuse me. Pardon. Sorry. Coming through. So sorry.' Mr Benson mutters as he shoulders through the crowd, apologising all the way, to people who don't care. Apologising in more ways than Marco knew were possible.

When they arrive, in what Marco has come to think of as protestor's corner, the crowd thins. It's as if the one, single, remaining protestor is somehow contagious. Marco breathes a sigh of relief and lets Mr Benson's hand drop. They made it. Benson straightens his smart, wool coat, the one that only ever came out on a Sunday, and wipes his face with a clean, pressed handkerchief, before folding it flat and tucking it neatly away in his pocket.

There's a barrier in front of the repatriation centre, a series of high, metal gates positioned behind it. When the gates open, Benson will walk through with ease.

'That's better. Thank you, Marco.' The old man raises his eyes to Marco's, and Marco realises with embarrassment that those old eyes, the seen-it-all done-it-all eyes that had watched Molly and Marco grow up, that had shouted *"get off my wall,"* and *"best get home before your gran catches you."* Those eyes that had always been so watchful, so on the ball, so much a part of Marco's community, are full of tears.

Marco has no idea what he's supposed to do. He's not good with emotions. Luckily, just at that moment, the siren rings out, booming its harsh, low, one-note drone over the plaza.

It's nine o'clock. The large light above the gates clicks to green, and people start to shuffle forward, forming themselves into ordered centipede lines.

Benson smiles sadly up at Marco, taking his bag and placing one withered hand gently on Marco's shoulder.

'Marco lad, you always were a curious child. Even though sometimes you were doing the wrong thing, your heart, well… can't say there was ever anything wrong with where your heart's placed.'

CHAPTER 5
THE SECOND WAVE

FIVE O'CLOCK. The day has been a disaster. The only good thing about it: it's over. Marco sits in a silver pod speeding high above the dark, wet city. He's trying to focus, watching the monitor tracking his heart rate. Trying to stop going over and over in his head how it's been one bugger up after the next. He didn't see Molly. She's no-show on the system. No-show is bad. But worse? He was so preoccupied, so messed up, so not in the zone, that he flunked five questions on the exam paper. It's taken a whole hour to calm himself down. He's just going to focus on practice, test papers, how he moves forward. First things first, getting that old lung capacity nailed. He's been holding his breath for four minutes. His heart rates at twenty-seven BPM. Despite the trauma of the exam, this is a personal best. Then, just as it's all going oh-so-well out of nowhere, he feels a sharp, swift slap across the head and his lungs expand with a loud, involuntary gasp.

'Not working, bro. Your ear tips - absolute crimson.'

It's Tee. Sometimes it feels like Tee is Marco's own personal shadow.

'Nutter,' Marco mumbles, embarrassed. 'Course they're pink. You just belted me.'

The slap may have been playful, but that doesn't mean that it doesn't sting like hell. Luckily nobody's noticed or, perhaps more to the point, nobody's interested. Marco's convinced that Tee lives permanently in some kind of cartoon world - drop a character out of a thirty-storey building and they'd stand up with birds swizzling around their head, and an imprint of their body immortalised in concrete – always the joker.

'Before, man…' Tee laughs. 'Those ear tips were tingeing pink before. Has to be *no external signs of stress when holding your breath.*' Tee can quote the regs like a parrot.

'I know. I know what there has to be.'

'Well then? I tell you there was steam coming out of those ears.'

That great big ever-ready grin plastered across Tee's face suddenly fades. He's getting the picture, or at least remembering the context.

'Sorry, man, about Molly,' he says, and shifts around a bit, like there's something hot under his feet. 'What do you think happened?'

But Marco has no idea what happened. More to the point, and maybe a more pressing question – *what the hell happened in the exam?* But right now, Marco does not want to go there. Marco had deliberately taken a later pod to avoid Tee. Marco does not want to go out tonight. Marco does not want to discuss Molly, or his results. Marco needs to get his head sorted.

'Hey, dude, you sore about the exam?' Tee says, gently. 'Look, man, seventy-five percent it's still…'

'Nowhere near ninety.'

'It's a pass.' Tee shrugs an *it-is-what-it-is shrug*. 'It's a blip. They'll see that, man. Everyone has blips. You're streets ahead of me. Grade A in your exams. Good enough heritage. Lung capacity … well, that could do with work. But hey, you're trying and just remember, mate, the test for humanity, that's an ongoing practical.'

Marco scowls, 'What's that even supposed to mean?'

Tee looks sheepish. 'Something I heard Molly say once.' His face falls. He's getting the picture. He doesn't even want to use the M word again. It's guaranteed to make everyone uncomfortable.

'Hey!' He comes back, trying hard, bright-eyed-and-sparky. So, I was thinking, tonight…'

'How many times! 'No. Tee! The whole weekend is off.'

'You can't cancel the weekend, man!'

Marco says nothing. They're supposed to be the same age, so why is it that Marco always feels like he's got a hundred years on Tee?

'I mean the Molly thing, mate. I mean,' Tee sighs. There's no avoiding it. They have to air it in public. 'Look, man. I mean that's bad, that's… Look, no one liked Molly more than me, but just… There's nothing you can do about it.'

Marco knows this is true, but it doesn't stop him from feeling sick to the stomach.

'And the tests? Next time, you'll bounce back. It's not a big deal. Just an hour at the Rec? It's Friday night.' Tee is not giving up. The next test is a whole week away.'

Marco can see the shadow of the levee wall approaching. It stands two hundred and fifty feet high. A stark fortress rising out of the waves. If he gets off now, he can walk home, avoid Tee, clear his head. He stands and moves towards the panel.

'We're walking?'

Marco lets out a sigh. How many hints does this guy need? It will have to be sledge-hammer tactics. 'Tee. I need a bit of space.'

Marco presses his palm against the service panel.

'Levee.'

At his command, the pod slows. The door slides open, and Marco steps out. Tee doesn't move a muscle, just stares out of the window at Marco, hangdog expression on his face, as the pod ferries him away into the gloom.

The damp air seeps through Marco's clothes like a wet flannel. The levee is empty. It's way past dusk. The sharp, white LED lights have already kicked in, showing the levee in all its brutalist glory, a massive grey, sloping wall, with three levels of walkways. The top path stands tall above the sea. It's too risky to walk it at night. The wind can be *playful*. Either side you go over, city or sea, you're dead. Marco picks the middle path. It's empty but sheltered. People tend to avoid the levee at night. It's the barrier between life and death, but it's also where the flood ducts are, and nobody wants to get caught out. Is that what happened to Molly? Marco wonders, as he lets his fingers slip into the knot of his academy tie, holding on to it like a security blanket. It's silk, real silk. But it's so much more than that. No one inside the city will mess with him if he's wearing the tie. But how long will they let him keep it if his grades slide?

He checks his phone. He's left countless messages for Gran, but she's not getting back. Maybe he should head over to the terraces, go see her? But if he does that, he just might get pulled into the investigation, and that's not going to help anyone.

He switches on his music. 'American Pie,' a track from the 1970s blasts out its own brand of pragmatic doom and gloom - Mother Nature taking *the last train for the coast, with God, the Father and the Holy Ghost*. It was a song Marco had on his system. He'd downloaded some of his dad's tracks after the disaster. It had been difficult to get a digital transfer. A lot of bureaucracy. Digital files were retina-encrypted, and a lot of retinas got lost. But Sanderling pushed it through, managed to get at least some songs out. It was only music, most of it out of copyright. He played his dad's mixes all the time. Sometimes he heard them on Gran's funny radio, too. A lot of the words meant nothing to Marco, meant nothing to anyone anymore. What the hell was a fandango? He had no idea. But he listened anyway, singing words out loud that he didn't understand. It was comforting to have this bridge between him and his dad. But the music did more; the music reminded Marco that even back then, even when there were fields and bees and fruits. Fruit you could pick off the trees; even <u>then</u> everyone thought the world had gone to the dogs.

Marco's arrived at one of the windows, vast concrete holes cut into the wall. It's noisier here. The sound of the hydroelectric turbines giving the wind a run for its money. The great blades sit directly between the windows in the levee. Marco thinks the powers that be could have thought about this a bit better. People have been known to throw themselves off, get caught up in the blades. He feels an ice-cold hand grip his gut. Molly? This is no good. Everywhere he looks, he can see nothing but tragedy for his friend. It would be better to know. Wouldn't it? Anything, anything but this.

'For Christ's sake.' He brings his fist down hard on the window edge.

He has to think she's alright. Think that it must be an admin cock-up. Because if not, the other possibilities are endless, and brutal, and turn his stomach upside down. He takes a deep breath, hardly able to catch the salt wet air in his mouth. It's so pushy. Admin. Leave it at that.

He can just make out three dark, horizontal floats, thirty feet by twenty, bobbing out to sea. His Clause Herbit project. He was working on creating floating fields. Not just desalination plants that took up acres of space. These fields would desalinate themselves. Usually, it fills him with pride, looking out over them. It reminds him he's part of the solution. But tonight, the floats look forlorn in the blue moonlight. One of the tethers has broken, so they're no longer neatly lined. Instead, they're being buffeted by the wind and tugged by the water. Two powerful elements that have decided to go juvenile; fighting like kids about to tear a favourite doll in half. In agreement, the sharp salt air slaps him hard around the face, stinging his ears and filling his nostrils with a dose of saline. A cold shiver slips down his spine. He shouldn't be here. It's not safe. The water is crouching in wait like a hungry monster, just on the other side of the wall. Marco's never quite sure of its shape, or where it keeps its eyes, its arms, its teeth. It morphs and swirls, giving the impression that it's all just particles. All just bits of H20 strung together. But Marco's met it before. Once, and once was enough. Is it getting closer? Is it slipping away? Maybe one day, maybe soon, it will just leap over the barrier in one great swoop and gather them all up.

He glances back inside the wall. He can see the neat pathways that make up the city, everything lit, everything orderly. But just outside the lights, another waiting body of darkness; the Glaire, all the bits that the city would like to leave behind. Everything in the world has been trashed. You can just about ignore it when you're inside the bubble. When your light switches on, switches off. Your room smells or lavender or honeysuckle pumped to perfection by an electronic spray, and long-dead birds wake you every morning with their sweet song. But outside everything still smells of water, and the dark, damp forces waiting just below the surface. He's going to have to be more careful if he wants to keep his feet dry. Sure, he thinks to himself as he walks down the steep, concrete steps away from the front, seventy-five percent is a pass. But things are never exactly black and white. Suddenly it hits him, and he smiles wryly at the irony, because isn't that what it might all, eventually, boil down to if things don't work out?

CHAPTER 6
THE NEWS

THE STACKS: thin, monolithic concrete slabs, tower above Marco like boney, shadowy fingers trying to pull themselves up into the dark sky. Each one houses six hundred of the city's *displaced but dynamic*; the loners who are said to hold the future of the planet in their hands. He scans his retina into the door panel. With an automated swish, the door opens, and the automatic lights flicker into life down the long, grey corridor.

He'll relax over dinner, then run through some test papers. He's already practised his breathing on the pod. Tee. Sometimes, that guy! Four minutes. Marco's never got past four minutes. If Tee hadn't… Marco makes a mental note to give Tee a wider birth. Tee is T for trouble.

He lets himself into his own hamster cage. It's not what Texicom call it, but if the name fits… It's all grey walls and furnishings: ten feet by fifteen. Everything a person needs to live out a *modest life*. That's what it says on the Texicom advert. *Modest*, not exactly what your average seventeen-year-old is after.

Despite the fact that this place is so small you can barely get away from yourself, and all cat-swinging is right off the agenda, Marco suddenly feels absolutely alone. Molly. He flips the 'secret' drawer under the breakfast bench. It's not much of a 'secret,' all the units have them, but that's the way they describe it in the brochure. How can you advertise a secret? Sometimes Marco despairs. But ironic or not, the name kind of stuck.

Inside is a small metal box, a picture on the lid of some kind of biscuit, one that's long since got soggy and forgotten. He pulls open the lid. There's a photo of his parents standing outside a church, all smiles and fancy clothes. If they had any idea what was around the corner, they'd have stopped smiling and got praying. Not that Marco believed it would have done any good. God had *form* on the flood front. There's a CD of his dad's, labelled 'Disco Nights (1980's),' an old alarm clock with bells and a wind-up key: first thing Sanderling had given him. Marco sets it going. Tick-tock, tick-tock. Tick-tock, tick-tock. Sweeter than music. Then there's the watch. The same style as he made for Molly all those years ago, bits of tin and metal salvaged from Sanderling's floor. It used to have this simple kind of movement, that's what they call the heart of a watch, the mechanism that drives the hands. When they were thirteen, on Molly's insistence, Marco had tried to 'upgrade' the watches. Molly thought it would be fun if they could communicate through them. They'd grown out of Dr Krypto, but *waste-not-want-not*. So, Marco re-appropriated the two-way radios, taking out the cogs from the watches and putting in digital connections. It kind of worked – if you were standing close by. But that also *kind of* defeated the purpose. The watch part worked okay, though. But then he'd moved into the academy, and he'd had to leave all that kind of thing behind.

He slips the watch into his backpack. Okay, so maybe they

can stop him from wearing it, but they can't stop him from carrying it.

Marco stamps Sanderling's number into his phone. Just like Gran saved Molly from the water, Sanderling saved Marco. Sanderling was like a… not a father figure. No, that would be wrong. Marco didn't want to replace his own father. But a granddad? Yes, maybe that. Sometimes on a weekend, when the academy kids with finance trusts were all being taken to the aquarium, which Marco hated more than anything in the known universe. Or the Planetarium, which was cool but had a pricey entrance fee, or the Museum of Human History which, let's face it – if your face didn't fit, you weren't part of the story. Well, on the weekend, when his Gran and Molly cleaned the corporate offices, Marco would go help Sanderling. At first, it wasn't like in the dream: Marco was not allowed to touch. He'd pester Sanderling with the whys and wherefores of the universe, and Sanderling would just continue his work, sometimes answering, sometimes not. All the time wearing that telescopic lens that made his eye fishbowl-out. Carefully placing cogs next to one another, lining them up so they were all just touching. Then he'd wind the mechanism, and one cog would turn the next, which would turn another, which would turn something else. Till all the moving parts got shunted into action.

'Just like people,' Sanderling would say. 'Get the right one moving in the right direction, and everything else will just fall into place. All the cogs need is for someone with the big picture, to realise what the end game is.' Sanderling could make the cogs tell any story, fit any words of wisdom.

'My boy.' Sanderling's face appears over the screen on the wall. His soft blue eyes set in a field of wrinkles.

Marco can hear the ticking, even through the airwaves. Tick-tock, tick-tock. So much louder than even his own alarm clock. And he feels his pulse drop slightly, like Sanderling's clocks have somehow been wired into his heart.

'Long time no see.'

'Actually, it's only a week.'

'Nope, ten days. Got it all in the diary.'

There's no point in arguing. Besides, Sanderling is bound to be right. 'Had a dream about you.'

'Doesn't count. Not like a personal visit.'

'That wasn't what I…

'…meant? Sure it wasn't. What were we up to in that dream of yours?'

'It was that first time you let me build a watch.'

Sanderling smiles, amused by the memory. 'Everyone has to start somewhere. You eating okay?'

Marco nods. 'I've got a carton of Turkey Dinner. Have it later.'

Sanderling shakes his head. 'You shouldn't eat that muck. I have fresh salad for you here.'

Over Sanderling's shoulder, Marco can see all the hydroponic tubes full to bursting with trailing green plants.'

'I know. I'll come over soon.'

'Always soon,' Sanderling replies, but there's no real reproach in his voice.

A life-size, copper-plated automaton of William Shakespeare, moving jerkily, puts a mug of tea down in front of Sanderling.

'As you like it,' Will says, and Sanderling laughs at the exact same moment as Marco sighs; it's all so predictable.

Sanderling used to supply the Museum of Human History with what were called *witnesses*: jerky automatons in the shape of the world's famous and good. But technology has moved on. Now the witnesses are holographs. Sanderling had rescued a few of his automata from the scrap heap, but most had been melted down, repurposed. William made good tea.

But this was going nowhere fast. It was one reason why Marco rarely visited Sanderling. Go in for a quick chat, and it could easily be a few days before you got out.

'Sanderling, you heard from Molly?'

Sanderling shifts his gaze to the floor. 'I saw she's a no-show.'

'She was heading to see you this morning?'

'You spoken to your gran?'

'She's not returning my calls.'

Sanderling nods his head, sagely. 'Molly will turn up. How did those tests go?'

Now Marco wishes he hadn't called.

'Seventy-five percent.'

'What are you doing talking to me, then, you man? You need to get those books open.'

It wasn't Christmas. It wasn't even December, and there was absolutely nothing to celebrate. But, just like Tee had said, it was Friday night, and there had to be some kind of upside. So, Marco warms a small slurp-carton of Turkey Dinner in the microwave. He knows it will be a lot more *cranberry* than *dinner*, but beggars can't be choosers.

Suddenly there's this god-awful BANG BANGING on the door.

'Marco! Marco!'

Tee. There's no need to bang; there's a bell. That was Tee all over – physicality rather than thought. Marco wouldn't be surprised if he opened the door to find Tee using his head as a battering ram. And Marco was hoping for a quiet night!

'Marco!' Another loud BANG on the door. Marco sighs. The sooner Tee's in, the sooner Marco can get him back out again.

'Open.' At Marco's command, the door slides back, revealing an agitated Tee.

'You seen the news?'

Marco shakes his head. 'I'm trying to revise.'

'Well, you'll want to see this.' Barging through the door,

Tee starts shooting commands at the wall panel. 'News, man. News – tex.'

On Tee's orders, the screen flickers into life.

'This is irritating. What happened to privacy? Tee!'

'<u>This</u> is important.'

Then Marco sees, and his heart sinks. The screen is filled with a montage of iconic landmarks, each one in the throes of destruction. Tower Bridge is now an underwater walkway. St Paul's looks like it's going to be quick to follow. London is going under. Tee flicks to another channel. More images of the same thing. So that was why they'd done the early repatriation; the city wanted to make more room.

'I guess…' Marco mutters, 'we always knew it would happen.'

'God, man, and I thought you were supposed to be the bright one? Okay. Think. London sinking – what does that mean for us?'

There's an image of boats on the screens. It's uncertain where the boats start or where they end because the picture is carpeted with a tight knot of scared, bedraggled people.

'Most university and industry staff were saved,' the newsreader tells them.

'See. See.' By now, Tee is practically jumping up and down.

'So? They always do universities and science industries first.'

'Wait…' Tee has his finger to his mouth. 'Just listen.'

The newsreader's voice fills the room. 'Despite Thursday's unprecedented repatriation, the Government has warned they may have to look again at the criteria.'

'You get that?'

And of course, he does, but Marco's trying not to think of the worst-case scenario. Besides, Tee and Marco are 'professionals' That's what the academy does. His grades are fine. At least, he can get them back up.

On the screen, a smartly suited, steely-eyed woman descends the wide, civic steps of the repatriation centre. The text in the corner reads 'Chief Officer Kendal.' But they know who she is.

A red-light blinks in the corner of the screen. A text bubble reads *friend in area.*

'You got someone there?' Tee asks.

Marco shakes his head. 'Tex. Identify.'

A small portion of the screen highlights. The next moment it's enlarging, zooming in to a medium shot, a clip of the crowd. It just looks like a bunch of civvies. The government made the announcement late. The timing's no accident; the *powers that be* want to minimise reactions.

As all this flits cynically through Marco's brain, the screen continues to hone in till it catches a glimpse of wild, red hair, and the name *'Portia Reynolds,'* flashes up.

Portia Reynolds is not what Marco would call *a friend,* but then, technology can't tell the difference between 'friend' and 'acquaintance.' She's a GK: a golden kid. To be honest, years ago, he kind of fancied her. But she's ocean sciences, not soil and … if he had to be straight-up about it, he's not keen on the company she keeps. She just so happens to be in with some of the most loathsome people left on the planet. A group of kids who think the world owes them a living. Probably she thinks that as well. Surely there would be no reason to hang around with them if…

'Man. Reynolds, her lung count, it's to die for,' Tee's saying.

And Marco marvels at the extent of Tee's one-track mind.

'Yeah, that one's got it all,' Marco surprises himself at how bitter his words sound.

'Well, not really. I mean, she's bright. She's got money. Part of the GKs. But it's not like she's got parents.'

'What's she doing sticking her nose in…' Again with the bitterness?

Tee shakes his head. 'She's ocean sciences, but she has this thing about journalism. Tried to start a free paper one time. You remember that? Anti-censorship.'

Marco didn't remember. Truth be told, if it's not soil sciences, Marco doesn't take a huge heap of interest.

'That's what her dad was, a journalist. Abe Reynolds. Well, he owned the last free newspaper. Got taken out in the second flood. He's in the Museum of Human History.'

Marco whistles in appreciation. You have to do something pretty major to get in there. But then … he feels that old bitterness creeping in yet again; if you're part of the old-boy network, it's not difficult to do *major* stuff. Portia Reynolds and Marco, they're not from the same mould.

'Tex, alter status.' Marco's just about to downgrade Portia out of his life, when…

'Wait.'

Fresh-face Portia has a mic pushed up close to Kendal's face, and for a moment Kendal's smiling; this is all so cosy, the elite interviewing the elite.

'So,' Portia smiles, 'what will the next criteria be?'

Kendal's face falls hard and cold as an avalanche.

'Yes!' Tee punches the air with a fist. 'Straight for the jugular.'

At Portia's words, the whole crowd goes quiet.

'The criteria?' Portia repeats. She's not going to let her question drop.

'We'll be announcing it tomorrow.'

Kendal pauses for one moment, just enough time to give Portia the kind of look that says *don't go to sleep – I'm after you.* Then she's off. Those clip-clop smart shoes are on the move. Suddenly, there's a loud, electronic whine and Portia's voice comes out amplified above the crowd. She's got some kind of tannoy app on that mic.

'But are professionals safe?'

There's a moment, just a moment, when nothing happens. Silence spreads over the screen like a virus. No one breathes.

'All departments are currently under scrutiny.'

The noise of the crowd swells like a wave. Marco can't hear what they're asking, but he can guess. Kendal is disappearing fast behind bodyguards and security. But Portia just will not give up. She must be part limpet because that mic is on again.

'Apart from level two and above? Apart from GK? apart from Relies?' Portia Reynolds is no longer asking questions. She's stating facts. There's a whole strata of people who, despite the criteria being widened, are still home and dry. 'Their names will not be entered on to the leaderboard.'

Then the image cuts out, as the broadcast controllers try to regain control.

'Wow! That girl's got balls.'

Easy when you're home and dry, Marco thinks.

'I reckon I'm safe.' Tee's saying, biting his lip.

Marco's not so sure. 'To be honest, mate, your test scores. Look, I could help you revise. I'm happy to.'

Tee's shaking his head. 'Man, don't you get it? It's not all about that. There's only one person above me on lung count. You seriously think they'll let go of one of their prize lab rats?'

Marco thinks of his bad test scores. He thinks of the people he saw this morning being herded like cows into the repatriation centre.

'Tee?'

'Hmm?' Tee grunts.

Marco knows one thing for sure – he has to make sure he's as valuable as is humanly possible. 'You got the keys to those tanks?'

CHAPTER 7

PRACTICE MAKES PERFECT

THE NEXT MORNING, Tee insists they catch the first pod in. It's five thirty, not even light. The streets are shrouded in wet mist; the sun hasn't even had a chance to burn it off. It's the weekend, and Marco slept badly. Not even setting that old ticking clock up right next to the bed helped. Molly is still running around in his brain, as were his bad grades, as was the fact that this evening new repatriation criteria are going to be unveiled. Criteria that could well have been widened out to include him.

All in all, the week is beginning to suck, and the tanks are not exactly Marco's idea of fun. A couple more hours in the sack and he would have maybe felt a bit more up for the challenge. But Tee had said they needed to be on-site and ready to go early. Everyone would have heard the news last night, and Marco and Tee wouldn't be the only ones devising survival strategies. So, early it is.

Marco hates the tanks. He feels that, surely, if you drowned once, you should avoid unnecessary exposure to over-ambitious volumes of water at all times. It never ceased to amaze him that some WUs spent all their spare time dunked over their heads in saline solution. He had thought they had a screw loose, that perhaps they were trying to resolve some deep psychological issue. But now he's not so sure. Maybe, just like Tee, they realised lung capacity might be more valuable than knowing applied trigonometry. Marco's just going to have to get on with it. Besides, he has another reason for spending his hard-earned Saturday back at the academy; the computer in the tank room logs into the mainframe, and the mainframe is faster and more up to date than domestic portals. If there had been an update on Molly, it could well be buried somewhere in that mainframe system.

Inside the wide, marble entrance hall, it's quiet as a grave. Tee smiles at the security guard.

'How's Claudie?'

The guard makes a so-so face.

'Two more weeks. She'll be glad when it's done.'

'Claudie?' Marco hisses.

'Stan's wife. She's having a hip replacement. Man, do you ever look up from your abacus?'

'It's a calculus program. You know that.'

'Yeah. Well, I'm not a science star, remember? But you should know about Claudie.'

Marco looks puzzled.

Tee sighs, 'Not literally. Not just Claudie. Be nice to the people you meet on the way up; you may have need for them on the way down.'

Marco's beginning to realise something about his friend; Tee sees things differently. Tee doesn't have the comfort blanket of academia to cling to. But despite his pranks and give a f*** attitude, Tee is making his own plans. And who's to say which way is going to work best?

But when they get to the door for the tank room, they find themselves locked out.

'It always works.' Tee presses his hand once again on the control pad.

'Maybe we're too early?'

'Hey, I get here this time every time we don't have lessons.'

'Call it in.'

'No one will answer, not at this hour.'

Waste of time – Marco thinks to himself. He should have stayed in bed.

'Damn.' Tee presses his hand once again against the control pad. 'You're good with stuff like this, Marco.'

'Not electrical circuits. Not really.'

'Better than me.'

There's no way out of this. Marco is going to have to show willing. Besides, he's awake now.

'You got a pen, one of those with the metal clip that you hook on to a pocket?'

Tee looks confused. But he pulls one out of his bag.

'What you going to do, write out of order?'

'Maybe.' Marco says, pushing Tee gently out of the way so he can get to the controls. 'No promises.'

He pulls the metal clip flat, then pushes it gently into the casing.

'Don't break anything.' Tee says nervously.

'You want me to do this, or not?'

Tee says nothing. Marco slides the clip into the gap just a little further. The panel jolts slightly before sliding off.

Inside, it's basic circuitry. A thin red laser runs from the control panel to the locking system. But the flow has been broken.

'Here,' Marco removes a small piece of card. 'Primitive way of locking people out. Disrupt the connection.'

The red laser picks up its natural course, flowing towards the locking mechanism once again. They hear a soft automatic click as it reconnects.

Marco presses the panel back on and hands Tee back his pen. The clip sticking out at an awkward right angle.

'It'll just take a moment to update.'

'Who would do something like that?' Tee presses his hand against the pad. 'I mean, it's sabotage. It's…' But the chatter dries on Tee's lips as he stares wide-eyed at the information panel. 'We've got company.

'One of the professors?'

Tee shakes his head as he hits a few buttons. 'It's not a code I recognise.'

'So, someone is already in there?'

Tee nods, 'and trying to keep us out. Level two access?' He reads from the screen.

'No keeping those guys out.' Level two access is in limited supply. They have gold wristbands and access all areas. If you've got influential parents or are part of the council, you tend to get level two, no questions asked.

'Ezra Clark,' Tee reads, as the display panel spills out a little more information.

'Clark! Oh, boy.' Clark is one smug-arse individual that Marco has no desire to meet. He's a pit bull of a person. Fed on protein and privilege and always on the lookout for a way to rub a person's nose into his God-given sense of entitlement. He should be out working on the docks, unloading boats, but because his dad's high up in the pecking order, Ezra got his feet under the table on the next Mars mission. And more, Marco has no love for Ezra, not just because Ezra is a pain in the proverbial. But soil sciences and space sciences, they're kind of polar opposites, instinctively natural enemies; think about it, they're after way different end results. If you've got a fancy new space station, do you really need that old planet?

'Let's leave it,' Marco says, turning to go.

'He shouldn't be here,' Tee mutters. 'This is my area. And

he tried to bugger up the controls. Ezra Clark can come back later.'

In truth, there should be enough room for all of them: there are ten tanks. But they both feel Ezra has kind of cramped their style.

'What's he doing here?'

Tee shakes his head.

'Practice?'

'Ezra?' Tee lets out a short *and-pigs-fly* snort.

And Tee's right. Ezra won't need the practice. Being related to a council member means you get a kind of get-out-of-jail-free. Most of the Relies are as thick as two short planks. But they're indigenous, and never on any repatriation lists. So, if Ezra's not concerned that his name's going to be on the list, why would he be doing early morning tank practice?

'Maybe he's trying to build up lung capacity?' Marco tries. 'I mean, it's got to be useful for space travel. There's no oxygen on Mars.'

But although the explanation is plausible, neither of them finds it convincing. Knowing Ezra, it's more likely that he's up to no good.

CHAPTER 8
EZRA

THE ROOM IS BATHED in the same blue watery light it always wears, and since it's so early, the only sounds are the constant slap slap of water. Like a slow sarcastic slap. It's almost like the tanks are mocking Marco. He can't help but shiver as he stares up at the gargantuan vats. Four are empty. Their temperature varies, but very little else: the induction tanks. Then there are the practice tanks. These have obstacles in them. It might be the cross-section of a boat or building, or maybe just shopping carts, old shoes, pretend bodies. The three furthest tanks even have pirates' treasure chests. When the WU were kids, they liked these tanks best. Now, no one bothers visiting the chest. Texicom soon got bored of sending divers down to hide *delights*. For the past seven years, they've been empty. You have to use your imagination and imagination applied to anything other than survival is in short supply.

The last two tanks are the 'organic tanks.' The first has weed and a few small fish, nothing over a metre. The final tank in the room is the one that really puts shivers down Marco's spine. The designers got just that little bit over-ambitious when it came to day ten of tank creation. It's interactive.

The far wall is backed by a steel shutter and can be raised or lowered. On a day-to-day basis, the wall is down; but when they want to do 'simulations,' the metal shutter gets taken up. It's a vast doorway to the outside; the world beyond the Levee. It doesn't go directly out to the ocean. There are always barriers within barriers. Supposedly, the first area is defended, kind of like a swimming pool fed by the sea.

Marco has always avoided going in this final tank. It's not just the proximity to the sea that bothers him; there's a giant octopus in there. Six feet long, last time he heard. The octopus can leave if it chooses, but somehow it never does. Marco often wonders if perhaps the octopus has an ulterior motive, if it doesn't like watching the 'show.' The last throes of humanity. *Roll up. Roll up. See human destruction from the comfort of your own personal ringside seat. Now you see them, now you don't.*

Despite the readings from the wall monitor, there's no sign of Clark.

'You think maybe he forgot to sign out?'

Tee shakes his head. 'The operating system logs you out automatically.'

'Well, he's not here now.'

But Tee's not happy. 'Then his name shouldn't even be on the panel. Ezra!' Tee calls out into the dappled gloom. There's no reply. Just the steady, gentle lap of mechanised waves.

'What the hell!' Tee snorts to one in particular as, irritated, he walks off down the row of tanks, glancing in at each one, scanning the narrow passageways between the giant vats.

'Look, Tee, if it's all the same to you, I'd rather go in one of the induction tanks.'

'Sure. That's what I had planned.' Tee glances around the room; there's no one there. 'Okay. Let's get you signed in.' He pulls two swivel chairs up to the last desk in the room. They sit, backs to the water, but Marco can't help giving a sly glance over his shoulder.

'Is the octopus still in there?'

Tee nods. 'Finbow. Named after the CEO, though don't tell him. The director that is - you can tell the octopus anything. Lots of similarities, an arm in every pie.'

Marco looks into the inky, deep-blue water behind. He can't see anything, but he's pretty sure that's because it doesn't want to be seen.

'Right, blood pressure first,' Tee announces as he brings up a practice screen..

Marco hands over his wrist with the wristband on, and Tee puts Marco's arm into the reader. Immediately, Marco's vitals appear on the screen. Tee runs an expert eye over them.

'You need to lower that a bit.'

'My blood pressure? I thought it was…'

'Normal? It is. On the button. But we're aiming for low.'

Marco nods.

'Running will do it. Treadmill. You need to put down that calculator.'

'Actually, I'm…'

But Tee's not interested in the soil sciences project. He likes to be able to pigeonhole people. Maths geek is where he wants to put Marco, so for the moment at least, that's what Marco will have to be.

'Okay,' Tee relaxes back into his chair, entering the last bits of information. 'All looks fine. I think first we should…'

But Tee's words are cut short by a sound at the entrance. Footsteps.

'You hear that?'

Tee's on his feet. 'Wait here.'

'But Tee?'

'Just hold on. Five minutes.' Tee walks back down the length of the tanks. 'Yeah?' he's calling out into the empty room. 'Hello?'

He disappears out of sight.

'Great,' Marco mutters under his breath, gazing at the

screen in front of him, hoping this will not take long. He can hear the murmur of voices from the other side of the room, but the content of the conversation is swallowed, muffled by the tanks. He could go and look but ... There's a laugh, a short, sharp, sardonic burst. Ezra, Marco thinks. He has no desire to get involved. Instead, he stares at the screen. This is a waste of time. He should be back home doing revision. Then he remembers, he had something else he wanted to do. He can get into the mainframe. Molly. He tucks his chair tighter under the desk and types into the screen: *Repatriation Log*, then stops dead as the last repatriation file opens in front of him. Row after row of disembodied names. He had been so preoccupied with Molly; he hadn't fully realised the scale of the operation. But surely, Repatriation must know what they were doing. This was their department. If the numbers were up, well, maybe that's the way things had to be. Maybe. He scans down the list. There it is: Molly WU.

And on the repatriation file, the box next to Molly's name is empty. She's a no-show. This is what's bothering Marco. It just doesn't make any sense. There's nowhere for her to go. No-shows are normally found pretty quickly after the initial repatriation process. Sometimes it's accidents. Other times, people top themselves. There were always a handful who went Off Grid. But it was a minority. The fear of plague kept people away from an Off Grid existence. Plague was supposedly rife in the OG community. But it's unusual for a no-show to stay present on the file for a full forty-eight hours.

Marco opens the video channels. All those repatriated can be contacted for two weeks after they leave. They're in the holding centres on the ships. Maybe there's been a computer error, and Molly is already there? He looks down at the video list. Around sixty percent of the repatriated have already been active; they've had some kind of communication with a loved one. Then he notices – Molly's name is on the list; she's available for broadcast. So there is a glitch! She's gone through the system, but they've forgotten to mark her off. He feels a sense of relief flood over him. Nobody wants to be repatriated, but nobody wants to end up out of the system either.

It's early, only just seven in the morning. Marco can hear Tee talking to Ezra down by the entrance. Tee does not sound happy; they could be a while. Marco presses his finger against the ID pad. There's time for a quick chat. He ticks the box next to Molly. 'Activate.' He hears the dial tone ringing out from some speck in the middle of the ocean. At least she'll be able to tell him what it's like. She's the first person Marco's known well enough to be chosen as a nominee for their communication list. Everyone can allocate up to two people. Molly had picked Marco and Gran.

'Molly?'

The pixels form into Molly's familiar face. Even at 7.00 in the morning, she's ready to take on the world, made-up and full of fire. He's not sure if it's something she was born with or something that got fanned into existence by Gran. Either way, staring at this confident young woman on the screen, he can't quite believe he's been worried sick about her – Molly can take care of herself. But there's something odd – her clothes.

'Hey, Marco!'

He sighs 'What's with the sack?' She's wearing a shapeless beige tunic.

There's an uncertain pause.

'Your clothes. Sack?' Still no recognition. 'Not your style. The clothes.'

'Oh, standard issue. Saves on laundry.'

'Really?' Molly is no way a 'standard-issue' clothes kind of a girl. 'That's coming from someone who used to personalise her pants?' It was true. Magic marker slogans, before the magic markers all ran dry.

Again, that slight delay.

'Sorry?'

'You know when you got the magic markers and...' but she's looking blank. Besides, there's a delay to his voice, and this is no way what he wants to be talking about. 'Girl, you really had me worried.'

'Oh?'

'You're no-show on the system.'

'Right?'

'But you're okay?'

'I'm doing good.'

'Great. What's it like?'

'Fine. Kind of sunny out here ocean-side. We haven't been processed yet, but they're treating us well. We have real food.'

'Not cartons?'

'Real deal.'

The sound of a high-pitched alarm blares in the background.

'Look, Marco, I've got to go. We've got inductions in half an hour.'

'Right?'

'Yeah. Lot of bureaucracy.'

'Some things never change.'

'But, Marco, I'm really happy.'

'Great.'

'Don't you go worrying.'

And with that, the image fades. Molly pixelates into a thousand pieces, and the screen goes dim.

She's happy. They're feeding her. The sun is shining. Yet despite the contact, Marco can't help but feel ... dissatisfied. Odd that she didn't mention gran? Maybe they had already spoken? But then, on the communication list, it states that Molly hadn't had any other contact. If you're not on the mainframe, it's unlikely that you'd get through. Somewhere deep inside, he can't help feeling uneasy. Marco stares into the inky blackness of the sleeping monitor, then realises – the screen is not black. There's something in the centre, a swirl, an image, a figure, a girl. There's a girl moving in the darkness. He can't make out all her features, just an angelic face, swirling in a mass of ribbons. As he watches, she lets one finger stretch out towards him, as if pointing at him. Then suddenly he realises; she's not on the screen. This is a reflection. There is a young woman in the tank behind him, pointing right at him.

He turns sharply towards the wall of water. There she is – dappled light playing across her body. She's like a mermaid but without the tail. Luminous white and framed by a mass of red wispy hair: the ribbons. Her hand is extended towards the tank wall, and him. Marco moves closer, captivated. She has the greenest eyes he has ever seen. The light plays in white bands over her body, which is wrapped in a skin-tight one-piece the exact same colour as her pale face. He puts his fingers against the glass so that their hands touch. The girl smiles, a bubble escaping her pink, etched lips. He's seen people swimming before in the tanks. He must have seen thousands of kids submerged, but this girl is wearing no weights. She appears so natural in the water, like she's a part of it.

Suddenly, there's a loud metallic clank; the lift gate is being opened. A hard ripple passes through the tank.

'No way. This is completely against all the rules.' It's Tee. His voice laced with hardcore irritation. Marco can't see him, but he's guessing that Tee is getting into the lift.

The girl swims effortlessly away without a backward glance, and Marco feels his heart sink – who is she?

'I can do what I want. The tests are just for people like WU.' There's someone else getting into the lift with Tee. Marco would know that voice anywhere, Ezra Clark, arrogant as always.

There's a second loud clank as the lift door closes. Why would Tee and Ezra be going up in a lift together? There's a mechanized whir as the lift mounts to the standing platform.

Their voices are lost. Marco walks quickly along the edge of the tank, peering up. Wondering what the hell is going on?

Then he sees the girl again. She's floating right beside him. Her head held at an angle as if listening to something far above. He would love for her to look around again, to move to the glass, to press her hand once more to his. But he's not even sure she's aware that he's there. Suddenly, a tunnel of bubbles appears through the water. Someone is in and sinking down fast towards the girl. When the bubbles clear, Marco realises that it's Tee. He's standing on the bottom of the tank, fully dressed, a couple of weights held in his hands.

He says something to the girl. You can communicate underwater. They all do basic training: submerged communication. It's not like regular conversation. They use a limited vocab, so it's more a case of listening and recognising, rather than having in-depth conversations. Marco doesn't need to have studied it much to know that a vertically pointed index finger means 'up.' And a vertically pointed index finger, thrust three times up in quick succession means: 'get yourself up now, quick.' The conversation, though, is very one-sided. It's all Tee and, despite the water and the tank and the distance, Marco can tell Tee's not happy. The girl doesn't talk back. No words, no gestures. Marco has no idea how long she's been down there, but there's a good chance that she's low on oxygen. So the fact that she's not talking doesn't mean that she doesn't have plenty she would like to say. He can see this much clearly in her eyes.

Marco runs to the lift. If there's a problem, he's on the wrong side of the glass.

He can still see the tank. He can see as Tee holds out one hand to the girl, but the girl shakes her head in disdain. The girl is refusing to surface. Marco wonders, as he presses the ascent button, should he call someone? But he can see Ezra's feet planted on the metal grill of the platform above. If there's a problem, surely Ezra would have called it in?

The lift whirs into action, carrying Marco up just as Tee lets the weights drop, grabs hold of the girl's waist and, hugging her tight, swims back up. The girl struggles, but Tee only holds on tighter. Must have been taking lessons from that octopus, Marco thinks, as he breaks through to the standing platform; breaks through at the exact same time as Tee and the girl arrive at the surface. She barely takes a breath for oxygenation. She's filling her lungs, which Marco has no doubt must have an impressive capacity, and flinging out insults.

'You idiot. You know how long I've been under?'

'Thirty minutes, doll.' Ezra says, clicking off his timer.

'I'm not your doll,' she says, the words barely audible. The anger has taken most of the volume out of her. Tee and the girl lean arms and upper body on the platform, like ship-wrecked sailors. The girl's breathing coming in short, sharp, hungry bursts.

'You cannot go down if you don't have a support network. Not in that suit.' Tee's voice is calm, his words enunciated, but Marco can tell he's seething.

'Funny,' Ezra says, a sneer on his face, and everyone knows that there is nothing about this situation which is in any way amusing. 'Actually, I can do what I want.' Ezra stares arrogantly down at the two wet bodies in front of him, his lip curled as he addresses Tee directly. 'WU, you have really overstepped your jurisdiction here.'

He's using WU as an insult. People like Ezra often do, but Tee has a thick skin. He also knows he's in the right. 'I've overstepped! No way. She's not even in the system,' Tee says, a note of utter disbelief in his voice. 'You have to log in. And that suit...'

The girl has pulled herself out of the water, and Marco realises that the suit is making a strange hissing sound.

'They're prototypes. Someone has to be with her at all times.'

'Hey, I was…'

'You went to get a coffee! And you jammed the door. You jammed the entry door!' Tee shakes his head in disbelief.

'Why don't you mind your own business, Tee.' The girl grabs a towel, and Marco suddenly realises who it is. It's Portia Reynolds. His mouth must have fallen open just a little bit too far, as the very next second she's turning her anger on him.

'And what in the hell do you think you're gawping at?'

'You just look…

'Don't tell me… you didn't recognise her without her clothes on,' Ezra sneers.

'Really?' Portia shoots Ezra a withering gaze, but he just laughs.

'Sorry, I just…' Marco tries to explain, but what is wrong with him? He's falling over his words, stuttering. He remembers how Molly used to stutter, and his gran would say, *take a deep breath, let the words out slow and simple like a train, all those carriages in line.*

'I just didn't recognise you,' he mumbles, embarrassed.

'Yeah well,' Ezra bites back. 'Recognise us next time. If we're in here, you two aren't. Come on Portia, let's leave the losers.' Ezra slips a protective arm around Portia's shoulders, and they walk towards the lift, leaving Tee huffing and puffing in anger, muttering to himself about protocol and regulations, and it not mattering who you are. But Marco just watches them go, finding it difficult to take his eyes off the girl. And he can't help but feel a wave of satisfaction when Portia pulls away slightly from Ezra like she wants to put a bit of distance between them. She may have been diving with Ezra, but Marco gets the feeling Portia is on nobody's team.

CHAPTER 9
FORGOTTEN PHONE

'TAKE NO NOTICE.'

This is new. This is a total role reversal. Marco reassuring Tee? They're beside the practice tanks. Marco's been diving all morning. He's exhausted, and he's only got three minutes. Not even up to his four-minute all-time best. So surely, it's Marco who should be feeling low? Surprisingly, he just feels irritated. But Tee? Tee is so moody he can barely crack a sentence, let alone a smile.

'Ezra doesn't have the authority,' Tee says bitterly.

Marco sighs. They've been going over the same ground all morning. 'Look, why don't I try one of those suits, the kind Portia was wearing?'

Tee laughs, and for once Marco's glad to see Tee hasn't lost his sense of humour, even if it is at Marco's expense.

'That's advanced stuff.'

'Where are the weights?'

'In the fabric. The weight's activated by water. Deactivated by air. They allow much more freedom of movement, but...'

Tee looks irritated again. 'It's a two-person job. You go down there; you can't physically get yourself back up. Someone has to go in after you.'

'And Ezra went to go get himself a coffee?'

Tee says nothing, just raises one eyebrow in irritation.

'You stick to the hand weights, Nautilus.'

'But it just doesn't sound safe – suits you can't activate yourself?'

'Part of the problem with diving is trust. The body doesn't want you to drown. It's hard-wired to get you back up, get more air into those lungs, whatever the cost. When you're in the air-suits, you know that isn't an option. A whole mental possibility gets taken out of the equation. There's no way you can get back to the surface. You have to become part of the water.'

Marco remembers the organic way Portia had moved through the tank. How at peace she looked. How, somehow, right.

'And when you want to come up?'

'You give a sign. Then your buddy goes down and hauls you up. And Ezra had gone to get himself a coffee!' Tee shakes his head in frustration. 'Idiot. Anyway, this is getting us nowhere fast. Down you go Aquaman; one more for the road.'

Marco sinks down, grabs the weights, and gets himself into lotus, then he clears his mind, pushes it all out, every little last bit of thought has to go. He thinks of Sanderling's workshop, of the sound of the clocks, that ever-comforting tick-tock, tick-tock. Of being safe and secure, and home. The next time he looks at the clock outside the tank, it reads five minutes. He's done it. Tee signals a quick thumbs-up, a wide grin plastered across his face: Marco has beaten his personal best. A weekend of study and he could get those grades back up. Marco is still in the game.

•   •   •

'You did good, man.' Tee calls above the drone of the showers.

'Good! Tee, five minutes! That's got to be more than *good*.' Marco grabs a towel and sets off to the dressing rooms.

'Man, we all change here. More sociable. The instructors hog the dressing rooms anyway, especially Vikdendar.'

Marco bristles at the name.

Leila Vikdendar was one of the few female ocean sciences instructors. Second-generation Norwegian. Her parents had all been Olympic medalists. How old she was, well, that was anyone's guess. She'd pumped herself so full of the latest must-have face filler that she kind of looked like a pumpkin, her eyes sinking back into her skull. Rumour had it, she was so buoyant she couldn't dive any more. Some of the other WU's thought she was beautiful, with her long blonde hair and ice-blue eyes. But Marco isn't convinced.

'Fine by me,' he says, toweling off. He's in no hurry to meet the ice dragon. She has the body and stamina of an action hero, the kind you meet in a game and hope is on your side.

'You still mad at Ezra?' Marco asks, rubbing his hair dry.

Tee says nothing.

'Report him.'

'The son of a council member. That'll go down well.'

'He shouldn't have been here. And jamming the door! He was working against protocol.'

Tee picks up a weight that's been abandoned on the floor; it's not one Marco used. Tee glances at it with mild disgust. 'And this. Couldn't even be bothered to clear up after themselves.'

'Let me dry off, and I'll help.'

'Not the point.'

Tee pulls a towel from a bench, and as he does, a handset goes skittering across the floor.

'Damn.' He picks it up. Luckily, it wasn't smashed. 'Yours?'

Marco shakes his head.

Tee presses the com button. *Portia Reynolds* flashes up on the screen.

'Well...' Tee shakes his head, irritated. 'If they think I'm running around town after them.' He glances at the pulsing dot, telling them exactly where Portia is. 'Museum of Human History.'

And it's out of Marco's mouth before he's given his brain a chance to catch up. 'I could just drop it over on my way home.'

Tee shoots him a *'really?'* look, but says nothing, just passes the handset over.

Phone in hand, Marco's heading for that door.

'Oh and, Marco?' Tee calls him back. 'Museum of Human History?' Tee gives him a long hard stare. 'On your way home?'

CHAPTER 10

HUMAN HISTORY

THERE ARE three museums at the plaza: Planetarium, Aquarium and Human History. According to the large sign at the base of the plaza, each and every one is currently sponsored by Texicom. The ubiquitous logo shines out in silver lights through the grey mist. It used to be the council logo, but it seems to Marco that the council is losing interest in pretty much everything these days, everything apart from repatriation.

Maybe Marco hasn't visited the museum before, but he knows the score. The Planetarium is the large, white dome, reminiscent of a nuclear power station.

The Aquarium has a tank on the outside; some days you can see a baby whale shark swimming sadly in the window. The Museum of Human History is a large, sealed box with no windows.

It's quiet here, nothing like the throng of the public areas. The plaza is zone-protected: green wristbands and above only. Maybe that's why he's never been. If he'd tried to get into the plaza with Molly or Gran, their wristbands would have given them that short, sharp electric shock. It's how the posh areas kept *posh*. Yellows could get in overnight. Well, someone had to clean the place, but Gran and Molly cleaned council offices, so they'd only seen the museums in pictures. Though he probably wouldn't have come anyway. 'Not a black face in the building,' according to Gran.

Marco puts his tie on the outside of his shirt, and even though it's raining, he takes down his hood and smoothes his hair flat. He doesn't want trouble. At a brisk jog, he takes the wide, stone staircase, glazed and shimmering wet like a smeared mirror, as it winds up towards the Museum of Human History. He knows he's supposed to be impressed by the sheer size of the thing, its gravity-defying design; the building is elongated at the top, so the closer you get, the more it looms out over you till, eventually, it blocks out a portion of the sky. 'Look at us,' it says all over its blank face, without one word of inscription. 'Aren't we clever? Aren't we big? Aren't we here for the long term?' But Marco knows the jury is still out on that one.

Checking Portia's phone as he moves towards the building, he sees that, according to the small red dot, Portia is still there, standing static somewhere in the museum. Without even thinking about it he does this odd, berky thing, he puts his thumb gently over the dot. Like he's drawing her closer to him. Like? What an idiot! He has to stop that kind of stuff before it starts. She's out of his league. He doesn't like leagues. He doesn't believe in them. But that doesn't mean that if there were leagues, she wouldn't be way out of his. He could put a call out at the desk, have her name tannoyed across all levels. He's not slowing his pace. The building is coming up quick. He could. He could do all of that non-contact stuff. Equally, he could just get a grip. Besides, if he hands the phone in, it kind of defeats the whole purpose. Its job is done, and Marco's wish to give Portia her phone back is not really, not exactly, not anything to do with getting the immediate job done. He just can't help himself. She's heart-rush blood-pumping addictive. He wants more, more contact, more conversation, more Portia.

Inside the vast atrium, glad to be out of the drizzle, Marco flicks through the museum handbook. He soon discovers Gran was wrong about the collection; there are in fact five persons of colour on display. One woman, four men. One football player, one astronomer, an oncologist who discovered a cure for bowel cancer, a nutritionist who currently dictates all the city's nutritional requirements, and Elena Cobey.

Elena Cobey predicted correctly that on March fourth two thousand and thirty, two meteorites would graze the earth, and knock it marginally, almost imperceptibly, off its trajectory. She should have been hailed as a hero, but sadly for Elena - and the rest of the planet – no one listened.

If he takes the lift, he should hit the media section without too much trouble. He heads towards the shiny, steel doors, puts his ticket against the reader, and the lift door slides open.

'Second floor. Media,' he announces. At this point, the doors <u>should</u> slide shut. The map of the building <u>should</u> be displayed, and the little green dot that is the lift <u>should</u> be seen shooting along, right, left, and up two floors. But instead, the lift gives a lurch and drops down two levels.

'What!'

The doors slide open, revealing the basement cold, dark and devoid of life.

Marco presses his ticket against the reader again.

'Please take the stairs,' he's informed by the operating system in a syrupy-tech, disinterested voice.

'Actually, I wanted to take the lift,' he mumbles, pressing the ticket once again on the reader.

'Please take the…'

It's futile.

'Yeah, I know, stairs, stairs.'

Reluctantly, Marco steps out into the basement. It smells of trapped, long forgotten air. The sweeping statement stairs of the atrium have gone. This is all second staircase stuff, spiral, thin and dark, like an afterthought. The only way out is at the other end of the room, about twenty meters away. To get there, he needs to walk down a winding pathway through a series of *witnesses*: holographs; portrayals of the great, the good and the famous, all set neatly in their very own personal diorama type affair. It's kind of creepy. They're illuminated, moving just a little, like ghosts trapped in sealed bottles. You need to press the button to activate them. He could do without any of this, but *what the hell*, Marco thinks to himself. He's paid for his ticket. Might as well get his money's worth.

He follows the path through darkness the colour of stewed tea, glancing at the witnesses' faces. He's good at history. It's not exactly hard, just people, places and dates, mixed up with a whole shedload of interpretation. But even though he's always had a fair-sized grip on the subject, he doesn't recognise any of these guys. The basement must be where heroes go to be forgotten.

The holographs were installed about four years ago. Originally, the witnesses were automatons. Some made by Sanderling. Despite himself, and his ingrained loyalty to Sanderling, Marco can't help being impressed by the new, improved witness design. Sanderling's automata, although strangely beautiful, has an awkward, jerky movement which kind of makes them look surreal, like some primitive kid's toy trying to spout words of wisdom. The content seems way too fancy for the container. The holographs, in comparison, are as seamless as human beings. Perhaps more so. They don't stutter or get distracted. They use real clips of speech, though often these have been edited, the waffling bits, hesitations and false starts left out. There's a slight translucence on the bodywork, but stand two meters away, and you would be hard pushed to tell a holograph from a human.

He's midway through the room when he sees her, stuck right in the corner, in the dark: Elena Cobey. The woman everyone failed to listen to. She's long dead now. These days Elena is a 4D holograph. According to the blurb on the electronic ticket, she's switched on at nine every morning but Sunday and switched off at five thirty p.m. every day. Apart from Thursday, when she can be persuaded to talk until eight. Though, being basement level, and occupying the darkest corner in the room, Marco feels that, in an ironic twist of fate, Elena's words are still easy to miss.

'Elena. Still lacking an audience, I see?' Marco mumbles, stopping bang-smack in front of her and leaning forwards to press the green button because, although he knows the story inside out and upside down, he's curious to hear Elena's take on it.

'It doesn't work.'

Marco jumps out of his skin. Only being held in by the fact that he's so embarrassed, bordering on terminally mortified, to be caught talking to himself!

He turns sharply. There's a woman sitting in the shadows behind him. She's half-hidden in the darkness but, even so, there's something familiar about her.

She gets up slowly and walks over to the barrier so that she's standing beside him, her shoulder in line with his. The dim light from Elena's exhibit catching the woman's face. She's around five eight, neatly turned out. And Marco knows her, he is sure he knows her. But he just can't place her.

'You familiar with the story?' she asks, and he wonders if she's a curator, here to help when the projections fail.

Marco nods. 'Sure.' He's all too painfully aware of the mundane-and-many *investigations* into how Elena's predictions could have been so fatally overlooked.

'Studied to death, first year of high school. *Lest we forget,* type stuff.'

'If the council had listened to Elena, missiles could perhaps have been engaged and might, perhaps, have exploded the comets before impact. Which could, maybe, have averted the current situation.'

She's doing that 'neutralising history' thing, slipping in all those 'perhaps' and 'maybes' and codiciled 'could haves' – museum staff, Marco thinks to himself.

'I'm Mia,' the woman says, fixing him with her soft, green eyes.

'We've met before?' Marco asks uncertainly. At this point, he hopes she's going to jump in, give him a clue. But she says nothing, not even bothering to affirm, deny, or question.

'You lecture at the academy?' He asks. Maybe that's it. Maybe she's history.

The woman smiles a small, wry smile that Marco is left on the other side of the non-understanding side.

'I've read the white paper,' Marco adds. 'The one the council commissioned.'

'To discover why Elena's voice got... overlooked?'

He nods.

'Sometimes it's not enough to just listen. It's important to hear. It's important to act.'

Marco suddenly feels uncomfortable. Are they still talking about Elena and the council? He's not so sure. Besides, the gallery is completely empty, and this woman that he can't place but knows for sure he has met before, well, her tone... it's kind of... odd, unsettling.

'I should go. Meeting a friend,' he says, which is kind of true.

The woman takes a headscarf from her pocket and fixes it around her head as she wanders back towards the lift.

'It's out of order,' he calls after her. 'Have to use the stairs,'

But the woman doesn't seem concerned.

'It was good to talk. Next time we'll have longer. We could do with someone on the inside. Your work – Landersly's work – ocean terraforming, it's of interest. When the time comes, we may call on you.'

Now he is really lost.

'For the museum?'

She smiles knowingly as she presses a pass-card against the lift panel and, oddly enough, the lift arrives.

'We'll tell you what we want you to do.'

'Sorry I…'

'We are living in a bed of lies, Marco Obademi.'

He feels his jaw drop. Standing fish-mouthed is not exactly a look he's trying to perfect, but sometimes the moment will let you do little else. No one has called him Obademi, not even Gran, not for years.

'Wait, how did you…?' He moves towards her, but the lift has already opened its wide-mouth doors behind her, and she's stepping in.

'Sooner or later, it will be time to wake up. You're either with us, or…'

She doesn't fill in the last part, and she doesn't need to, because he knows where it goes. The lift doors slide shut, slicing between them, and suddenly he remembers she was the protestor at the repatriation ceremony! She was the woman chaining slogans to the railings. But what the hell is she doing here? And more to the point, how does she know his name? And even, how come the lift is suddenly working?

CHAPTER 11
ALL THE GOOD MEN

WITHOUT THE LIFT, finding the media section is not exactly easy. Add to this the fact that Marco's brain is still in a free-fall spin from the basement encounter, and Marco is getting nowhere fast. The walls of the museum are semi-permanent, taken down, replaced, or twisted into any and every which way with each new witness arrival.

Sadly, Marco appears to have found himself in the space sciences arena. And who should he have the misfortune to bump into but Marty Clark, Ezra's uncle. The only plus side? It's not the real Marty. Marty is still alive and kicking. *Persons of note* are awarded witness simulation during their lifetime. Despite himself, Marco can't help being impressed by the likeness; the witness is every inch as smug and superior as the real deal. There's Marty standing at his desk, itching to show off the designs for <u>his</u> space station. Truth be told, Marco has zilch interest in Marty and his plans. He gets way more than enough *guardians of the universe* rubbish in the cafeteria and feels an irresistible temptation to lean forward into the exhibition and flick Marty's ear.

The display has Texicom logoed so liberally over it, it's like wallpaper, the suit, the desk, the monitor. Space sciences had been the first place Texicom 'officially' put their money. Forward looking, that's how Texicom liked to think of themselves. Forward-looking, opportunistic-in-the-event-of-disaster, spookily on the ball, unnervingly ready to pick up the pieces. All of the above. Marco doesn't need to read the blurb to know exactly what space sciences, and Texicom, have on the agenda – exodus, though maybe not of biblical proportions. Moses' ideals for the egalitarian movement of the masses have kind of gone out the window. If you're not bright and brilliant, there's no place for you on the Marty transit. The academy was also funded by Texicom. The government seemed to be handing the city over bit by bit. And that was bad as far as research was concerned. Texicom ploughed way more resources into Space than they did Soil or Ocean. So, the results were warped. It looked like space had this great future that was almost within their reach. That wasn't the only bit that got to Marco. The bit that really gets Marco, the bit that sticks in his throat like a shattered glass sandwich, is that the earth is marked as disposable. That's the fundamental difference between earth and space sciences, and it's major. Marco's seen pictures of how it used to be; the forests full of plants and animals, the oceans teeming with life, polar bears living way far out there in no-man's land, just them and the penguins. Shouldn't mankind be trying its hardest to get it back, to reverse the damage, rather than escape?

He looks at the handset. The red Portia dot is still pulsing. Yeah, yeah, like anyone would seriously ask him for his opinion anyway. He leans in and flicks Marty's ear.

———

The media display is even more of an afterthought than the basement. It has an unloved, unwanted feeling like it's no longer relevant. There are a few artefacts; an old printing press, a typewriter – the kind with keys you press and a ribbon that spools from side to side. Some original newspapers, printed on real paper, though they're behind glass cases now, illuminated by special light frequencies that won't bleach the ink from the page.

The witness section itself stands in a cramped corner, annexed out of sight behind a partition wall. Marco glances again at the handset. Yup, he's almost there. He feels his heart quicken, and suddenly his knees feel more jelly than bone and cartilage. What does he say to her? 'Here's your phone,' 'thanks,' end of. He didn't come halfway across town just for that. He wishes he'd had the chance to do a quick overhaul in front of the mirror. He takes off his tie, stashes it in his pocket, takes a deep breath, cupping his hand over his mouth, breathing into his palm to check for toxic. It's A-okay. This is it. But as Marco draws closer to the annexe, disappointment shreds through his veins. He can hear two voices; a young woman – Portia? and a man – Ezra? They were together this morning. His heart sinks. Doesn't it just stand to reason they would have headed from the tanks to the museum together? Of course. Looks like Ezra got himself a day pass. *Why don't you come meet my dad* - type deal. Always the same. Isn't it just always the same with these people?

If Ezra is there… Marco fingers the phone in his pocket… maybe he'll just turn back. Head out before he's seen. He can leave the phone at reception, get them to do the whole tannoy-call thing. He has no intention of getting another dose of the Clark fraternity, not today. He'll just peek from the shadows. He rounds the door with a mountain of contingency plans race-tracking through his brain. But in an instant, all his head noise has its plug well and truly pulled; there she is, looking more beautiful, more ghostly, more haunting than ever. And even better, miracle of miracles, there's no Ezra. But he doesn't rush in. There's something about her manner that says do-not-disturb. For starters, Portia is on the wrong side of the barrier. She's actually in the exhibition, so her father, Abe, is walking around her, sometimes through her. And there's something about her face, the sadness Marco sees in it, that makes him think he's stumbled on a moment so intensely private, like catching someone sleeping or praying. He feels, if he steps forward, her whole world might shatter into a thousand tiny pieces that he will never, ever, be capable of putting back together again.

So Marco loiters behind the partition, watching, while the witness that is Abe Reynolds delivers his speech in a voice so filled with gravel it could have re-tarmacked the entire planet pre-disaster. Abe Reynolds is the kind of man, even in simulation, that it's difficult to ignore.

'Democracy,' he's saying, 'is not always a good thing.'

Marco wishes he'd caught the earlier bit. It looks, from the timeline illuminated on the display panel, as though the speech is heading towards its finale. Then Marco notices something else, something underlying the soundtrack. To his surprise, Marco realises that Portia is not listening to her father. She's kind of mumbling something, coming in quick and sharp after Abe's words. He strains to catch the content.

'It can destroy a citizen's sense of community,' Portia mumbles. 'Even though we live in a democracy, as individuals, we must not abdicate our responsibilities as citizens.'

She barely finishes before Abe starts up again.

'There are other models. The East India Company, and now Texicom, offer alternatives.'

Texicom? Marco's not sure he's getting this. Can Abe Reynolds really be advocating rule by corporation?

He waits for more, but the lights on Abe begin to dim. The button on the barrier starts to blink. The show is pretty much over. Abe has finished his speech. Portia remains in situ, continuing quietly, deliberately, her words barely audible. 'Corporations are not citizens. There is no place for the buck to stop. They do not have souls. They should not be trusted.'

'Oh, I get it.' Marco could kick himself. He didn't mean to speak. It was just kind of a eureka moment, and the words were out of his mouth before he could put a zip on them.

Portia's face pales even whiter than the sheets of paper her father was so passionate about. She had no clue Marco was there hiding in the shadows like a… (and he has to be brutally honest here, seeing it all in a blinding instant from her perspective)… like a creep. Suddenly he feels foolish. She's embarrassed, not even meeting his eye. Plus, the fact that it looks like he's been stalking her, following her all day, two steps behind since the tanks.

'Get it? Somehow, I doubt that,' she mutters as she stands, zips her backpack and flings it across her right shoulder, climbing back over the barrier.

'I'm at the academy. Soil sciences.'

'Big-shot then.'

'I saw you this morning, in the tank.'

'And now here you are again.'

And she's turning on her heel, heading out of the door, carried off in a wave of disdain that will never allow him to be anything more than undesirable. He can't let her go.

'They edited his words.' Marco blurts out. 'Your dad.'

Portia slows. She doesn't turn she doesn't look at him, but the slow is one hell of a good start.

'He's supposed to be giving a warning,' Marco continues, 'not advocating corporate rule.'

She's stopped, she's not moving towards him, but she's not moving away.

'Sorry,' he offers. 'I didn't mean to startle you. Here…'

She turns to find his hand outstretched, her phone clutched loosely in his fingers. 'You left this at the tanks. In the changing room.'

'Oh, right.' Embarrassed, she leans forward to take the phone. Then it happens, just for a brief moment, a rush, a joy, a sensation that flicks through his body, carrying more electricity than a line of Tesla towers. And by the way she pulls the phone out of his hand. The way it slips, almost hitting the floor, the way she smiles when he dives down to catch it, he can tell she felt the spark too.

'Thanks ... again.' She's blushing, not meeting his eye, looking at the handset, as though it's got all the answers to just about everything.

'If you want to go in again, into the tanks, you should go in with Tee. Ezra's too...' Marco suddenly realises he doesn't have anything but insults queued up, ready and waiting on his tongue.

'Too much of an idiot?' Portia offers, staring right at him now with a challenging look on her face.

'No. Well...' he hesitates. 'Actually yeah... what you're doing, it's kind of... could be dangerous and Tee... he knows the ropes. Ezra...'

'Yeah, I know,' she smiles ironically. 'Ezra can be a total jerk. Okay. Next time I'll go with Tee.'

Interaction done. She's heading for the door. Helpful. That's all he is. That's how she's going to think of him: getting her phone back, apologising, giving her advice. He can work with *helpful*. Then it dawns on him – what a first-class idiot. What an absolute berk! He's just managed to get the girl he fancies a date with his best friend?!?

'Wait!' it maybe comes out just that tad too loud, too desperate, but it does the trick. She stops.

'I thought what you did, it was brave,' he blurts.

She looks puzzled.

'The question about the repatriation criteria, I thought it was brave of you to ask.'

'Oh right,' she sighs. 'Someone had to.'

'But... you mind me asking, why you?

She looks puzzled. 'Sorry?'

'Why...' he stumbles over his words, wishing he had thought it through, wishing he wasn't jumping both-feet-in unscripted. 'I mean you; you're safe. You don't need to draw attention to yourself. Why do it? Why ask?'

'Because we need to know.' She glances back towards her father, trapped inside his sealed ghost-bottle of a display.

'Dad … Dad would have asked. Freedom of the press… it's important. People have a right to know what's going on.'

She holds the phone up again and smiles sweetly – the pink-lipped variety. A genuine eye-flash, heart-racing, honest-to-goodness electric-charged smile.

'Thanks.' And she's gone.

CHAPTER 12
WAVING OR DROWNING

'MOLLY IS STILL no-show on the system. But she's on the mainframe.'

Gran looks blank.

'No doubt she'll be up on the domestic portal in the next couple of days.'

'No doubt.'

Marco's surprised there's not more interest. This is Molly they're talking about, Gran's all-time favourite subject. He's sorting through boxes; knelt on his knees in Gran's dark narrow hallway. The smell of stale food hanging in the air, cold long-forgotten pockets of dead happiness.

'Help yourself to whatever you think is worth the effort.' Gran shouts from the kitchen.

Is that it – no more Molly talk? Maybe it's Gran's way of coping.

'So, you finally did it…'

She's lost him now.

'…Went to *that* Museum of Human History?' Gran gives a full-body-shiver of disapproval.

'Actually Gran, it was okay. Saw Elena. They've got her in a bit of a tight corner.'

'Some things never change. That the reason you went?'

'No, in fact she wasn't working. At least … I think she wasn't working.' He pauses for a moment. Had Mia lied? He lets a pack of cards slip back into the box, which, in turn, sets a toy off on its lonesome chime from the past. They used to have it in the garden as kids. It had large windmill spokes that caught in the wind and wound the mechanism inside. London's burning. That was what it played. Could certainly do with a reboot!

'You sure you want to get rid of all this stuff?'

Gran just shrugs. 'Most important bit's gone.'

He couldn't argue with that. His fingers fix on a large, transformer style doll.

'Ha! Dr Krypto. Remember this?'

She raises one eyebrow. 'Remember, they cost me two weeks' wages a piece. You and Molly, you just had to have them. Then you slice the damn things open; stick the workings somewhere else.'

He looks at the back, the heads are open, the transmitters taken out.

'I put all the working bits in the watches,' he says.

'That be the thing you stopped wearing?' She puts a cup of bladderwrack tea down beside him. The warm, salty taste giving his nostrils a kick-start. He takes a sip. No one makes bladderwrack tea like Gran.

'And while you're at it.'

She hands him an old toaster.

'Promised Mary Wimbley down at number 44 you'd fix it.'

'Hasn't she got a toast-a-wave?'

Gran snorts. 'You think she's born of money? Can you do it or not?'

He looks at the toaster. Holds it to the side.

'You got any power sockets?'

She points to one on the wall. 'That one still works. Just about.'

He plugs the toaster in and slides down the lever at the side. The metal cages inside just bounce straight back up again like nothing's holding them.

'Probably the cord. I reckon it's not getting any power.'

'You can fix it?'

Marco shrugs. 'Need to take it home; it's easy enough. But Gran…' Why is she always pushing odd jobs his way! 'I'm supposed to be saving the planet, not…'

'How long will it take you to fix the toaster?'

'I don't know, get a new wire, half an hour maybe.'

'Then you got time to do both, save the planet, fix the toaster. Everyone's happy.'

Gran, she's got an answer for everything, which reminds him.

'You know any protestors?'

She fixes him suspiciously with her deep brown eyes.

'At the repat ceremony, there was this woman putting out placards. Then I saw her again in the museum.'

'White woman. Dark hair, five eight, forties. Blue headscarf?'

He nods.

'Saw her on the TV the day Molly was…' Gran's voice drops like she hasn't got the energy to keep the words up and running. She grabs a handkerchief from her pocket and disappears into it. 'Damn those synthetic onions! Been cooking with them all morning. You'd have thought some of your fancy boys would have been able to take the sting out of the damn things.' She puts the handkerchief back into her pocket. 'Mia Polanski. The woman you were just asking about. You went to see her at the museum?'

'No, she was just there.'

'Mia Polanski's never *just there*. You see her again, walk the other way, quick. She's trouble.'

'I had to drop a friend's phone back, she left it at the tank.'

'Oh?'

He wishes he hadn't started this now. 'Portia Reynolds.'

'Abe Reynolds' kid?'

'Yeah.' He's finding it hard not to smile; having to bite his lip down at the corners, even at the mention of her name.

'Friend?' Gran asks, half question, one-whole skeptical.

'She's at the academy. Ocean sciences.'

'Seems to me that girl's becoming mighty high-profile. On the TV just the other night.' Gran sniffs. 'Skinny white kid, asking questions.'

'Not questions, Gran, <u>the</u> question.'

But Gran's not having any of it. 'Causing trouble,'

'But people have a right to know.'

Gran gives him her long, seen-it-all done-it-all knowing eye. 'Marco, people don't go having any rights, not these days. An' those that aren't affected by repatriation, they sure as hell don't have the right to go asking willy-nilly about *our* destiny. You suppose those questions are important for *Ms Reynolds*?'

She says the Ms Reynolds in a way that sounds like there's someone on the inside of her nose, squeezing her nostrils together, hard – Gran's impression of posh. 'More like she's running her mouth off 'bout things that don't concern her. Trying to cause some kind of *sensation*.'

'I don't know, Gran. I think…'

But Gran's not listening. 'Portia Reynolds, and all those people like her, all the Golden Kids, Relies, Level Two access, council members, just about anybody I clean up after, 'cept my God damn self, they can afford to be mouthy as hell. You. People like you, people like me, we can<u>not</u> afford to be caught in the crossfire. We can't afford to have opinions.'

Marco snorts, not have opinions, that's rich coming from Gran. But his laughter's cut short.

'You listen to me, Marco, and you listen good. I choose when and where to open out my… opinions. I got a filter on my mind so tight, none of you science boys can get a look-in.

But I got to warn you, there are people flooding in now. The powers that be, they're going to be looking for scapegoats. Any reason to get you repatriated, they will use it, Clause Herbert...'

'Herbit,' he corrects. She always gets it wrong! He should have invited her to the awards ceremony. He'd ummed and ahhd about it, convinced himself she wasn't interested, but maybe he should have let her make her own mind up about that.

'Whatever.' Gran waves a dismissive hand. 'Point is, that award is not gonna help. Portia Reynolds, she'll be up there on the levee waving you goodbye with her pressed white handkerchief, nails all a painted, and her pretty, little, white feet warm and dry in those cashmere socks. Whilst you, you're heading out on some boat going God knows where. Stick with your own kind. Can't afford to lose anyone else. They try and repatriate you, you go to Sanderling. You understand? Straight to Sanderling.'

'I should go see him, anyway. It's just so busy at work.'

Gran snorts. 'You young people, too busy to live half the time.'

'Gran?'

'Marco?'

He has to ask, because it's weighing heavily on his soul.

'You think you're safe from repatriation? I mean, I was...' and he can't help but let the worry creep into his voice.

Gran looks up from her cup, a large grin shining like a sunrise across her face. 'Safe as houses.'

Marco's gobstruck by her confidence. This is a woman who flunked school. She's the lowest of the low on the operative list, but she's so certain she's safe?

'I put in for refugees. Molly's gone. You're not around. I've got room for two easy. Though, by the looks of the newsfeed, all those people pouring in, I'm betting they'll give me ten. Someone will need to look after all those kids.

Marco's amazed; it looks as though everyone has their survival plan in place. Everyone but him.

'Don't you go worrying about me,' Gran says, filling his teacup once again. 'You just make sure you keep those grades up.'

CHAPTER 13
THE REC

IT'S early evening and Marco finds himself standing at the long bar of the rec – recreation centre. A bright-lit, warehouse style, leisure hang-out. It's part of the academy: a restaurant, live music, the odd film. Bar stools cluster around high tables. There's even a basketball net on the wall. It's the default hangout for most academy students and staff.

It was set up to enhance cross-discipline cultivation, the idea that serendipity and inter-disciplinary contact can do wonders for free-wheeling innovation. Maybe it works, maybe it doesn't. Marco's heard that the toilets are bugged, and there are mics under all tables. But he doubts this. Not because of any moral issues, invasion of privacy stuff. More to do with manpower. If conversations are being taped by the great, the gorged and the land-grabbing, it's unlikely that there is anyone left on the operative work ladder to listen to the reels and reels of oh-so-pedestrian dialogue that a single hour at the rec is likely to generate.

Marco glances across the packed bar as he waits his turn on his drinks order. Most bars were automated now, but the rec, in keeping with its serendipitous high ideals, still has human bar staff. Not that this is an advantage as far as Marco's concerned. Getting hold of a drink on a busy night is near-on impossible. There's a pecking order, one that has absolute zilch to do with first-come-first-served. At the other end of the bar, Ezra Clark is ordering drinks for his mates. Ezra's in good spirits, his loud laugh projecting off the walls like a Barnes Wallace bouncing bomb. The fact that he's queue jumped, the loud laugh, the obscenely large round he's casually buying with his father's points, all of this is cause for irritation. But the real problem, the one that sticks in Marco's throat big time, is the cause of Ezra's glee. There was an announcement on the central intercom system late that afternoon; due to southern territory evacuation, a second repatriation would be facilitated. The leaderboard would be available that evening.

This was unusual: two repatriation lists in under a week. But Marco had seen pictures of the docks on the news; boats packed with live bodies. This was just the beginning. Maybe the authorities were thinking that a swift, sharp blade was better than a slow, blunt knife. Give people time to stew, and they might well serve you up a revolution.

So tonight, the rec is crowded to bursting. No one wants to be on their own when the news comes through. Most of the faces he recognizes, but there's a number he's not too sure about. There's something fresh and naïve about these new faces. They're not the pale forgotten features of those hidden away somewhere deep inside the compound, heads down for years untangling geo-scientific problems. These faces are all wide-eyed, washed and groomed, their mouths inadvertently held slightly open, goldfish style, as they listen intently to a 'buddy' – a member of the faculty staff that they might as well be physically attached to.

These are the *Gold-Sifted*. The threat. The first trickle of arrivals from the southern territories. The privileged few who are so renowned that they don't even need genetic verification. They're engineers, professors or promising students that were already on the city's *wish list*.

'They look innocent enough.' It's Professor Landersly, the head of soil sciences and Marco's supervisor. He's one of the youngest supervisors in the city. Tall, thin, a shock of still dark-brown, tangled hair. But these days, he looks permanently tired as if he's having to will himself each and every hour to try standing vertically for a bit. Landersly takes his drink from the bar and glances around the room. 'New talent. All wide-eyed and thankful.'

'I guess.'

Landersly smiles sadly to himself, 'But we both know they're far from innocent. They're survivors. These days, you're either one side of the survival dichotomy or the other. If you're alive, then chances are someone else paid for it.'

Landersly's wife, Katya, died around six months ago, washed over the levee in a freak storm. Her disappearance had left Landersly with a bitter gash in his soul. She'd been having a kid. They were one of the few couples who had been granted permission. You had to be pretty important to get the okay on a reproduction of any kind these days. IQ's in the genius realm. But all that brilliance was gone in an instant. Marco had only met her a few times, a sweet woman, golden-blonde hair and a kind smile. He guessed she was Polish or Slavic. She had one of those accents. But the heritage thing wasn't really a concern. She was bright, the regular star of the IT department. One day she was there and Landersly was all excited about the baby and his wife, and how they were going to create this fantastic world for everyone. Next minute, she was gone, as was Landersly's hope for his brave new world.

Marco loved working with the guy, but social gatherings and Landersly were no longer a good mix, not since Katya's untimely exit.

Marco glances around the room. It's painfully obvious that the old talent is giving the new talent a wide birth.

'Don't worry, Marco,' Landersly sighs, 'you're safe.'

'I don't know; my test scores weren't exactly brilliant.' Marco finds it hard to conceal the irritation in his voice; he chose one hell of a week to slip down the ladder.

Landersly nods, slowly. 'It was atypical. They can see that. You were the youngest winner of the Clause Herbit award.'

'Only because of your advice.'

It was true. Marco had been following this mad scheme. It was embarrassing to even think about it now. He had completely ignored all the reverse osmosis research on desalination membranes and ploughed ahead with single-atom materials that could be operated using tidal flux. Landersly had gently steered him away from it. Got him into terraforming with rubber frames and reverse osmosis, and the Clause Herbit award was sealed and sorted.

'All my department should be safe,' Landersly says, not taking his eyes off the room. 'Without us, where would Texicom's plans get a hold? We're cheaper than space sciences. Besides, you've got my backing, Marco, if that counts for anything.' And he winks at Marco, a small, sad in-it-together wink, before he disappears off into the room, glass in hand.

'You seen how many people they let through without testing?' Neil, a tall, skinny, currently terrified-looking guy, is saying by the time Marco gets back to his table. They're old friends. Neil came in on the self-same wave. He's the kind of guy who looks as though he grew up in a room without enough ceiling space' permanently bowed, as if attempting to excuse himself for something he probably hasn't had a chance to do, on account of the fact that he's too scared to do it. Cowed, that's how Marco's gran would describe it. She's always banging on about how it's something to avoid. *'Always stand tall, then you've got room for the knock-downs.'*

Tonight, even by Neil's standards, he's looking nervous.

He works in Ezra's department, which is part and parcel of the problem. Working with someone like Ezra would have that tortoise effect on anyone, with or without Gran's coaching. Where Ezra's concerned, if you aren't one of the *Golden Kids*, you need to have an ever-ready shell to shrink back into.

'I counted twenty new faces,' Tee says, eyeing the room.

'Thirty.' Marco takes a sip of his drink. 'Ten in here. Five went out as we came in. Three on the door. Four by the…'

'Okay, okay. We get the picture.' Tee laughs. 'Human calculator.'

'If there's thirty here, there's probably at least another thirty who couldn't make it,' Neil adds nervously.

'And that's just the ones with special clearance. You imagine how many there'll be when they get through processing? Southern territories - they're bright.'

As soon as it's out of his mouth, Marco regrets it. Tee's academic test scores are mediocre at best. Neil's also on shaky ground. He's bright enough. Always has good scores, but there's the Ezra factor.

In typical Texicom manner, there was an *announcement* on the seven o'clock news, that there would be no *announcement* till later. Marco figures they're waiting for it to get dark. Get everyone off the streets. Avoid unnecessary riots. But the city has developed itself a kind of nervous, high-energy vibe which hangs in the air like a lightning charge. No one who is not level 2, a Golden Kid, part of the council or the relies, will be sleeping tonight. They're all waiting anxiously till that leaderboard goes up city-wide on all entertainment panels. Names of all those eligible for repatriation in the city will be flicked through and rated. Just like they were for Molly. If a person is not rated highly enough, they'll be out. Since the last batch has only just gone, word is that the next batch will be given five days to pack their bags, nominate two loved ones on their communication list, and say their goodbyes.

'I put your latest lung capacity scores through,' Tee says,

as if reading Marco's thoughts. 'Hopefully, they'll get processed in time. Should bump up your rating.'

'Thanks, Tee. My round all night.'

'You'll be fine, Marco.' Neil says nervously. 'Landersly's rock-solid.'

Marco sees Neil glance sheepishly at his hands before stealing a look towards Ezra, ensconced in his bullish party; mainly male, mainly attractive, every one well-dressed and built on protein and privilege.

'Hey.' A soft, clear voice breaks into the moment.

Marco turns to see Portia pulling herself up onto the stool beside them. She looks flushed and vulnerable, nothing like the irritated, proud Golden Kid who pulled herself out of the tank earlier in the day. More like the lost young woman caught speaking the forgotten words of her dead father. Marco realises she's selective as to when and where she adopts Golden Girl status; she finds it embarrassing.

Tonight, her red hair is pulled back out of her eyes. She's going all out for practical rather than pretty. She knows as well as Marco that there will be new recruits around from the southern territories. The admin wheels will be whirring. The powers that be will want to match the bright kids: intelligence breeds intelligence. Portia is prime stock. By the pulled-back hair and thrown on clothes, she's playing down her desirability as an asset. Or at least that's the game plan. But, for Marco, she only looks more effortlessly beautiful, more honest, more… out of his league.

Smiling, Portia extends one soft-pink hand towards Tee. 'I think we got off on the wrong foot.'

Marco can see Tee is totally knocked off-guard. Portia Reynolds seeking him out! Portia Reynolds should be over with Ezra's group. She's so-no-part of the rag-tag WU scene. Marco can't help feeling just a glimmer of amusement as Tee's cheeks flush scarlet like someone just turned a hot tap on inside his brain.

Then Portia sends that small, understated, pink-lipped smile Marco's way, and his heart flips. Kid you not, it does gymnastics in his chest. One woman in the mix and the whole thing's a mess.

She turns back to Tee and smiles. 'I wanted to thank you,' she's saying in that crisp, clear voice.

'You were right about protocol.'

The ground could swallow Marco up, and he would die happy. A girl like this? Saying sorry? Admitting she's wrong? Forget about terraforming the oceans or Mars, this really is unchartered territory.

'Hey,' Tee shrugs, 'it's just safety.'

'Yeah, well,' Portia fixes him with her soft green eyes. 'See, I can't get access without an operator. I'm not Level Two clearance. And Marco here…' she nods her head gently towards him, and he hopes he's not colouring up to match Tee.

'Marco says you're the best.'

Tee glances down at his drink. 'Well, I…'

'Can I practice with you? I know it's a lot to ask …I know you're busy, but the suits are fantastic, and I just think with a little more…'

'Sure.'

Her smile lights up the whole table.

'Hey, Portia!' The mood shatters. Ezra's call comes loud and clear across the room. Portia bristles instinctively. So, Marco was right. She feels the exact same way about Ezra as they all do.

'You can stay with us,' Marco offers, maybe just that little bit too enthusiastically.

'No,' Portia sighs. 'Ezra will just cause trouble.' She gets her bag together and slips off her stool.

'Guys, good luck for the leaderboard.'

'Good luck with the idiots.' Neil says, nodding his head

towards Ezra. Wow, thinks Marco, when that boy is out of his shell, there's almost no putting him back.

If Portia heard Neil's comment, she makes no acknowledgement. 'Tee, can we do tomorrow? Six a.m?'

Tee's puppy-dog eyes are open, wide and sparkling. 'You bet.'

Portia smiles and walks towards the guffawing.

'It's a date,' Tee says way too loudly and perhaps, Marco feels, overstating things just a tad in that over-optimistic way that Tee has.

Portia catches the comment and turns back, her bright eyes narrowing slightly, mock-serious, total amusement. 'Actually, it's more of a coaching session.'

'Date?' Neil gives out a short, quiet, skeptical whistle.

'Guys!' Tee can barely contain himself. 'Whatever it is, training with Portia Reynolds? Man, she is the best.'

CHAPTER 14
THE LEADERBOARD

WHEN TEXICOM BIG IT UP, they describe 'repatriation' as a new adventure. A great opportunity to 'broaden horizons,' to 'conquer a new world.' But when you're none too sure what kind of state the world beyond the levee is in, when the only images you see are of doom and destruction, when you never hear back from anyone that's been out, not after that initial two-week processing period, let's just say a person would be reluctant to get themselves on that repat boat.

By eleven pm, Marco's nerves are wearing thin. On the hour, every hour, there's been an announcement telling the city that there will be an "announcement" later. Portia left hours ago. Slipped a light green coat over her shoulders and left alone. It's more detail than Marco feels is strictly necessary, but he's finding it hard to put the girl down.

As the crowd dwindles at the rec, Marco realises he is no way up for giving Ezra and his entourage the satisfaction of witnessing the smallest hint of a reaction to the leaderboard results. Neil and Tee must be on the same page because when Marco suggests they head back to the stacks to catch the live broadcast, the others fall in line.

There's a chorus of jeers as they leave.

'See you tomorrow. Oh, wait, probably not.' And catcalls of laughter.

'Idiots,' Neil mutters under his breath. 'We get five days.' But even as he says it, the words dry on his lips.

Five days, Marco thinks to himself: not much consolation.

Within half an hour of arriving back at the flat, Tee has set his wrist monitor for five am and is snoring soundly on the couch. He's got an appointment at the tanks with Portia Reynolds, and he has no intention of missing it.

'You hear anything from Molly?' Neil asks, trying but failing to make his long limbs comfortable on the standard issue chair.

'Got through this morning.' Marco flicks on to the screen, bringing up Molly's repatriation file. She's been taken off *no-show*, the status is now *accounted for*. There's one pre-recorded video transmission available, the meeting Marco had with her this morning.

'She says it's sunny. They're feeding her real food.'

'Wow. Real grub.' Neil looks impressed. 'I always liked Molly. Feisty kid.'

'She's not dead,' Marco counters.

'Mind if we watch it? I've never been on anyone's communication list,' Neil shifts awkwardly in his chair, looking like Johnny-no-mates. 'Would be good to see how it's done,' he blusters. 'Might even be doing my own broadcast soon.'

'You'll be f…'

But Neil doesn't even bother to let Marco finish. He shoots Marco an ice-cold look; he's not fishing for reassurance. 'To be honest, Marco, I think all of us are on borrowed time. The cull's begun.'

'It's not a cull.'

'Call it what you like. But tonight is just the tip of the

iceberg. Twenty thousand displaced people came in from the southern territories. Maybe that's not even it. Maybe there are more on the way. The city can't support that kind of volume.'

'There are other cities.'

'Not worth going to. Word is they're lawless.'

Marco doesn't bother to reply. He's heard the same.

'Look, maybe you're safe with Landersly. Maybe Tee, maybe he's safe with his amphibious lungs. But me? Ezra hates me.'

'Ezra's not in charge.'

Neil says nothing; he just glances down at his hands.

'You want to call Molly?' Marco's keen to change the subject.

Neil nods. 'Maybe she's got a bit more info.'

Marco's kind of surprised that there's not a second recording. If he can access the file from the hamster cage, Gran should be able to access it too. But it looks like Gran has no interest in contacting her own personal *Golden Child*. But then Marco figures that even if he lives to be a hundred, he won't ever work out the intricacies of Gran's mind. Marco dials the repat number. The tone rings out once, twice. Then there she is, Molly. She's still wearing that odd shift thing, but her face has a touch of makeup on, and her hair's done up in some kind of weird and wonderful construction. He's seen pictures of it before, just the same, all over her social network. It's a style she was pretty impressed with. So, as always, she's trying her best to work the look.

'Moll!'

'Marco.'

'And Neil. Neil's here.'

She doesn't say hi, just waves at them, a short sharp acknowledgement.

'What's happening?' She asks.

'Leaderboard's back up.' Marco says.

'Two in one week. Can you believe that?' Neil's jumping in, keen to get all the dirt out from under the carpet.

'Well… I guess the government knows what's best.'

'Ha! First time I've heard you say that.' Marco snorts.

'They've got the whole picture. You've just got to go along with it.'

'Yes but…'

'Don't cause trouble.'

This is Molly talking? He can't really believe what he's hearing.

'They give you a lobotomy along with the hair-do?'

'Shh.' Neil grabs Marco's arm, squeezing it tight. 'Just joking, right, Marco? Always the joker.'

'Always.' Molly says, though Marco wouldn't really have described himself as a joker, not with Tee on the scene.

Suddenly, the siren rings out in the background.

'Damn.' Marco sighs. 'That thing, it's always going off.'

'It's busy here. I got to go.' She's standing, getting ready to hit the off button.

'Is there a better time to call?' He leans forward in his seat, like somehow, if he gets closer, it will hold her back.

'There's a lot to do, induction.'

'But there must be…'

'Just try any time. Can't promise anything but… Catch you later, guys.'

And she's gone.

'Lobotomy? Really? You know they listen to all those tapes?'

'It was a joke.'

Neil gives a snort. Marco says nothing for a moment, just drums his fingers on the desk. The whole Molly thing leaves him with a Quatermass pit of unanswered questions.

'So, she's available for two weeks?' Neil asks, cutting through the angst.

Marco nods, 'After that, I guess a person could be miles

away from a repatriation centre. It's just too difficult to keep tabs.'

Neil flips the play button again, the recording spools through once more. Neil lowers the sound. But there's something… Something not quite sitting straight. It still feels odd. Is it just because the interaction is kind of forced?

'What even is that?' Neil slides closer to the screen.

So, Neil's sensing it too; something's off. 'What?'

'The colour. That smock thing… Is it beige?'

They both stare at the monitor.

'Know what? I think it is.' Molly would never be seen dead in beige and now.

'Wow!' Neil stares at the image that he's frozen, then rewinds it backwards just for the hell of it. 'She can even pull that off.'

'She always looked good. You want a soda?'

'Why not.'

Marco grabs a couple of drinks from the machine as Neil hits play yet again.

'Odd,' he says as the tape runs to an end.

'What? You want ice?'

'Nope. Keep ice frozen. Even watching it melt in a drink gives me the heebe jeebies. No, it's just that she called you Marco?'

Marco looks at Neil, puzzled. 'That's my name.'

'Yeah, but… she kind of pronounced it odd. I mean, like in real life, Molly, she kind of said Macko, like Jacko. She missed out the R.'

Marco stops dead in his tracks. Neil's right.

Molly had a problem with R's when she was a kid. It took Gran years to get her to pronounce the letter. Moll used to stand in the bathroom every morning, toothbrush in hand, rolling her r's like a motorbike. She'd started off calling him Macko, and then even when she was perfectly capable of hitting the elusive consonant; it was all kind of too late because Macko had kind of stuck.

'But I mean, it's no big deal, it's…'

But whatever Marco is about to say is lost under the announcement.

A computer-generated, silky-smooth voice emanates 360 from the wall speakers. 'Citizens. The leaderboard is available for viewing.'

'Tee. Tee!' Marco nudges Tee into action and vaults over the sofa, leaving the drinks abandoned on the counter. They're all acting as though there's not a minute to waste, but they have plenty of time. They'll have to watch the results as they come in. Nothing is fixed yet. They stare at the screen as names appear and digits begin to calculate.

'I can't see me. You see me?' Neil scans down the list.

They've never paid much attention to it before, never had to. It's a confusing scheme. It was the only chance that Marco caught it on Thursday.

Fifty names are already up, and more are flowing in. The calculations are being done real-time. Everyone has a 'usefulness' calculation. That one's normally set on occupation. You can score 1 to 10. Then there's academic score, again 1 to 10. There's a citizen score as well. If you don't toe the line, if you kick up trouble, give the city any kind of grief (like spread rumours of lobotomies!!! Maybe?) you can go into negative numbers. Origin doesn't appear on screen. It's your base number, the number you enter the board at. That's pretty much fixed. Indigenous peoples are set at ten. British Isles are nine. Europe is an eight. African descent is a five if you're fourth-generation or less. There's never been lung capacity before, because professional classes are the only ones who train and, since they've never come under scrutiny, the LC reading has been redundant. This time it's there, on the board, glowing in bright red neon letters, and Marco lets out a deep sigh of relief – he's been practising.

The names flick up the board, continually changing places as digits are added. Some lucky names slipping off the board completely.

'Got you!' Tee screams in excitement.

Sure enough, Neil WU appears – entry level, at the top of the screen.

'At the top!' Neil's voice sounds gutted.

'Hold on, Mate. Hold on. They haven't done any calculations yet.'

A ten appears in the box. Neil's still looking worried, but his name shoots down the board.

'Wait! What?' Neil says.

'It's okay,' Tee explains. 'It's good. The aim is to slip off the board. The bigger your score, the idea is you just drop off the end. You never watched this before?'

Neil looks sheepish. 'If it doesn't affect you, it's easy enough to turn a blind eye.'

Marco doesn't say that he hasn't really paid a whole heap of attention either.

'Ten for Occupation!' Neil sounds ecstatic.

'Maybe Ezra doesn't like you at space sciences, but you've got someone in your corner,' Marco says encouragingly, as another ten appears in the box.

'Yes!' Neil fist pumps the air.

'Are we on yet? Marco asks, picking up the remote and flicking back to the top.

'Hey!' Neil's not happy.

'Just hold on, we can get back to you.' Marco continues to scroll through the new entries.

Tee shakes his head. 'I don't think we're there.'

The names and numbers appear so fast it's difficult to trace them through. Marco flicks down again, catching up with Neil, as his name sinks down the scoreboard.

'So, that's Academic.'

'Citizen scores next.'

A six appears.

Neil wrinkles his nose.

'Ezra,' Marco says, without raising his eyes.

'We on there yet? We must be.' Tee asks anxiously.

Marco shakes his head. 'There must be three hundred on there already.'

And since the names are continually shifting as calculations come through, it's difficult to keep track. Another six appears next to Neil's name.

'Lung capacity?' Tee looks impressed.

Neil's name slips to the bottom of the board and disappears.

'Ha! What?' There's a brief pause before it dawns on him. 'I'm safe. Guys, I'm safe!' The relief is all-consuming.

'You nailed it.'

'Wow, guys. Look at my hands.' Neil holds his hands out rigidly in front of him; they're visibly shaking.

'Home run.' Marco punches Neil playfully on the shoulder. But the celebration is short-lived as Tee calls out, 'That's me. I'm up.'

His name is on the board. Straight away, he's got a ten, and the bright red digits of his name are slipping down the leaderboard fast. Tee breathes a sigh of relief.

'Academic's going to be bad.' He bites his lip.

Six comes up. He nods his head as if weighing it up. It's a fair shout. There are others far worse off than Tee. His name continues to slide down the board.

'I'm up,' Marco shouts.

His name is at the top. Within nanoseconds, a straight ten appears next to it, and the name slides towards Tee's.

A three appears next to Tee's name.

'No way!'

'Citizenship?' Neil looks puzzled.

'No way! I keep my head down. I am Mr Helpful. My middle name – Helpful.'

'Ezra,' Marco says bitterly. They all know it's true. 'The run-in this morning.'

Tee sinks back in his chair, rubbing his face in his hands.

'You've got lung capacity to go. You'll be fine,' Marco says, as a six appears next to his name.

'Damn! Told you I did badly in that last test.' Marco could kick himself.

But there's barely enough time. A ten appears for citizenship. He nods to himself. Okay. He can work with this.

'You're almost off the board, both of you.' Neil's rapt, sitting on the edge of his seat, his eyes glued to the screen. 'Know what, this is actually quite exciting.'

'Lung capacity – twelve.' Tee's eyes light up.

'Can they do that?' Neil's incredulous. 'It's only up to ten?'

'What can I say? When they want you, they want you.' Tee smiles.

His name is the last on the board. One more shift and it's off. He's home and dry.

'Wait, I'm on LC,' Marco shouts as the numbers change.

'You got it, mate. I entered all the info good and early.' Tee stares transfixed at the screen. Marco's fingers are crossed. Say the new LC results didn't get through in time? Say there was a glitch with the processing?

The number eight appears next to Marco's name. The digits compute. He's got thirty-eight. As they're cheering and congratulating themselves, Marco's name low jumps Tee's and exits the board. It's then that the smiles freeze on their faces. The red light has appeared in the top right corner. The pulsing digits have stopped. The board is frozen.

'What's going on?' Tee jumps to his feet, staring at the screen.

Marco checks the connection. 'It's working.'

'Then what?' A look of terror crosses Tee's face.

Suddenly, the apartment is filled with absolute silence, as

the leaderboard is displayed, big, bold and red as blood on all four walls.

'The announcements have been made' the syrupy voice announces 360. 'Since there has already been one recent repatriation, exit times will be reinstated. All those repatriated will have the customary five days. Please…'

But they're not listening. Marco has hit the off button.

'You didn't make it, Tee,' Neil says into the silence.

CHAPTER 15
SORRY

THE FOLLOWING MORNING, when Marco lays his palm across Tee's doorbell, he's informed by the silky-smooth operating system that Tee WU is not in the building. This is weird. It's Sunday, they had one hell of a night, and it's still only six thirty a.m. Then Marco remembers – Tee had said he was going to practice with Portia. Surely after all that happened, tank practice would be the last thing on Tee's mind? But then, this is Tee, Marco's thinking about. And when Marco asks the operating system if there's a fix on location, sure enough, he's informed that the tanks are exactly where Tee can be found.

Marco feels like he's left his eyes out to dry in a wind tunnel next to a line of Peking ducks. He didn't sleep most of the night. Not even the tick-tock of that old clock helped. He nodded off eventually at dawn for a tortured half hour in which everyone he loves including, for a reason he fails to understand, the giant octopus in tank ten, is being dragged to the bottom of the sea by a vortex of laughter let loose by Ezra Clark.

Curiously enough, Marco was going through this bizarre REM weirdly vivid state, at just the exact same time that Tee would have been slipping on his hoodie, heading out of the stacks alone, and walking through the ever-grey morning mist towards the academy. Marco is so filled with self-loathing he can't even look at his sad, sorry reflection in the glass pod windows as the pod slides to a halt in front of him.

Thankfully, it's still early. The city had a late night and is still curled up, licking its wounds. The pod is empty. He would like nothing more than to hunker down under his duvet with all the other 'lucky' winners and cancel the whole day. But he's not exactly feeling *lucky,* and self-loathing is guaranteed to give a person a heavy shot of insomnia. He's already spent far too many years pouring over his books, avoiding the awkward questions as to why so many faces disappear every couple of weeks. He's been head-down thinking of the future, while the rest of the world has been struggling to digest the present. It might be too late for him to do anything about Molly. But it's not too late to do something about Tee.

Guilt hangs heavily on Marco's shoulders. It feels like he's done something so underhand that, despite the knowledge that he didn't engineer the situation, and there is nothing in the world that would induce him to hang his friend out for the vultures, the net result remains the same: Marco has signed, sealed, and delivered Tee's deportation papers. If Tee hadn't bumped Marco's LC count up; if Tee hadn't had a run-in with Ezra - because he was training Marco; if Marco had done exactly what he said he was going to do, stayed home and read through practice papers, this would be a whole different ballgame.

'How's Claudie?' Marco asks as he walks casually past Stan towards the entry barrier. Stan looks at Marco like he's got *IDIOT* marked up over his forehead, and Marco wishes he'd kept his mouth shut.

'You get repatriated?' Stan asks.

Marco presses his hand against the entry panel.

'No.'

'Lucky.'

'You?'

Stan shrugs. 'Not this time. Been a slight job shift, though. They're moving me out of the academy.'

'Oh?'

'Not a problem. Maybe it was time for a change. It's still security. Guess they need bodies in different places. Not such a success story for your man, I hear?'

'No.' Marco drops his eyes to the floor, wondering if Stan knows the full story.

'Shame,' Stan says, oblivious. 'He's a nice guy.'

'Not something you get points for,' Marco says bitterly.

The security button bleeps. Stan glances at the screen, pushing out his lips in a thoughtful pout, before raising one eyebrow.

'You don't have clearance.'

Marco sighs. Tee isn't answering his phone. There's no way of getting hold of him. But Marco has to tell Tee that he's serious; he's not going to let his friend take the rap.

'I can't get hold of him.'

At this, Stan nods his head slowly, doing that pillar-of-worldly-wisdom routine. 'Maybe he just doesn't want to talk.'

Marco sighs. 'It shouldn't be him going. It should be me.'

'You think telling him that is going to make any damn thing any bit better?'

Stan's got a point.

'Just half an hour. I've got a plan.'

At this, Stan throws back his head and laughs. A deep resonant, spontaneous roar into the vast empty forum.

'A plan. I like that.' He laughs again, though a bit quieter this time. 'Not sure anyone under Level Two is allowed to have 'plans' anymore. Think we're all just part of somebody else's *'plan.'*

'Please?'

'You're not going to cause trouble?'

Marco shakes his head. 'I'm just in and out. No one will even know I'm here.'

'Apart from the CCTV guys.' Stan glances up at the cameras positioned four corners of the room.

'You think they're still watching?'

Stan shrugs. 'Wouldn't like to test it out.' But he steps back anyway.

'Last day on the job, might as well give you a bit of slack. Cheer him up, you hear?'

———

'Take a break now, then try it one more time. You can get that heart rate down.'

'Seriously! Any lower and you sure I won't be dead?'

'Think pearl divers.'

'Pearl divers, bloody pearl divers,' Portia mutters. A whole symphony of irritation laced through her words.

The disembodied voices float down towards Marco as he hurries towards the final tank. They would have to be in tank ten!

'Tee?' Marco can't see them from where he's walking below the platform, but as soon as he calls his friend's name, an icy, stone-cold silence descends. Nothing human remains, just that slap, slap, slap of waves. But Marco knows they're up there. He heard their voices. Besides, where else would they practice? Who would want to bother with a nice, clean, weedless tank when they could go swim with a monster-sized octopus?

'Tee?' he repeats.

Another pause, then he sees Portia's face at the edge of the platform.

'He says he doesn't want to speak to you.'

Marco nods; that figures. 'Tell him I know. Tell him…' Marco sighs, running his hands through his short, cropped hair, 'Tell him I'm not going to let it happen.'

There's another pause.

'Okay.' Portia's voice again, but this time she doesn't bother looking over the side. 'He's coming down.'

Marco hears the heavy mechanical clunk of the lift-gate as Tee steps in and the lift whirs into action. Then something else, the sound of someone plunging back into the tank. Portia descends, locked in a spiral of white bubbles, her sad, luminous face appearing the other side of the glass. She must think he's a traitor. She must think he's lower than low. She must think…

'So?' Tee's standing right behind him. A look of burning rage plastered across his face. 'You planned it all.'

Steam would not look out of place coming out of those ears. But this is no joking matter.

'Well?' Tee asks, irritation biting hard into his words.

But all the apologies, all the words, each and every sorry utterance evaporates from Marco's brain.

'What?' is all that he manages.

Marco meant to say sorry. First off, the first thing out of his mouth should have been an apology. But his brain has been addled. He's not thinking. So, all he can manage is a stupid, mind-numbingly banal *what.*

Tee storms off, Marco running after him.

'Look I…' Marco's hand reaches out for Tee's shoulder. Then Tee swings around and hooks his right fist hard under Marco's chin. Reeling, Marco stumbles back, falling against the tank, folding into a heap.

'What?'

Again with the 'what?' Though, this time, at least it was

fitting. Marco rubs his chin. He wouldn't have thought Tee had it in him. But he can't say that he doesn't deserve it.

'I know, I know…' at last the words are beginning to form. 'It should have been me.'

'Ha!' Tee shouts triumphantly. 'See, you admit it. You had it all planned!'

'No, that's not what I…'

But Tee isn't listening. 'Will you just listen to yourself? *It should have been me,*' Tee mimics cruelly. But the words soon dry on his lips, the fun draining double-quick time out of the mimicry. Seriousness descends, bringing with it all the anger and frustration and sheer unadulterated terror that is bubbling beneath the surface.

'One thing I know for certain,' Tee says, not even bothering to look Marco in the face, 'It should not have been me.'

His stance is one of boundless energy, as if he's hoping Marco will get back to his feet and take him on. As if he's just itching for that very opportunity. But Marco's done enough damage already. He remains slumped where he's fallen.

'I know. I know.' Marco sighs, grabbing a handkerchief from his pocket and dabbing it on his nose. There's a tiny speck of blood. He presses his fingers against the cartilage. Nothing appears to be broken, but his jaw is on fire.

'It's all my fault,' he mumbles. 'Sorry.'

'Sorry!' Tee scoffs.

'Yeah. Really sorry. It should have been my name on the board.'

Tee lets a brief snort escape. 'Like that's going to do any good now.'

'It will. Honest. I swear. I'm going to take the blame.'

Tee looks at Marco curiously, not quite fully understanding.

'I'm going to go in your place. I'm going to…'

Suddenly, a plume of ice-cold water comes flooding down over them from the top of the tank, streaming over Marco's hunched body. He gasps, trying to get his breath, struggling for air, uncertain as to what it is that just happened. Then he hears it, a sound that is like music to his ears. A sound that this morning he thought he might never hear again. Tee is laughing.

'Well done, Finbow.' Tee's holding his sides and roaring with laughter.

The heavy arms of the octopus can be heard from above, breaking the surface like a walrus at a fair; taking its applause before it propels itself back down into the depths.

'Wow, you see that?' Portia calls from the top of the tank. 'That's the best spout he's ever done.'

Marco glances behind him into the tank. Finbow, the octopus, looking as satisfied as it is possible for an octopus to look, floats down towards him. One eye held wearily open, fixed on Marco.

Marco holds up an arm in surrender.

'It's okay. I admit it should have been me. Finbow, Tee, Portia...' he calls out into the room.

'...I should be going. I am going.'

When Marco turns back to Tee, Tee's holding a hand towards him; a hand to help him to his feet, but of course, so much more - a peace offering. Marco reaches up to grab it. A backlash of water goes flooding down his sleeve, and Tee is off – laughing uncontrollably yet again.

'I feel like I'm wearing the tank.'

'Man, you look like you're wearing the tank.'

'I'm sorry about everything. I won't let it happen. I promise.'

'Like, how are you gonna stop it?' Tee sighs. This whole situation is hopeless.

'You know those *friends met on the way up*?'

Tee nods, not sure where this is going. 'My contact list?'

'You got any working for Kendal?'

CHAPTER 16
KENDAL

AS IT TURNS OUT, they don't need Tee's contact list, not with Portia on board.

Monday morning, Portia and Marco get exeats from the academy and head over to the repatriation centre. Landersly's not happy, advising against the visit, claiming that Marco's putting himself at too much risk. But at heart, Marco figures, Landersly must get it: it just doesn't seem fair.

The vast entrance hall is up-to-the-brim out-to-the-edges stuffed with people and noise. The zone restrictions on wristbands must have been lifted at the repat centre. It's a free-for-all. Everyone and their uncle has had the self-same exact idea; they've all come to plead their case. Only, by the looks of them, most of them have been camping outside all night. And from the weary expressions on their faces, Marco can tell that though the body is present, there is a total absence of any kind of hope.

The hall's old, a vast echoey atrium, used for trading when there were things to trade. These days a gated iron barrier runs through the centre, slicing Joe-public off from the admin staff. The powers-that-be are not taking any chances.

'Take my hand,' Portia instructs, heading into the throng.

Marco doesn't need a second invitation. There's something reassuring about being pulled through the crowd. Like he can divorce himself from it; they're not his responsibility. Portia and Marco have their own mission.

'Don't let go,' she calls back over her shoulder.

'Grow old with you attached.'

He feels a prickle of joy when she laughs.

There's a gate fixed into the iron railings; two security guards on the people-packed side, and two on the cool-as-a-cucumber empty bit. Portia's heading straight for the gate.

Maybe it's something about her confidence, or maybe it's the fact that they're both washed and dressed, academy blazers buttoned, ties on full display. People kind of bunch up out of the way, leaving a thin-cut Moses-style pathway to let them pass.

'I want to see Kendal,' Portia says to the guard, when they get close enough to be heard.

Want, Marco notices, not *need*. Her voice is clear and calm, filled with an entitlement that only comes from a life of absolute privilege. Marco stares around him at the dirty, miserable faces that could so easily have belonged to him, or his gran, or Molly. All these people, they'd all come to see Kendal. The difference, Marco realises, as Portia flashes a short, superior smile at the men in uniforms, and presses her slim, silver wristband on to the ID tablet being offered up through the bars, is that all these others will not, in a million years, make it through that barrier.

The gate slides open. There's a brief surge forward from the crowd, and the sharp buzz of an electric circuit as a yellow pushes too far. The dense, warm smell of burnt-human hair spikes Marco's nostrils, as a large man thuds to the floor. It must have been some voltage.

'Stand back.' The guard shouts. 'There's no medical care if you get yourself fried.'

The crowd cowers. There's a sharp tug as someone

attaches themselves to Marco's coat. He shakes the coat loose. He's finding it difficult to breathe, the crowd is crushing in, the smell of burning and body odour is thick and acrid in his nose, making his eyes sting. He turns to Portia, noticing that she's acquired someone too; a small, scared black woman tugging away at Portia's coat.

'Miss, my son…'

'Portia, we got to go,' he says, but the woman's not giving up.

'Benjamin. My son. Please.' She pushes a note into Portia's hand. 'He's only little. Please.'

Marco brushes the woman's arm away. But her other hand fixes itself to Portia's sleeve. She's like a bloody octopus.

There's another buzz, a young lad this time. He yelps in pain like a wounded dog and falls to the floor, whimpering, cracking his head on the unforgiving marble.

'Back,' shouts the guard, but the crowd has learnt its lesson. There's absolute quiet, just the sobs of the boy. Cowering, frightened eyes fix themselves with pure hatred towards the fence.

'We can't do anything,' Marco says to the woman attached to Portia's coat, knocking her hand away, but as he does, he notices her other hand slip the note into Portia's pocket. He's not sure if Portia's seen, but the woman is backing away.

'You coming in?' The guard barks.

Marco pulls Portia forward. But her free hand drops down, gently fingering the pocket. Barely visible, she pushes the paper down deeper.

'Bless you, mam,' the woman mutters, before disappearing off into the crowd. It was all done so efficiently, so effortlessly, that Marco hardly has time to process what he's seen.

There's another sound of someone being zapped.

'Quickly, please,' the security guard sounds major-league-pissed-off. Marco can kind of understand why. With a brief nod of thanks, he pulls Portia through the narrow opening.

The gate swings shut behind them. The hands of the people press through the bars once more. Marco can't help himself; a shiver passes over his body.

'Bloody animals!' The guard mutters.

'Come on.' Portia says, striding off across the hall, aiming for a large lobby, with its bank of grand old-school wooden lifts. Marco's in hot pursuit, glad she knows where she's going, but then…

'How come you know where you're going?'

Portia stops in front of one of the large teak lifts and presses her wristband against the call panel.

'Let's just say, me and Kendal, well, we've kind of had dealings before.'

Marco's not sure whether this is a good or a bad thing. But when the lift arrives and they stand inside, and those doors slide firmly shut, he feels thankful for it all. They're special. One step removed from the 'many' outside. Is it okay to think that? Isn't that just part of the trap? How easy it is to get sucked in.

'I couldn't have done that without you.'

She just nods; she knows all of that.

'But now, I go in on my own.' He doesn't want to get her into trouble.

But Portia just smiles a like-that's-going-to-happen smile. 'Not really my style.'

She hits the button for the 30th floor, reaches for her pocket and takes out the note.

'What's it say?'

'Her son, Benjamin.' She scans the letter. 'He's thirteen. Thirteen! Earmarked for repatriation.' She shakes her head like it's all hopeless. 'How can I help with that, Marco. Seriously?'

Marco sighs. 'After we're sure Tee's okay, I'll mention this.'

'Look what you're doing… What you're trying to do is really… honourable.'

She lays her hand on his shoulder, and as she does, he feels that charge shoot through his body. Not the kind you get from going somewhere you're not supposed to go. This charge is all about finding yourself in the exact right place you need to be.

Her cheeks flush. She's trying to ignore what just happened. She glances down at her shoes like suddenly they are oh-so-fascinating.

'It's honourable. But you can't do it.'

The lift slides to a halt. Marco's lost for words. This is not part of the plan. A chill runs through his blood; he's being sidelined. She's put herself into some kind of pseudo-parental role. She's pulling rank, and that is really guaranteed to get up his nose big time. It's his friend they're talking about, and they've only got one chance of getting it right. The door slides open, she's stepping out. He presses the ground-level button and pulls her back in.

'Hey!' She's not looking happy.

'We agreed.'

She sighs, shaking her head. 'To be honest, I didn't agree to anything. Apart from agreeing to get you in.'

What the hell is she up to? Gran was right; you can't trust people like this.

'The point is,' she says, in a quiet, calm, assured tone, the kind of tone that only those who've grown up in an environ-ment in which they're listened to, can afford to use. 'If I hadn't been there, none of this would have happened.'

Marco hadn't even thought of it this way. He'd only ever seen it from his perspective: he had been in the wrong place. If he had only stayed at home with his books. It was him that had put Tee in danger. But it worked both ways: If Ezra and Portia hadn't been diving.

The consolation's short-lived. Ezra's Level Two. Level Two can be almost anywhere they choose at any time.

The lift doors slide open on the basement. But Portia hasn't finished. She presses the button to hold the doors. 'I've got to take the fall. If you just act as…'

'Wait, what?' This is so far from the plan; they're going to need GPS to get them back on track!

'I shouldn't have been there, unsupervised. Ezra complained about Tee because of me. This is my fight.'

She presses the thirtieth floor again. The doors slide shut. This is in danger of going on all day.

'Where would they even send you *back* to?' He can't help it; his voice is rising in frustration.

Portia shrugs, 'Doesn't matter. They always manage to find somewhere. Look, Marco, all I need from you is a character witness on Tee.'

She says it like she's asking someone in admin to open a door for them, while she shakes off her umbrella. He can't help it; it stings.

'Who said it was okay for you to just pull rank?'

Even as he says it, he knows there's something ridiculous about the whole thing. Now everyone is putting themselves up for repatriation, and he's developed a chip on his shoulder? But the dig seems to float way over Portia's head. She just sighs as the doors slide open again.

'You weren't even on the list.'

Now he hits the button so the doors can't close.

Portia shrugs. 'They can make an exception. I've been causing a few pain-in-the-arse problems for them recently. I challenged Kendal about the repatriation criteria. Most days I'm at the Museum of Human History trying to defend my father's freedom of speech.'

She steps out of the lift, but Marco can't let her go; they need to get this sorted.

'Portia!' Marco grabs her arm, her jumper so soft, her arms thin and fragile as a china doll's. He wishes they could stay here forever, just him and Portia, going up and down in the lift. Trapped in their own personal time bubble. Safe and dry, forwards and backwards, before the storm kicks in.

'Be realistic. There is no way they'll repatriate you. If we go in there arguing, we'll never get what we want. We have to unite on this. It's me that goes.'

A tear glints at the corner of her eye. But hot on the tail of sadness comes a flicker of irritation; this is one girl who would rather gouge her eyes out than look vulnerable. She turns her back on him and pushes out into the hallway.

'You see. It all stinks. The whole thing. It's just my luck. Find people I like, and the system will just clear them out of the way.'

She likes him. She said she likes him. This whole thing is going from romance to tragedy in a single act.

'So, we're agreed?' he says, his voice cut sharp as a crystal.

She nods. It's a reluctant nod, but it's a nod.

'Okay,' her voice comes quiet as a whisper. 'It's just… the wrong time, then.'

He reaches out and touches her face gently. She doesn't push him away instead; she places her hand over his.

'Next lifetime?' he says.

'You're on.'

And there they stand, outside the lift, his hand over hers. And time seems to go just a little bit slower, like it's trying for once to be on their side. And he leans forward, leans in and kisses her gently on the forehead. It feels like the world is exploding out wide and crunching down quick, all at the same time.

'You getting that?' he laughs. 'The…?'

'Spark thing? Yeah. Mad. What is that?'

'Hmm hmm.'

They turn to see a security guy clearing his throat.

'Oh, hi.' Portia's face glows beetroot. 'We're here to see Kendal.' She flashes her wristband.

'I do the talking,' Portia mumbles, barely audible.

This time, Marco just nods.

'If she's mad, her face won't show it.'

'Indoctrofix?'

'With a bit of cement thrown in for good measure.'

Marco smiles.

'If she's in a bad mood, she has her fingers interlaced. If she is in a foul mood, she taps one line of fingers on the desk.'

He raises an eyebrow.

'Like I said… been here before.'

'What about good mood?'

'Doesn't happen, not these days anyway.'

'Ms Reynolds?' An aide announces as the door to Kendal's room swings open. 'The administrator will see you now.'

Turns out, Kendal is tapping all ten fingers on her desk. The full quota.

'So. Ms Reynolds? To what do I owe the pleasure?'

It's a big desk, solid and uncompromising. The whole room has the same feel. High ceilings and serious. If it's meant to intimidate, it does the job nicely.

Portia takes a deep breath. 'I've come to apologise.'

Marco's surprised. He hadn't expected Portia to have a strategy.

'I shouldn't have questioned you on the steps,' Portia says, dropping her head as if in abject atonement.

For a moment, the finger-tapping stops. Kendal nods, then glances at the information-screen propped open on her desk.

'You're one of our star pupils. Highest grades in exams, and Lung Capacity, twenty-five.' She nods appreciatively.

'Actually, I hit thirty yesterday.'

'Hmm. Thirty.' Kendal gives a satisfied grunt, then glances back up at them, the hard glaze returning.

'So, what exactly is it that you want?'

'I've got someone in trouble. A young man called Tee. He works in tank operation. He's a skilled trainer. There's no way I could have got to thirty if...'

But Kendal simply holds up her right hand, indicating silence. 'I take it he's on the repatriation list?'

'Yes.'

Kendal sighs like this whole business is so utterly tiresome, before glancing down at some paperwork. 'We have quotas.'

'I know, but...'

Again, the hand comes up. 'We are having to absorb a lot of skilled people arriving from the southern territories. Which means we're in the uncomfortable position of having to lose people who have skills that we do value. But ... are replaceable. It's not personal. It's just ... unfortunate.'

'I thought I could go in his place,' Marco blurts.

'We don't do that.' Kendal spits back, sharp as a toad catching a fly.

'But his rating was a mistake.'

'We don't do that either,' she pauses for a moment, taking her glasses from the bridge of her nose and giving Marco one long, hard stare. 'And who, exactly, might you be?'

'Marco. Marco WU.'

'Hmm.' She nods at the WU, as if to say *wouldn't you just know*. She flips the glasses back on and reactivates her information-screen.

'Soil sciences?'

Marco nods.

'You won the Clause Herbit award last year, 'Prototype of floating soil made out of rubber.'

'It's more molybdenum disulphide. The rubber's just a flotation device. The MoS_2 desalinates water so...'

Kendal nods slowly to herself. 'You do know that rubber comes from trees?'

'We would, of course, have to initially grow the trees.'

Kendal smiles indulgently, as if Marco has just said something oh-so-stupid.

'So, we would, of course, have to have somewhere to grow the trees.'

Marco's met this objection before; he knows it inside out, upside down and, more to the point, how to get out of it. 'The rubber's not the main thing. And besides, initially, many of the new fields would be taken up with low-lying rubber plantations. It's a case of initial investment, long-term returns. We would have to...'

But Kendal holds up that hand again, and Marco pulls on the brakes.

'Thank you. I'm not after your *school* project.' With an unmasked look of acute boredom, Kendal glances back down at her screen. 'I see that you only just scraped through this time?'

'Yeah, I had some... my test results were atypical.'

Kendal scrolls down the screen. 'So it would seem.'

'Tee, my friend, he really is brilliant. Maybe just this once you could?' Marco despises the note of pleading in his voice, but if it gets the job done.

Kendal shuts the device with a firm, sharp slap.

'Mr WU, you have to understand that we are in a finely balanced situation here. Over the next few weeks, we will be getting more people in from the southern territories. Not as many perhaps as arrived yesterday, but what we are currently experiencing, this is only the first influx.'

She stands. The meeting, it appears, is coming to an end.

'Atticus, could you show Mr WU out?'

A member of the security detail steps out of the shadows.

Marco hadn't even realised he was there. If she carried on with the repatriation plans at this scale though, Marco was pretty sure security guards were going to be one profession on the keeper's list.

'Hang on a minute. You're missing the point.' Marco blurts as the security guard edges into position, level with Marco's shoulder. 'I'm willing to swap.'

And Kendal laughs. It's semi-spontaneous but not exactly kind. 'Can you imagine the administrational nightmare if we started to 'swap' people? It would also mean that we're not left with the skills that the city needs. The whole idea of *swapping* is contrary to everything we do here.'

'So, this little exercise has been absolutely pointless.' Portia's finding it hard to hide her irritation.

'Not at all. You're both on my radar now, and that's always a good thing.'

Portia's face flushes a shade of red, which can only be described as furious.

'Come on, Marco.'

They turn to leave.

'Wait. Not you, Portia. You can meet up with your little friend later. I'm not done with you.'

CHAPTER 17
CLEANING UP

MARCO CAN'T STOMACH the entrance hall again. Not straight off. He needs to collect his thoughts. Installed in the bathroom, he stares at his sorry face in the mirror. He could swear that he's aged thirty years in the past few days. Worry is etched on his forehead like it's been carved there with permanent marker. The bathroom is dark panelled wood, small orange sconce lights on the wall are fighting a losing battle against the darkness. It looks like something left over from a Dickensian 'gentlemen's club.' Which only serves to rub salt into those wounds - if you're not in the club, you don't stand a chance in hell. Tee is lost. Molly has gone, and now Marco's set himself up on Kendal's 'radar.'

Suddenly, a shot rings out.

'Shit.' Marco stares at the door. What the fu**! The washroom is empty. He's right out on display, like a sitting duck at a carnival show. Another shot. He has to get somewhere safe. Grabbing his backpack, he dives into a stall, raising his feet up from the floor. Another shot. He should have locked the door. Why didn't he lock the door? He leans forward slowly, his hands shaking, his breath coming in short, panicked bursts. Thank God Portia's not waiting for him outside. She's still with Kendal. They've got security. She'll be okay. He slides the bolt across. Done. He edges back on the seat, holding his knees uptight. Where was it coming from? Was it above? Was it outside? Then suddenly it cracks out loud and clear again. BANG. BANG. BANG. Three shots. But… He stares, incredulous, at the bag squashed onto his knees; the shots are coming from inside his backpack?

He sticks his hand in, feels around. Is it his handset? He draws it out, shakes it. Presses it against his ear. Nothing. He pushes his face up close and personal to the bag. That can't be right. He holds it even closer, so close he's practically wearing the damn thing. He can hear running. Someone is running in his backpack. He tips everything out onto the floor, scrabbling down on the hard tiles after his books and wallet and then he sees it. The tin watch, the one he'd made to match Molly's. There's a light on. It must have auto-charged from his handset. The faint green light pulses. He presses the back of the watch to his handset; the battery is years old; it needs all the help it can get, then wedges his ear close to the display.

Breathing. He can hear breathing. Short, sharp inhalations, and the pounding of feet, over…? What is that? It's not the tiled floors of the repat building. It's a thick heavy thud, then a slight splash. Thud, splash. Someone is running over a platform on the water. Another pant, a deep inhalation. No, not someone. It can't be. Another inhalation. Molly! Molly is running.

'Molly.' He shouts into the receiver, wishing he'd upgraded the damn thing. There had been years in-between the initial plunder of Dr Krypto. Years of way-better technology that could have been housed in the watches. 'Molly!'

But if it is Molly, she can't hear him above the sound of her own pounding feet.

'Molly!' he shouts again, louder this time.

Another gunshot. A brief cry. A scream of pain. Then, then…

'Molly!'

Nothing.

'Molly.' He shakes the watch. 'Molly!' He screams.

'You alright?' There's someone outside the toilet.

He catches his breath. What the hell just happened?

'Hello. You okay in there?'

'Yeah,' he manages, but he's not. He is the furthest from okay he's ever been.

He stares at the watch, hoping it might cough out some answers. But now it's succeeded in getting his full attention, it remains obstinately silent. What does it mean? She's supposed to be on a boat.

He opens up the back of the watch, takes out the transmitter, shakes it. Ties it back in, checks the connections, twists one thin metal coil just that tiny bit tighter. But nothing. Just white noise.

His head is so full of thoughts fighting to get aired, it's like a battery-hen furnace in there. Feathers and squawking and panic. He goes out of the toilets. There's a guy at the wash-stands, the guy who asked Marco if he was okay. He's squeezing soap into his palms. He stares at Marco, looking for an explanation.

'Dodgy slurp-carton,' Marco says. 'Stomach playing up.'

The man nods. 'Not sure what they're putting in them these days. Can't always…'

But Marco's in no mood for small talk. He needs some air. He's out through the doors before he realises something's not right. He's exited the Men's the wrong way; there must be two sets of doors. He's about to go back when he realises where he is. He's in the records building. Molly used to clean it. Even in broad daylight, it's quieter than the other council buildings; it houses the archives, a hundred shades of business done and dusted. Presided over by an old guy Molly called 'the Owl.' On account of the fact that the man never slept. Spent all his days, all his nights, filing away the city's hard copies. The building is less grand than most of the other council buildings. More akin to the Dickensian toilet Marco just walked through, than the high-ceilinged, in-your-face, brutalism of the repat building. It's like stepping through into a different age. Corridors for walking down. Rooms for working in. Only, by the lack of bodies, it looks like they're on operation skeleton staff.

Molly brought Marco in here on some of her shifts. After 10 pm, her wristband got switched to access. He stuck a bit of foil under his, so the tracer didn't work. It was an old trick he'd picked up from Sanderling, but a good one. He'd come in to help Moll. Well, help a bit, and mess around a lot. He'd seen this corridor before; its long windows overlooking the docks. They'd stood and watched the boats coming in, going out, cutting dark trails in the water. Bobbing like Christmas trees in the endless black. Molly's boat would have been long gone by now. But the transmission? He's still holding his handset, the watch attached. Was there some kind of problem on her boat? Pirates? How would he know? How could he help? The boat must have been attacked. He glances at his handset and tunes into the news station. Tips on how to make a curry using seaweed. A lot of other stuff. Most of it mundane. Not one mention of boats lost.

Back against the wall, Marco sinks to his knees, staring down the long, familiar corridor. Molly. It seems like yesterday that it was just the two of them, in this exact same spot. They used to grab a couple of swivel chairs from the offices and have chair Olympics. Fun and games down this very carpet. Him pushing her, her pushing him. Or sat shoulder to shoulder, scouting along with their feet.

'Come on, Macko'

He can almost hear that voice, conjure it up. Only this time he knows it's in his head; memories called into play as inevitable as a CD put into a reader.

'Chicken, cluck cluck.' She'd be throwing out her arms, bending them into short stubby wings. Typical Molly.

'I just think if Nan.'

'Oh, Macko!'

And she fell to the floor, just like he'd shot her. A big flop: body first, legs comedy style up in the air, then coming down hard-thud on the carpet.

She was so loud. How did she get away with being that loud? Is that what tripped her up in the end? All that joy-of-life that somehow it was impossible to squash.

Then she'd be grabbing his leg, and he was over in an instant, and Molly rolling on top of him, waggling his cheeks, pinching them between her fingers.

'Oh, poor little Macko. In trouble with Gran?'

He'd push her off. 'It's fine for you. You can get away with anything.'

She rolled over onto her back, and they lay, looking up at the ceiling, comfortable as if they were laying out on gran's rooftop garden.

'You know Gran, she likes it really.'

'What?' Molly had lost him.

'When people push. Gran likes a bit of push in a person.'

'Yeah, well.' And he couldn't help himself, sometimes it was tough being the outsider. Three's a bad number. Someone is always on the outside. But in that corridor, chair Olympics, it was just the two of them.

'It's got castors,' she'd said. 'The chairs, they've got wheels.'

'You mean yours has got wheels?'

'Come on. I'll let you choose.'

Then she stared at him, those big Molly eyes, mostly daring, but a little bit of pleading mixed in for good measure.

'Okay.'

'Yes!' her voice echoed off the walls.

'The Owl's out tonight. He told me. We've got the whole place to ourselves.'

And they would rush like a freak wind down the wide corridor into the library, which was a different kind of space altogether. It had a kind of hush to it; as soon as you opened that door, you could feel years of silence come seeping out, but none of this stopped Molly.

'Come on, which one d'you fancy, Macko?'

She'd go pulling out all the chairs, lining them up in a chaotic fashion. 'World's your oyster.'

He would eye the line critically.

'Can I have five minutes to check it over?'

'Like I was born yesterday. Five minutes, Mr Fancy fingers and you'll have re-designed the whole thing: put in pneumatic tyres and spin-faster spokes.'

He'd smiled, because of course she was right.

'Take it or leave it.' She'd said, spinning the backs of the chairs so they started to swirl like crazy carousels. 'Buyer beware.'

'Okay.' He chose a low-backed chair with wheels that could lock and managed to get in one spin. Then it was out in the corridor again. Molly drawing a starters line with a thin trail of paper clips, before hollering out a deafening 'one, two, three, go.'

They would spend all night. All night lining up the chairs and fighting for supremacy. Then, after their stomachs were sore, bruised black and blue with laughter; Molly would manage a ten-minute dust. Marco did a quick throw-around of the Hoover, and they were out. Nobody ever knew. But that was all in the past, a different world from the here and now.

· · ·

Marco peers down at the docks below, and suddenly his heart sinks. More people than he can count are pouring out onto the quay. They look like ants as they clamber off boats, rafts, dinghies - anything with enough buoyancy to support itself and a smidgen or two of life. Wet, sorry, sad shapes shuffle into rigid lines far below. Marco's glad he's above it, glad he can't see the hopeless expressions on the faces. Most of the migrants would never get past the customs gate. But that didn't mean that those who did wouldn't upset the city's finely tuned apple cart. The situation was even more desperate than he'd thought. Okay, so he hadn't been on the latest repatriation list but, after his run-in with Kendal, there was not a doubt in Marco's mind: he'd be on the next one.

He feels a sharp stab in his hand and realises he's still holding the watch, crushing it tightly in his palm. Molly. Something just does not stack up. The device had never had a wide broadcast range, and Molly had been gone days. How much distance was that? He's not sure, but it had to be more than Dr Krypto could handle.

'You are not supposed to be here, young man.'

He jumps out of his skin. The watch falling from his hands.

'Sorry, I...'

There's an old guy standing there, snow-white hair. Almost as round as he is tall, which is a difficult feat to pull off these days. And dressed in this odd tunic thing with baggy trousers underneath.

'This area is restricted access,' the man says.

'My band didn't...'

The man glances at the green band.

'It's not all about colour, dearie. Some places are just no-go unless you have an invitation. And I did not *invite*. Security has to phone me from the lobby.'

'Oh, sorry... the door was open in the toilets and I just...'

'Just, just…' The man bends down, grunting as internal air gets trapped somewhere between knees and stomach tyres.

'Blasted interns. Well, you best *just* get back out the way you…' he picks up the watch, turns it through his fingers. 'Where did you get this?

'I made it.'

'I don't think so, sonny.' The man's eyes narrow. His short, stubby fingers tightened like a cage around the watch.

'I did. I…'

Then the man's face suddenly alters, the frown disappearing into a cheeky school-boy grin. 'Marco?'

Now it's Marco's turn to look confused. 'Yes, but…'

The man smiles, opens his hand, and slides the watch back towards Marco. 'I'm the Owl.'

CHAPTER 18
THE OWL

'SO YOU SAY the transmission range is short?'

'Yeah, I mean we haven't used the things for years, but the range was never good.'

The archives office has the heavy tang of leather hanging in the air. The smell is so dense, Marco can almost see the cow. Each wall is covered, floor to ceiling, and then some, with books and files. All of this would be impressive enough. But the room is like two stories high. There's even a little ladder hooked to a golden-brass rail sailing 360 around the room.

'Mad,' Marco says.

'All the planning applications for the last two hundred years, all safe and stored,' the Owl tells him proudly. 'We don't get many now, of course. The only people allowed to build are the government/ Texicom. And Texicom / government. Space is not exactly easy to come by. Horizontal real estate is not always safe. People in the Glaire kept building vertical structures, but none of it was stable. Up, up, up if you can't go out. Does not work: you block out light, or the whole damn thing falls and … Well, you have to have regulations, laws. Safe and practical, that's the buzz words today. Everything safe and practical. So, the archive, well, it's a bit of a treasure; a comprehensive picture of how our city developed.' He depresses a button on a wooden cabinet and out slides a drawer packed tight with neatly filed, beautifully penned architect's plans. 'And I like to think that we're not only informative, but we are rather pretty to boot.' The Owl smiles at the room, as proud as if he had birthed it himself.

'It's amazing,' Marco says. 'I went into the library, but I can't believe Molly didn't bring me here.'

'House rule, strictly no chair Olympics.'

Marco laughs.

'Not safe, not practical. And you may find it amusing, young man, but it was me who had to stick the wheels back on. This one here ...' he slides a chair across the floor. It rattles, sharp and bickering as an arthritic, old lady. 'Never recovered. Besides, I dread to think what you two would have done to my ladder.'

Marco eyes it wistfully: hanging there on the rail, wheels attached and ready to go. The Owl has got a point.

'Tea?' the silver-haired man asks, holding out a bone china teacup. The warm scent fills the air. Marco inhales.

'Is this…?'

'Real? Everyone has a weakness. Mine is tea. Now, back to business. You say Molly was no-show?'

'Well, technically, she wasn't.'

The Owl cocks his head to one side and gives Marco a beady, inquisitive look. Marco wants to laugh out loud – he may be an insomniac, but there are a host of other reasons as to how this guy got his name.

'She wasn't marked on the system as no-show, but I was at the re-pat centre. She didn't turn up.'

'It gets crowded. You could have missed her?'

Of course he could, but Marco shakes his head. 'I was up on the steps, had a good vantage point. It's unlikely.'

'But possible. And there's been a transmission on her comm-list?'

Marco nods.

'So, at one point in time Molly was on that boat, but now because the transmission range for your watches is so short, you think she must be back in the city?'

'Got to be.'

'Okay,' the Owl sucks in his breath, then sighs out like he's a balloon deflating. 'Well, needle-in-a-haystack is an expression which springs to mind.'

'Yeah,' Marco is fully aware.

'Terrible waste. I miss her already. She was...' he searches his mind for the right word.

'Not safe or practical?'

'Lord, no,' the Owl laughs. 'If she came in to clean, I'd have to do it after her. No, not safe, not practical. But... you see that's part of the problem with life. Safe and practical are all well and good but leave out the fun and terminal tedium will finish you off.'

The Owl picks up the watch once more and turns it slowly around and around, as if somehow it might be hiding answers behind that tin exterior. 'So, take me through it from the top. What did you actually hear?'

'Running, panting, gunshots, a scream.'

"Hmm, doesn't exactly sound good, especially not good on the gunshot, scream combo. And ... what did it sound like?'

'Sort of AHHHH.'

The Owl looks at Marco like he's really lost the plot. 'Actually, I meant the transmission. What did the transmission sound like – the running, any background noise?'

'Sorry?' Marco's can't see where this is going. He's also feeling more than a bit stupid after the scream. It was so embarrassing. Why did he have to...

'Concentrate. The sound of the footsteps. What did they sound like? And please don't demonstrate, just tell.'

Marco closes his eyes tight shut and tries hard to think back. Thud. Thud. Thud.

'The quality. We're looking for the quality here,' the Owl says, placing one arm on Marco's shoulder as if he can draw the experience back out, and suddenly Marco understands.

'On wood. Footsteps on wood, so it could easily be the boat.'

'Uh, ha.' The Owl shakes his head in a slow know-it-all side-to-side all-the-time-in-the-world fashion. 'The re-pat boats are all metal.'

So not a boat. 'But there was water. Like the wood, like it was being slapped by water?'

'Floating on, maybe?' The Owl quizzes.

'Like a raft? You think it could be…'

But the Owl is already smiling. 'No Marco, no, I don't think it's a raft. One, because that's just silly. Where would you run to on a raft? and two because… because I think it sounds like a wooden platform. A platform that's laid across the sea. I think it sounds like the levee.'

Marco sighs. This is getting nowhere fast. 'But that's concrete.'

'M M M.' The Owl is doing that shaking head thing again, but now he's got one single finger going in the same direction, windscreen wiper style. 'There's a wooden platform on the outside of the levee. In fact, spookily enough, that's what the last planning application was for. A refurb. Most of the time, the platform is under the water. And a lot of it's rotted through. The only bit still standing strong is on the east side of the levee.

The Owl slides open a drawer and starts rooting through papers.

'Wow! Is this…'

'Yes, yes. Real. But not tree 'real.' Tea paper. It's bleached and mushed and … well, whatever else. I'm an archivist, not a… a tea pulper. All I know is… does the same job, easier to get and… Well, let's just say I get well supplied as a sideline. Here,' he pulls an A1 sheet of parchment out and lays it across the top of the desk.

'Like I said,' he runs his finger across the diagram. The pencil line is broken. 'See the gaps? I'm pretty sure that's all gone. But the east side, it's kind of looking okay. If the scope of your search is narrow,' he rattles the watch in the air 'because of transmission limitations. And if it was wood, you heard her running on, my bet would be that our young Molly is just the other side of the levee. Problem is, of course…' and he takes a moment to let out a thoughtful sigh, 'how on earth do you get there?'

CHAPTER 19
ANYBODY OUT THERE?

'BUT WHERE WOULD YOU START?' Portia's been pouring over copies of the Owl's plans for a solid thirty minutes. Problem is, the Owl had a 'plan' for everything. And since he very rarely got visits, and never slept, and had a soft spot for Molly, he was maybe bordering on the over-helpful side. Marco ended up with way more information than he can realistically make coherent sense of. And not just the levee, but the whole city laid out on tea-paper. Portia's right – there's just too much.

'I'm not even convinced it's where she'd be. I mean, the broadcast you heard,' Tee says, turning the tin watch over and over in his hands. 'It doesn't mean she's in the city, or just the other side of the levee. We all had that Dr Krypto thing. Everyone was broadcasting on it. Now … well, the frequency that radio's working on, it's pretty obsolete. Only thing that's broadcasting these days is you and… well whoever it was you heard,' he says, flipping the switch and listening to nothing but white noise.

'Did you hear her voice?' Portia asks.

Marco shakes his head. 'A scream.'

'Her scream?'

'I don't know. I thought so.' But everything he 'thought' he knew is dissolving faster than sandcastles at high tide. 'Maybe.'

They're sitting in the tank room on the platform of tank ten. Tee claims it's the only 'safe' place to talk, since Finbow (the octopus) keeps squirting the recording devices.

'Maybe the watch was stolen. You've seen the broadcast, man. She was on the boat. She must be okay.'

'To be honest,' Marco mumbles, 'I'm not sure if any of us are 'okay' anymore. You should have seen the docks.' He shivers at the thought of it. 'Kendal was just a waste of time.'

He glances over at Portia, who's still pouring over the plans. 'What was she ear-chewing you about?'

Portia looks embarrassed. 'Oh, you know…'

They don't.

'Asking her awkward questions: humiliating her on a live broadcast.'

'Slap wrist time.' Tee says, he knows all about that kind of thing.

'Sort of.'

'She is one spineless monster,' Marco sneers.

'She's not that bad, not really, she's just confused.'

'Confused!' Marco is no way letting this one go. 'Because of that woman, everyone I care about is being shipped out.'

Portia sighs. 'She means well she's just… to be honest, Texicom are giving her very little room.'

'The way people are coming in,' Tee snorts. 'No one's being given much of that. Look, guys… you tried. None of this is your fault.'

But whatever Tee says, Marco will always blame himself. Some blame you can't just back-peddle out of.

'Come on,' Tee says, smiling, 'can it really be that bad? Maybe the city… I mean maybe they're bigging themselves up here. You really, honestly believe that the whole world has been wiped clean and that this is the only place to be?'

'No... but what we do know, what is not even up for dispute, is that it's grim out there.'

'And who profits from that? Who's set to gain from the fact that the entire world, apart from our city, has gone down the tubes?'

Marco shakes his head. 'Nobody profits.'

Tee snorts. 'Really? Jeez, man. Follow it through.'

But Marco and Portia are still looking blank.

'I thought you two were...'

'Bright?' they both chime in together. Both hitting the exact same wearisome note at the exact same moment.

'You got something, Tee?' Marco says, feeling irritated. 'Spit it out.'

'Okay. Listen. Someone always profits. Texicom, they're...

'...Not the government, they're a corporation.' Marco is getting really irritated by the way everyone keeps blurring them together.

'Bingo,' Tee shoots Marco his very best gotcha-wink. 'Texicom is a corporation. But over the past few years, Texicom and the government, well, they've kind of segued.'

So, Tee's feeling it too, but he's not stopping there.

'And corporations have an agenda; they want to make profit. All those bright-spark people coming in from the territories, who's been sailing off like Prince Charming and picking them all up?'

'We have. Our city.'

'The brightest people with all the very best skills.' Tee nods slowly, looking smug, like he's nailed it. 'Looks to me like our very own city, that's the one profiting.'

'But there's no money in all of this.' Marco just cannot see what Tee's hinting at.

'Yet,' Tee says, leaving the word hanging. 'No money... yet. Take all the best people, tell them there's nowhere else to go, what are they going to do?'

Suddenly, Portia's eyes light up, she's got it. 'All those

bright, homeless people, they're going to stay with you. Work for you.'

Tee smiles. 'A brain-drain, only kind of more of a brain fishing net. No, more of a...' he continues, scanning his mind for a neater handle.

'Factory?' Marco offers.

Portia nods slowly. 'One where you've already clocked in, and there's no clocking out unless Texicom decides they want you out.'

Marco mulls it over, feeling out where it leads. 'You get all the best ideas, and everyone willing and able to work for the *greater good.*'

'There have to be other places,' Tee says, a grin plastered across his face, 'and maybe our Molly is already halfway there.'

'Hey, rewind just one moment,' Portia's rolling up the plans. 'Before you go off on your grand tour, don't you think we should just check in on Molly? See if there's any explanation as to where she is on her comm-list? If she's gone AWOL, it will say.'

They cluster around the monitor, their bodies bathed in the eerie blue light from the tanks. Marco doesn't expect Molly to answer because he doesn't expect her to be there. He'd heard the shots, heard someone running, heard the scream. But there are no notes next to her name. Within seconds, the transmission clicks through and to his absolute amazement, there she is, large as life. No bullet holes.

'Marco.'

'Molly!' he allows himself one gargantuan sigh of relief; repatriation may not be great, but it's better than being shot at. 'I was worried about you.'

There's a slight delay in her voice.

'I'm fine.'

She looks fine. He glances at her wrist; the watch has gone.

'You've lost your watch?'

'No jewellery allowed. Get it back on arrival.'

He remembers the gunshots, the running, the scream.

'You sure you're okay?'

'No worries, and real food. You?'

'Yeah, you said. I mean, about the food.' He's not sure Gran would be too pleased about all the hype she's giving the catering facilities. 'Tee's here, and my …' he hesitates over the word *friend* 'My Portia.' – _my_ *Portia* – what kind of an idiot says that!

'Hi,' Molly says.

'Hi,' they chorus back.

'I just wanted to ask you a few questions about…'

An alarm cuts in.

'You have got to be joking!'

'Sorry. Marco, you always ring at a bad time. I got to go.'

She starts to get up.

'But…'

'Bye.'

The screen goes black. For a moment they sit in silence, the words robbed right out of their mouths. Yes, she's safe, but the whole thing is about as satisfactory as a no-tasting tour of a chocolate factory.

'So, the watch thing…' Tee glances at the tin husk in his hands.

'Must have been stolen?' Portia offers.

'Well, one thing's for sure, it wasn't her broadcasting.' And Marco's pleased, seriously he is, only…

'I mean,' Portia says, scrutinising the screen, her pretty green eyes scrunched like she's trying to decipher a semiotic code which may not even be there. 'I didn't know her before, but she looks okay.' There's a pause before she adds, a little embarrassed, a little in awe. 'She's actually really beautiful.'

'Thank the powers that be, she has no clue on that one,' Marco says. 'Modesty is not something Molly exactly suffers from.'

'And real food,' Tee's digesting the very thought like it's been freshly baked from the oven. Marco knows how Tee's brain works. Swimming makes people very, very hungry. There's not a waking hour goes by that Tee doesn't infuse with the idea of food, the reality of food, or the desire of food.

'But she always called me Macko.' When Marco says it out loud, he suddenly realises that it sounds kind of childish, petulant. Like somehow, he's wounded by the loss of familiarity. Upset that his friend, with her new life with its real food and sunshine, has cast him to one side sure as a freshly-minted teenager leaves an old toy under the bed.

Portia shrugs. 'So, she used your real name. It's a more formal environment.'

'That works,' Tee offers sagely. 'How about we try calling her later? I still have a shedload of questions.'

Marco nods, it seems like a plan. 'And that delay thing, it just makes it difficult to...' He leans forward, hand towards the screen, about to close it down.

'Wait!' Portia's voice rings out sharply, echoing around the room just as Marco's about to swipe *close* on the screen.

'Look.' Portia pulls herself forward, sitting so damn close to the screen Marco can hardly operate the controls.

'Rewind.'

There's a sense of urgency to her voice that Marco hasn't heard before. She's spotted something.

They play the recording again, none of them making a sound. Only the water carries on oblivious, with its constant, quiet chatter chatter. But, despite the scrutiny, Marco can't see one thing that doesn't work. It's the same Molly, bright-eyed and confident. She's calling him Marco, not Macko. But she did that, sometimes, occasionally, rarely. The room looks clean. The food sounds great. There's a delay but...

'There!' Portia points to the spot, her finger hovering over the wall clock 'Zoom in.' Tee instructs, and it's done.

'Rewind,' says Portia.

Marco does as he's told. A couple of seconds skirt back double-quick, but just a couple because no sooner has he hit the rewind button than Portia's grabbing his hand away.

She hits 'play' herself, and they sit rooted to the screen. Then they all see it.

'Sorry, you always ring at a bad time. I got to go.'

But they're not looking at Molly. This time, they've homed in on the clock. And just as the words *you always ring* come tumbling out of her mouth, the clock on the wall does something really odd. It moves backwards. Barely perceptible, but back it goes.

'This transmission, it's fake,' Portia says, rewinding the evidence just one last time. 'Molly's not really there. We need to find out who faked that broadcast, and why.'

CHAPTER 20
NEIL

'WHY SO INTERESTED IN SATELLITES?'

Neil was surprised to get the call. Having escaped the cull, Neil had earmarked a whole day of nothing-but-Neil-style celebration, and Marco knows exactly how that goes; a solid eight hours watching back-to-back reruns of old game shows. It's where he picks up general knowledge for his cat lines. It's supposed to make him look brainy and bright, but only serves to hammer-home the fact that he's a bit of an outsider. Something left over from another world. They're crowded into Neil's hamster cage. Same spec as Marco's, only smaller. Someone really has got it in for Neil. It would feel cramped with just Neil and Marco, but the whole entourage is giving it that sardine feel.

'Satellites? Hey man, I mean, who isn't interested in satellites?' Tee says, sounding only half-way convincing. They've decided that the less info Neil has, the better for everyone. But there's a problem. Neil is looking really puzzled because they have never, ever, not once, shown any interest in space sciences. Not since Neil's known them, which, as far as Tee and Marco goes, is pretty close to forever.

'Portia, she's interested,' Marco mumbles, hoping this will cover it, and that Portia won't have a problem with the lie.

Neil gives them a long, hard stare. The 'Portia thing' is forcing everyone to do a whole new re-frame of their *mates'* *scene.* Marco can tell by the way Neil hesitates that Portia's fuel for thought. No doubt Neil's figuring that if Portia is into space sciences, maybe, possibly, Portia might be into Neil. He takes a deep breath, filling out his chest so he's standing a couple of inches wider.

'Well, there was the millennium frame.' He smiles at Portia in a knowing, brainiac, secrets-of-the-universe-contained-between-these-two-ears, type way. 'That's every-thing up to the year 2030. But a lot of the systems got lost when we were nudged out of orbit. Now we've got four prin-cipal Texicom satellites.'

I'll bet we do, thought Marco.

'Tends to keep us covered.'

Portia's forehead creases into a frown. She's trying to think of the best way of getting the info without alerting Neil to the true nature of the problem. She's concentrating so hard it reminds Marco of those games he played as a kid. Gran had an attic full of retro. This game you had to run a metal hoop over a twisted wire. If the hoop touched the wire, there would be this buzz, and the lights would flash, and it would be *game over.* That's the kind of expression Portia's wearing, like there's no room to slip.

'Would someone be able to tell which satellite broadcast which video?' she asks simply.

Neil smiles in a sadly slightly patronising way, a way that just reinforces to Marco why Neil has such a problem finding girlfriends.

'Not from the video. From the central control panel? Yeah, sure. I mean, it's not really my area, but we were briefed on it during induction.'

Marco, Portia and Tee shoot each other a knowing look; they've struck gold.

'Could you do that on Molly's transmissions?' Marco asks, going straight for the jugular.

Neil looks surprised. 'Really?' He says, meaning really - *why*? Not really, *yes I really could*. It's got that sarcastic tinge that sometimes bubbles up out of the blue with Neil. Especially when he's on his space sciences horse.

'You know where she's heading? It'll be broadcast from whichever satellite was broadcasting from that region at that time.' End of, according to Neil.

'Yes, but …' Portia presses on, 'how could we find out?' There's a note of desperation in her voice that doesn't really fit with the casual *just popped over for a parlay on space sciences* dynamic. Luckily Neil's oblivious. 'Find out? Well, <u>you</u> can't.'

'Oh.' That's it, a small sad, pathetic word let loose and unattached from Portia, and Neil climbs down off his high-horse.

'I mean, a person could. But not you. You'd have to ask someone at the satellite team. Well, I say someone …' Neil corrects himself. 'It's a small team. Most of the time, unmanned. It's not like there's much going on out there. What's this all about?'

Blank faces all around as everyone adopts an expression of innocence.

'It's just something's bugging me about the transmission,' Marco says. And this much, at least, is true.

But Neil doesn't look convinced or interested. They're losing him.

'It's a fascinating area, satellite broadcasting. It would just be great to know more.' Portia's shot doesn't even get into the ball-court. Neil just blasts it down, unaware it was trying to get off the ground. 'Like I said, not really my field.'

'It would be really interesting to know where Molly's broadcast came from.' Tee's turn. 'Condemned man's last wish.' And for the final touch on this way-more personal attempt, Tee crosses his body as if he's about to supplicate in prayer.

'Sure,' Neil says. 'Got off lightly there. Would have broken you into the space sciences building if you'd asked. Last wish and all that.'

'Yeah, last wish.' Tee fist bumps Neil. But Tee's smile is all plastic.

Broken into the space sciences building!

Marco's wowed at the generosity, not normally Neil's style. Although, if they were going to spend last wishes, he thinks they should be wishing for a reprieve; a recount; or for all of those boats heading in from the southern territories to get lost, to find somewhere better.

But then, if there is somewhere better, shouldn't they all be looking for it?

As it turns out, the information Neil gets on the satellites is the kind of thing a desperate man might put on his last wish list. It's also the kind of information that could push a regular man quick-smart into desperate man status. Though it comes with strings attached. The main "string", which is more of an unpredictable noose now dangling around Marco's neck, is Neil.

Tuesday, the day after they've cornered Neil at his hamster cage, Neil returns the favour - cornering Marco on the pod on the way home. Neil, due to his size, is a difficult person to hide. He's also not exactly the best actor. So, as soon as Marco gets on to the pod after his shift, he knows that Neil has most likely been waiting for him on the platform for a couple of hours, and the way Neil is hopping from foot to foot also suggests Neil's trying to suppress a secret and a half. Either that, or he's itching for the toilet. But something about the irritated look written wholesale over Neil's face suggests that he's in possession of news that is way too hot to handle.

'Why don't we walk?' Marco suggests.

Neil glances nervously at the two cameras positioned either end of the pod before noding in a way which is supposed to say casually, *sure, why not*. But has *this is going to blow up in our faces, do you know what you've gone and asked me to do, you idiot?* etched all over it. You wouldn't even need a lip-reader, CCTV footage or a webcam stuck to Neil's fore-head to know that something dodgy is going down.

'This is not funny,' Neil says the moment their feet hit the platform. It's cold, and the air is wet. The LED lights are making everything battery hen style: wild-eyed and wakeful, especially Neil.

'Let's just get this straight.' He pushes a slim file towards Marco and, as soon as Marco has hold of it, Neil removes his hand's double-quick time, plunging them deep into his pock-ets, like the file is somehow toxic.

'I don't want any part of this, understand? Any part.' And with that, Neil gets on another pod, and sails off down the track with only his sense of betrayal for company. Marco is left completely alone. Alone and feeling bad, bad about everything. The cold night air seeps damp through his clothes. The neon lights shine bright and unforgiving onto the platform. Marco pushes the folder deep inside his jacket and takes the steep steps out of the station. He walks two hundred yards or so, his footsteps echoing off the high concrete walls of the levee. He walks till he finds a place with no cameras, no lights. There's a small bench cut into the levee wall. Maybe it was an early pod stop or somewhere for workmen to take lunch-breaks when the levee first went up. Marco's not sure, but he's glad to get out of the wet mist. Flipping his handset on torch mode, he tears the envelope open.

He's glad he's taken time to get out of view, because as soon as he stares at the stats, he knows. He knows why

Molly's broadcast didn't feel right. He knows why Neil is mad as hell at him. He feels a lump in his throat. The rug from under his feet has been well and truly whipped out from under him. What the hell does this all mean? He thinks of all those *broadcasts* filling into the city. Then he flips his monitor to communication mode and messages Tee and Portia, just one-word 'Practice?' then 'One hour.'

Marco hasn't got the whole picture. There are a couple of pieces in this jigsaw that he needs to get nailed in place, and a lot of unanswered questions. He turns his hood up and sets off at a jog through the mist. Right before she left, just before she disappeared, Molly went to see Sanderling. He quickens his pace. Sanderling. Gran told Marco to go to Sanderling if he ever got repatriated. He hadn't been repatriated, but his days are numbered, and Tee is on the list. It's eight o'clock. He could be there in thirty minutes.

CHAPTER 21
SANDERLING

'IT'S A HOLOGRAPH.' Sanderling peers through his gold-rimmed glasses at the recording. 'The outfit, it's what they cover holographs in before they put in the detail. And there's a slight transparency at the edge of the projection, marginal, but it's there. Then the lag on the dialogue. It's automated.' Sanderling takes his glasses from the bridge of his nose and puts them carefully, methodically, back inside his treasured leather case. The case with the curious logo that Marco tried to ape on Molly's watch, a circle with a hammer, a map and a pen. A craftsman's guild, that's what Sanderling had said. Leftover from a time when each person was excellent in one thing and one thing only.

They're sitting in Sanderling's workroom, surrounded by stacks of neatly filed cogs, wheels, and shiny automaton body parts. It smells of old wood mixed with water, but fresh water. It's where Sanderling keeps his hydroponics. The constant glug, glug of the water pumps and the chatter of clocks, makes sure there's not a moment's silence. Tick-tock, tick-tock. And somehow, those rhythmic noises seem to weave into the consciousness, become a part of a person. Every time Marco drops by, he always feels like his heart, his breathing, even his movements slip into Sanderling's syncopated beat, like he's a part of it. This place has always been Marco's sanctuary. A haven where he could pull up a seat at the bench and work on his studies, shoulder to shoulder with the stand-in father-figure that he'd erected from the wreckage of his life.

And now, despite all the confusion, all the frustration, all the half-understood answers and undigested lies, Marco can't help feeling a sense of peace. Everything will be alright; he's with Sanderling, and Sanderling always has all the answers.

Only, now it looks like the man Marco has trusted for the best part of his natural, the man he has always thought was beyond honest, that very man has been keeping secrets.

'But you knew it was fake already.' Marco doesn't take his eyes off the old guy. If Sanderling has a tell, Marco intends to spot it. 'You knew there was no transmission.'

'You want tea?'

'No, Sanderling. No, I do not want tea. I want answers.'

Sanderling takes a deep breath, his cold blue eyes looking just about as unfathomable as the ocean. 'We're not one hundred percent sure about the repatriation scheme.'

'We?'

Sanderling shakes his head. 'Doesn't matter.'

'You're working with the protestors?'

'No,' Sanderling says, quick off the mark. 'The protestors have a different… agenda.'

Marco takes a moment to think. Maybe this is always the way Sanderling operates, just like one of those old clocks that he loves to fix, there are wheels within wheels at work, and Marco's on the outside of the mechanism. Why? Doesn't Sanderling trust him? Only one thing is for sure: the ground between Marco's feet is beginning to feel a whole lot shakier than it used to.

'So, who are you working with?'

Sanderling looks awkward but, for a man who is being

pushed into a corner, there's a kind of pragmatic confidence about him - Sanderling is holding all the cards.

'That's not important.'

Marco realises he's getting nowhere fast. He needs to change tack.

'So, tell me, what's wrong with the repatriation scheme?'

Sanderling sighs, a kind of tell-me-what's-right-with-it hopelessness attached to his breath. 'It's uncertain.' He says simply. 'These transmissions…' he indicates the screen with his hand. 'Doesn't take a genius to figure there's something wrong.'

'Was that an implied criticism?'

Sanderling smiles. 'No, Marco. No. You're bright enough.' All the genuine warmth, the love, the caring, it's all still there. If Marco's on the outside of the information, he realises he's there because Sanderling feels that *outside* is the safest place for him to be. But 'safe' isn't working anymore.

'So, there's a problem with the recording?'

'Coupled with the fact that we have people in Africa, Europe, America.'

Marco's finding this hard to digest. It's that 'we' again.

'The repatriated, wherever they're going, it's not where the council says it is.'

'Where's Molly?'

Sanderling shakes his head. 'You don't need to know.'

'But she's safe?'

Slowly, certainly, Sanderling nods.

Marco unzips his bag, takes out his watch, throws it down on the desk.

Sanderling smiles, picking it up and pulling open the casing. 'You know it's primitive?'

'I made it years ago.' Marco is no way about to apologise for shoddy workmanship.

Sanderling's glasses are back on.

'And this transmitter, two way, but the circuits are barely…'

'It's not about the watch! Molly had one too. I made it for her. You know all this.' But there was more; there was something Sanderling didn't know. 'It broadcast yesterday. I heard someone running. I heard shots.'

Sanderling sighs, easing his hand through his hair. 'Clever. The watch… very… But what can I say. She's safe.'

'I heard a scream.'

'I said she's safe. I didn't say it wasn't difficult getting her that way.'

'And Gran knows this?'

'Of course.'

'Just me on the outside, then?'

Sanderling shrugs. 'We need… we want… to keep you in the clear. Knowledge is a dangerous thing.'

'You saw the leaderboard?'

Sanderling nods.

'You know I only just managed to get off it?'

'It caught us by surprise, somewhat. We have contacts. Next time we can fix that.'

Fix that? Marco's unsure what he's hearing. But Sanderling hasn't finished.

'Next time, you'll be fine. You need to continue your studies. Your research is important.'

'Hang on a minute. The world is going to rat-shit, and you want me to focus on my grades!'

'Your research…'

'It's rubbish, hopeless, a pipe-dream.' Marco can't shake off the hard-edged sting of Kendal's scorn.

'No. We have a wider plan.'

There it goes again *we*. 'You and Gran?'

Sanderling narrows his eyes, but there's a flicker of amusement. 'No. Look, Marco, I'm not going to give you any more information. You have enough and, like I said, it's dangerous.'

But this was no good. This wasn't going to work at all.

'I've got to get my friend to safety.' Marco finds the words rushing out of his mouth, fast and cranky as one of those old-time freight trains. 'Tee, my best mate, he's being repatriated.'

But from the blank, impassive look on Sanderling's face, Marco can tell that he's getting nowhere. Sanderling is not listening. The doors to salvation, whatever these might look like, are closing fast. 'It should have been me,' he blurts.

Sanderling rubs his large hands across his jaw, a weary look hanging over his eyes. 'Repatriation is in three days' time. It's not possible.'

'What? You got Molly out. I have to make sure Tee gets out. I owe him.' Marco's not going to let this drop; he's going to badger and wheedle until... Then he glances at Sanderling's face and can't help but feel shocked. Sanderling suddenly looks so old, careworn, like life has dragged him over a boar-bristle rug and left him to rot on its doorstep.

'We were lucky with Molly. Now, it's not possible.'

Marco feels the walls closing in. 'But you've got to.'

Sanderling's just shaking his head. 'The timing's out.'

The Tick-tock, tick-tock that surrounds them seems to swell like a bitter chant in Marco's brain, like it's mocking him. *We're running out, tick-tock, running out, tick-tock... running...* His breath comes short, anger shreds through his veins.

'But it's my best friend. You know what it's like to lose everything? You know how long I've had to live with everyone I know being taken away. The timing's out!!!!'

Tick-tock, tick-tock. Tick-tock, tick-tock.

Sanderling just looks down at those large walnut hands that can normally fix anything.

'Marco, I'm so sorry.'

CHAPTER 22
THE PLAN

'SO MOLLY IS A HOLOGRAPH?'

They're looking at the clip. Zoomed in 500%, they can see the edge blur plain as day.

'She was no-show, right?' Portia rubs her forehead, trying to figure it all out. 'You think they're trying to cover themselves? Don't want to lose face?'

'It's possible,' Marco says.

But nothing stacks up. Marco hates working in the dark and this is like working in a lights-out coal-shed with nothing but a black cat for company.

'But...' Portia glances through Neil's stats, flicking the pages forward and back like she's missing something major. 'There have been no incoming messages from the northern hemisphere satellites this week?'

Marco takes a deep breath because that's just the tip of the iceberg. 'Actually, there are no messages. There's nothing coming in outside of UK waters, full stop. Ever.'

This takes some getting-your-head-around. For a full three minutes, no one talks. All they can hear is the slap, slap gurgle of the tanks.

'So, what did Sanderling say?' Tee's voice, when it comes, is hard-edged serious. It's Tee's life that's next on the line.

'Very little, just said Molly was safe.'

Portia scrolls down the repat list. Most of the names are shown as having had communication with loved ones.

'Is it all lies?' she mutters. She's going through alphabetically. There are so many names, so many communications.

Suddenly Benson flashes up.

'Stop, wait. I know him.'

'You and nobody else,' Portia says. 'Not one broadcast.'

Marco looks at the notes. Benson hasn't even bothered to assign anyone on his comm-list.

'What does it matter? It's not real anyway. All of it's fake.' Tee's pacing the room like he's going to wear a hole in the floor, get out that way.

He's got a point. Nobody on that ship's been communicating. But somehow none of that makes it any better. Because what's filling Marco's soul with despair is that in a world so hopelessly short on space, there's still plenty of room for loneliness.

'Even though sometimes you were doing the wrong thing, your heart, well, can't say there was ever anything wrong with where your heart's placed.'

The words come back to haunt him. He'd practically shoved Benson through the gate to God-knows-what, actually waved him off!

'If these people aren't being deported...' Portia bites her lip staring at the screen, trying to make sense of it all. 'Then what are they doing with them?'

'Generators. Putting them on the treadmills.' Tee says. 'The government's always looking for renewables.'

Marco shakes his head. 'Benson's old. If they were after people to physically help generate energy, they'd be going for the young.'

Tee says nothing. The thought of being chained to a generator for the rest of his days holding zero attraction.

'But Molly is *safe*.' Portia's eyes narrow, mulling over the implications. 'Because she wasn't repatriated. She was no-show. They got her out.'

Marco nods. 'Reading between the lines, that must be the gist of it.'

'They?' Tee asks.

'Not sure. Sanderling wouldn't say.' Marco feels frustrated again at his sad lack of info. Why had Sanderling shut him out? To keep him safe? From what? It wasn't like he was a kid anymore. People he loved, people he liked, people he grew up with were being earmarked for one hell of an uncertain destiny. Marco needed facts.

'These others,' Portia scrolls again. 'So … they aren't really broadcasting. No signals are coming in. Even though the comm-list is ticked, the broadcasts aren't happening. But that doesn't mean to say they're not on a boat.'

Marco nods. 'It just means the broadcasts are fake.'

'But why do that?' Tee's asking. 'Why go to all that trouble?'

'To maintain calm,' Portia clicks the screen off, she's seen all she needs. 'In a city as densely populated as ours, *calm* is a prime objective.'

Marco hopes so. He hopes that somewhere on the waves Benson is safe, setting off in his heavy wool overcoat for a new life.

'Okay, try this,' Tee says, still focused on saving his own skin. 'Could Sanderling be working with the protestors?'

Marco shakes his head; at least he knows this much.

'And I guess that's the Off Grids out of the equation too.' Marco remembers the square, remembers Mia, remembers the OG and the kiss. 'I get the feeling they work pretty much in tandem.'

'Look, this is all very, to be honest, all very completely

utterly unhelpful. The bottom line is – Sanderling got Molly out, can he get me out too?' Tee's asking the million-dollar question, and now it's Marco's turn to come back with the one-cent awkward answer.

'He can't, Tee.' Marco says, glancing down at his short, neat nails in preference to Tee's face. 'Sanderling says it's not possible. Something to do with timing.'

'Says the watchmaker.' Tee's lip curls in a bitter sneer.

'Look, I don't know the details. But I do know if he could, he would.'

There's silence again, just the continual, hypnotic slosh of the tanks.

'Maybe the OGs can get you out?'

They both turn towards Portia, wondering what she's got up her sleeve.

'You're right, Marco. The OGs and the protestors, they work together.'

How does she know all this? Marco's expression must be begging that exact same question because suddenly she's giving him answers.

'They give me info sometimes. That's how I knew the repatriation criteria were going to be widened.'

'Hey, hang on a minute,' Tee's looking puzzled. 'You knew that, and yet you still asked Kendal the question on prime-time broadcast?'

Portia shrugs. 'It's journalism. Everyone has an agenda, mine's truth.'

'Great,' Tee sighs. 'Currently, mine's staying alive – back to basics.'

'Look,' Portia says. 'I've got a meeting with the OGs tomorrow, about Benjamin.'

Marco looks blank.

'The woman at the repat centre, she gave me that letter?'

Of course, it had vanished clear out of Marco's head.

'Benjamin's only thirteen, but he's earmarked for repatriation.'

'What!' Tee can't believe what he's hearing. 'Thirteen years old? They can do that?'

Portia nods her head sadly. 'His mother feels if he gets repatriated, he won't survive. He's type one diabetic. She figures if he goes, no one's going to care about getting him his insulin. The OGs have stockpiled a lot of medical supplies. They've even developed a vaccination for the plague. Medically, they're in a good place. If Benjamin goes Off Grid, maybe his chances are better. And Marco, let me borrow those maps of the city. I can get the OGs to look at them. They might have an idea about Molly: where she went. How she got out.'

The meeting's over. Portia's gathering her things together. 'Tee, I can ask them about you as well.'

'Thanks, but no, I mean that's neat about this Benjamin guy,' Tee blusters. 'He's got a kind of additional need. But living OG, you serious? You know how long those people spend underground in the sewers. They're like living in the shi…'

'Okay, okay,' Marco says. 'That isn't going to work for you, Tee. But look, it's like you said, do we really think this is the only civilised place left? There must be other communities, towns, villages. We're near the peaks, high ground. There has to be something somewhere.'

Tee nods. 'Got to be.'

'Which is good because…' Marco gets ready to drop his atom bomb. 'Tee, I'm coming with you.'

'What?' Portia's voice comes out blanched and cracked like it's been broken in two.

'It should be me going.' No word of a lie; that's what Marco honest-to-God knows. The fact that he got off is pure fluke. 'Besides, I'm on Kendal's *radar.*'

'So, what's …?' she's protesting. Her face crushed as if her dreams just got trampled, and he knows exactly how that feels, but…

'I have to, Portia. Whatever's going on, I have to find out.'

She turns away, glancing into the depths of the tank.

'Hey.' He rests his hand lightly on her shoulder and wishes he could leave it there forever. 'I can be your source on the outside.'

'I'm neck-deep in sources. Tee will be *on the outside*. He can be my source.'

She turns her face towards him, and he longs to reach out and touch it, just like he did outside the lift by Kendal's office. But he doesn't. This is fitting, because their whole relationship is all one big, missed opportunity.

'You don't have to go,' she says, desperate, as though she's grasping at sand and feeling it slip through her fingers.

Marco glances over at Tee, who's looking oh-so dejected and alone. He thinks of Molly, already out there. Safe? He thinks of his futile academy project. His illusions: how he was going to save the world. His great, big hope binned in a few short sentences from Kendal. But that doesn't matter, not really. Because it's fast becoming apparent that he doesn't even know what this 'world' is.

'Yeah, I do need to go. We need to make this right. And if I'm in here, if I'm part of the system, that's not going to happen.'

CHAPTER 23
LANDERSLY

THE LIGHTS in the science block are out, all apart from one, soil sciences. Marco was right to think his tutor might be working late. He stashes his bag in the lockers outside, slips on a white coat from the hook by the door and presses his wristband against the entry panel.

Marco has no intention of telling Landersly what they're planning. Sanderling was right about one thing; knowledge can be dangerous. Tonight, it's all about getting extra pieces for the puzzle, pieces that might just help them survive on the outside. Landersly used to work in deportation, had been integral in designing the most recent transport ships. So, stands to reason Landersly might have some key insights.

'Marco?' Landersly doesn't even look up. He's sat at a bench, a pile of old tech and archaic screens laid out in front of him. Marco looks puzzled.

'Oh, this?' Looking just a little embarrassed, Landersly turns his swivel chair around so that he's facing Marco. 'You know … when Katya died, it wasn't just the loss of … a brilliant wife, a friend. A person who would have made the best, the absolute best mother. No. No, it wasn't just that. We lost all her research.' He sighs and turns back to the computer screen. 'She was so close. So close to finding an answer to the …' he hesitates, 'storage problem.'

Marco notices there's a small piece of plastic held tightly in Landersly's palm, like an earbud, slightly bigger, and with a sharp plug-drive sticking out angrily from one end.

'What is that?'

Landersly raises one eyebrow. 'Part of the answer. The other bit …' he taps the keyboard once again, then picks up an old electrical circuit board. 'Maybe it died with her, but maybe, just maybe, it's in here?' he mumbles to himself. Then suddenly, appears to shift gear, like he's remembered this stuff is classified. He pushes the circuit board and the earpiece to the side, like he wasn't really interested, anyway.

'So?' He turns back around and looks straight down Marco's eyes – full attention mode. 'You manage to save your friend?'

'No.'

Landersly shakes his head in a resigned manner, as if he hadn't really expected any other result. 'Too bad. What continent is he destined for?'

'Europe.'

'As far as I know, the European centre is working okay. Not that they tell me a great deal anymore. He'll be just fine.'

Marco shifts slightly, foot to foot; how can he ask what he has to ask without arousing suspicion?

'And?' Landersly asks, sensing there's more to come.

'I was just wondering, are there other places like here; I mean other functioning cities that didn't go under in the UK?'

'It's pretty grim out there. And now London's gone, it's set to get a whole lot grimmer. Sure, there must be other Mad-Max style communities.'

Marco was aware of the film, its vision of an apocalyptic mismatch of communities. The comparison didn't inspire much hope.

'But...' Marco knows this is no time for allowing trite

dismissals. '… there were other cities, other places higher than we are above sea level. What about Scotland? Scotland had mountains. There must be some places that are okay?'

'We were lucky. Texicom was based here. They'd already put some survival plans in progress on account of global warming. They diverted the river and the canals away from the city. You ever think about that? Thirty-five miles of waterways just re-tracked. What you might call forward thinking. 'Course, no one knew about the meteorites: that disaster could happen overnight. But as an area, we were just … just a fraction more prepared than the rest of the country. It's not all about being on higher ground; you need the infrastructure.'

'But there must be…'

Landersly shakes his head. 'You've seen the pictures.'

'Yeah, but…'

'Look, Marco,' Landersly sighs, 'I don't know what you're hinting at here; some kind of idyllic sheep-rearing utopia stuck out there on a hilltop? Honestly? Sure, there are some crazy tales, myths. People talk; it's human nature. We don't want it to be *just us*. But believing in Santa Claus doesn't make him real. There's no evidence to suggest there's anything else out there. Up until last week, we were pretty much a two-centre waterpark, London and here. But London's going under. Your friend's best bet is to get on that deportation vessel. Maybe central Europe's okay.'

Marco feels the hope drain from his body. Tee was wrong; there is no conspiracy. They are all just clinging to the last few options.

Landersly fixes his attention back on the old screen in front of him, and sighs. 'God, this is slow work.'

'Thanks anyway.'

'Sure. Anytime. All got to play our part, Marco. That's it. No more, no less.'

Marco's heading back towards the door when suddenly he remembers Kendal: the scorn. His shattered research.

'Kendal didn't think much of my project.' It's out of his mouth before he's had time to wonder if, present company accounted for, out of his mouth is the right place for it to be.

Landersly sighs and swivels his chair back around like he's preparing himself to break some dream-shattering truth to a favourite child.

'It could have worked, just … the time scale is out.'

Time yet again, why did everything revolve around time?

'Not just out by a bit, way out. Setting up forests? Growing the damn trees?

Landersly rubs his eyes wearily.

'Sorry. Maybe I should have talked you down a bit. Just didn't want to burst your balloon.'

Marco feels anger surge through his veins. Mia was right; they were all living in a bed of lies with a few false hopes thrown in for good measure. Landersly didn't need to worry about Marco's balloon bursting, it had well and truly popped.

CHAPTER 24
ESCAPE

HE'S BEEN a total waste of space for years. Mia and Kendal were right. Marco would have been more productive cleaning offices. His research, his delusional belief in a *better future*, all of it is a highway to nowhere. How could he have been so naïve, so gullible? When Marco gets back to the hamster cage, the fact that he is one huge, sorry waste of time has followed him home. But he's been working it through all night, and he knows one thing: everything is going to change. No more research. What's called for now is action. He switches off <u>all</u> electronic devices. He's working on a curious mix of over-hyped adrenalin-fuelled paranoia, gut instinct and just a smattering of scientific fact. If a signal got in, it could surely, always, possibly, get right back out again. Even the lights were on and off in an instant. Marco didn't want anyone getting a heads-up on his movements. Not tonight.

Sitting in a small pool of torchlight, Marco winds that old alarm clock, the gift from Sanderling. Usually, he has it stashed out of sight in his 'secret' drawer. His own personal museum of the outmoded. He can still remember the feeling of awe when he'd seen Sanderling throw it together in a matter of minutes, just from bits lying around on the workshop floor. Minutes that Marco had packed full of questions – why that there? Why not bigger? Why the spring? Questions, questions. And now he had a whole different set of questions for Sanderling, but this time Sanderling didn't want to play ball. Well, at least the training had paid off. If it hadn't been for Molly's tin watch, he would never have discovered just how off-track the world had been getting.

'This is adios, mate,' Marco mutters to the clock, as he winds the key one last time. He had meant the words ironically, a satirical goodbye to the hamster cage, the city, his life. But somehow, it doesn't come out like that. Somehow, the words have the taint of the condemned man. The game, whatever the game had been, is up.

Marco gently pushes the alarm hand to three in the morning. No bird's song for him tomorrow. He wanted to be sure that he didn't miss the call. Three had been unanimous; they all figured it was the best time to escape. Two o'clock and the night revellers might still be around. Four thirty and the city's skeleton crews would be waking themselves up for the day, staring out of dusky windows, armed with toothbrushes and glazed eyes. But glassy eyes still saw, and half-sleepy brains still asked questions. Three o'clock and the world would be theirs.

They had split up after the meeting at the tanks. Tee was going to raid the academy for anything he thought might prove remotely useful. Full-body dry suits were going to be essential: feet, hands, head, all needed to be covered. Marco had been assigned to *information*, but he'd fallen well short on getting anything halfway useful from Landersly, so he'd slipped back into practical mode. He'd put together a small bag – food, water, nothing too heavy. Wire cutters, always useful. Compasses, the old-fashioned type, waterproof but low tech. A couple of contour maps of the area. Chandler's Peak was looking hopeful. It was over two thousand feet above sea level. East of the city. According to the Owl, that was the side with the wooden walkway. The same side that Molly could have been.

He left a note for Gran on her kitchen table. He dropped by late after seeing Landersly and debriefing with Tee. The lights had all been off, so he guessed she was already in bed. He'd used his old key, the one she'd forgotten he had. The hallway was dank and dark, like the life was slowly ebbing out of the place. The door had rattled like skeletons in a cupboard when he'd closed it behind him. He'd stood for a moment, feet planted firmly on the cold floor tiles. He could hear Gran from upstairs, snoring peacefully in her sleep. He couldn't stay and look after Gran. In another world, that would be great, but he had to work with the world they'd been given.

He'd left the note propped up by the salt cellar, along with the mended toaster for number 44. Gran would have to pass the word on to Sanderling. Marco was still mad at Sanderling. Knowledge might well be dangerous, but ignorance had to be a whole heap worse. Tee and Marco were heading into this situation blind as mice chased by that old farmer's wife.

Was it okay to just leave a note? Probably not. It said what you would expect. It thanked her for looking after him. Said how he appreciated everything. Told how he didn't want to go, but felt he was destined for the next leaderboard. So, he would get out now, with Tee. He hoped she would understand. That's what he wrote. But deep in his heart, he knew that Gran understanding it all, that was just never going to happen. And he was secretly glad that he wouldn't have to face the explosion.

So, at three, he was guessing he would be ready as he was ever going to be. He wound the alarm clock just as far as the old key would let him. He wanted to hear it tick. He'd read somewhere that you could play babies' womb noises, and they'd fall straight asleep. He didn't know anything about babies. You hardly ever saw them anymore. But clocks ticking, well, that was his womb music. He'd sat so many years by Sanderling's bench. Heard nothing but tick tock tick tock. The sound had kind of seeped into his soul, become part of him.

Next morning, he woke to its shrill tin-can clamour. He was already dressed and packed. He knew he should have left the clock. It was just dead weight, but he stuffed it into his bag anyway. It was his one memento. The one thing that wasn't save-your-life practical. Everyone had to have something.

He slipped out of the stacks into the fog-filled gloom. His chest filling with damp cold air, etching clear lines into his lungs. In comparison, his ears felt dull, as if stuffed by cotton wool. There was not a sound. His footsteps seemed to scream, echoing off the tall concrete towers. Even though the pods that circled the inner-city district ran all through the night, he couldn't risk taking one. Young guy, with a black face, travelling the pod at night? Somewhere, someone, somebody, was going to notice. Besides, he was wearing his shoes. Running was what they were made for. It was unlikely the shoes would be coming with him for the whole journey, and it pained him to think that he hadn't got his money's worth. He made a mental note to enjoy the run and set off at a neat, paced jog.

The city might still be asleep but, although he'd barely grabbed three hours of rest, Marco felt every inch of his body pulsing with life.

He skirts away from the stacks keeping in the shadows of buildings, a thousand thoughts flitting through his head. He'd never been into the levee before, but he'd heard stories, none of them good. The levee had a labyrinth of tunnels inside, and it was all too easy to get lost or drowned. He hoped Portia had managed to make some kind of sense out of the maps she'd taken. But he figured all they needed to do was get out to the open sea. Follow any dirty water that was being pumped out. That should work.

By the time Marco reaches the entrance to the levee, he's feeling like this might well be a suicide mission. But curiously, more alive than he's felt in years. He's never done this kind of thing before: struck out on his own. It's scary as hell, but what choice has he got, when the system is built on lies? He's going to get out, get Tee to safety and see Molly again. The cold air hits the back of his throat, it feels clean and sharp like the whole world has been made anew. It's only as he draws closer and sees two shapes huddled in the shadows that he realises the full force of the situation. This isn't some kind of thought experiment about righting wrongs. This, whatever it is, wherever it takes him, is his new life.

'What took you so long?' Tee's laying out kit into two piles: the dry suits, waterproof bags, a couple of flashlights. His voice sounds edgy and kind of high. He's not joking around anymore, this is serious.

'Didn't want to take the pod.' Marco's words come out staccato as he catches his breath.

Portia smiles sadly at him. He wishes she didn't. He half-wishes she wasn't even here, because seeing her only serves to remind him that this could be, might be, is almost one hundred percent certain to be, the last time they're going to meet.

'I talked with the OGs. There's some high land, five miles to the east?'

Marco nods. 'Chandler's Peak?'

'That's the place. You got a compass?'

He nods, still trying to catch some air.

'And I did this …' Portia pulls the Owl's maps out of her bag, but now they're looking different. Like someone's been all over them on a felt-tip fiesta. It's all different lines, and routes and colours. 'This is the levee, the internal workings.'

Marco's face blanches. 'How in the hell did you map all this out?'

'The OGs helped.'

'Did they have any idea where Molly might be?'

Portia goes quiet.

'Portia?'

She sighs. 'They said if she's not on the boats, it doesn't look good. Although…'

'What?'

'Well, they said they had a boat stolen yesterday.'

Marco looks blank, not sure where she's going with this.

'And they said it was about three o'clock.'

Three o'clock, that's when Marco would have been in the washroom in the repat building. It's when the message came through.

'They were keeping their cards close to their chest, but they kind of pointed to the map when they were talking about it, and the bit they pointed to …' She lays the map out flat. 'Well, it was the east side.'

Things were all fitting into place.

'They shot at her?'

Portia shrugs. 'Maybe. She was stealing their boat. But from the way they were talking, it sounded like they didn't manage to stop her from getting away. They were majorly pissed off. They don't really like… how can I put this… letting go of people. Once you're down there, they like to keep you.'

'So, how'd you get out?' Tee asks.

'I'm useful to them. It's good to have me working up top. Though they've got a new leader and, well… he's a bit extreme. Charismatic, but… not really my kind of guy. If you two try to get out through the OGs, I'm not sure you'd make it. He's got a chip on the shoulder about academy kids. Besides, now they're on the lookout for breakouts.'

Marco runs it through his head. 'Main thing is she's out. There was no engine on the broadcast, just shots and running. So, if she stole a boat, it means she got away after the Dr Krypto transmission.

'If the closest high land is Chandler's Peak, I'm betting that's where she'll have gone.

Tee's not looking so confident. 'Only five miles away, it's not exactly secure. If that's where she is, we don't have much time.'

'Okay,' Portia says, sucking in air like she needs a run up on the conversation, before diving in. 'This is the entrance.' She points to a small grey tube on the map. 'It's currently dry. There's no rain forecast tonight, so you should be safe enough till here.'

'The OGs have used this way out before?' Marco asks.

Portia shakes her head. 'To be honest, I wasn't exactly broadcasting the fact that you two were going to make a break for it, so the discussion was kind of hypothetical. But they try not to use it. It's... well, it's not straightforward.'

Portia points to a small T junction on the diagram.

'That's mainly surface water. I'm guessing it's around a metre, a metre and a half deep.'

'So, no need for suits?'

'No. You need the suits on as soon as you go in. This junction here.' She points to an intersection of grey lines on the map. 'It may be less than two metres of water but, this time of year, it's cold. It's not just security guards, dogs and drowning that's going to be a problem. You're going to have to watch out for hypothermia. You get tired...'

Tee gives a fake yawn. 'We know the drill.'

'Well, make sure you stick to it; no clowning around.'

'Would I?'

They both shoot him a *yes you would* look.

'Okay. Then you've got to follow this tunnel to the right. Left goes back to the city, all the treated water. It's around a mile long. Here…' She points to another junction. 'This could be the problem. It's guarded.'

Tee squints at the map. 'How do you know? There's nothing marked.'

'It's an intersection. All the flood ducts meet here, but also, above it, you've got Texicom's headquarters. You seriously think Finbow and Co are going to leave that unguarded?'

Tee nods. She's got a point.

'This is the tricky bit. To get out, you're going to have to take this route here for five hundred yards, then there's what looks like a tank. You're going to have to drop down underwater.'

'What, you mean like fully under?' Marco asks. He's not liking this. To be honest, he's not liking any of it anymore. His hero complex appears to have jogged right off in the opposite direction. Forget adrenalin-fuelled excitement, now it's fear that's keeping him company.

'Look,' she sighs. She's picking up on the vibe. Trying to avoid eye contact. Wishing she had more info. 'I'm not entirely sure. I don't know anyone who's actually done this. But some parts of the journey, I'm guessing you're going to be fully submerged.'

'We got tanks?' Marco asks, scanning Tee's small pile of kit.

Tee just snorts. 'Tanks!'

'Yeah.' Portia leans forward and gently places her fingers against Marco's chest. 'Two of the best. Fully portable. Keep those safe. You understand?'

He did. He really got it.

'People?' Tee brings them back to earth with a bump.

'Okay. So then… you're almost home dry.' Portia gives a

wry brow-tilt at the irony. 'Almost, but there's this kind of flux thing going on with the water.'

Tee gives Marco a blank look. 'Flux?' She's lost them.

'Kind of like water could be coming in? Going out? Could be doing both at the same time depending on the level.'

'Right,' Marco says, not liking the sound of this 'flux' thing one bit.

'Get through, and there's a shoot that comes out, just about here.' Portia points to the edge of the map. 'East side of the levee. You've got a compass?'

Marco nods.

'And a couple of inflatables.' Tee holds up two five-inch by five-inch packages. He must have clocked Marco's sceptical look because he launches into explanation mode. 'It's okay, bro. These babies blow up to six feet by three, easily enough for one man apiece, two if we get into problems. What more could a guy need?'

Marco can think of more than a few things that might be helpful, but he lets it drop. 'Okay. Let's do this.'

CHAPTER 25
THE LEVEE

'SOMETIMES, mate, you just crack me up.' There's a tone of utter disbelief running through Tee's words, clear-cut as the name of a seaside town stamped through a stick of rock. Not that there was 'rock' anymore, but on-the-other-hand the only kind of *town* that was left was most definitely *seaside*.

'Hey, Portia, seeing as how you can't have my body could you babysit my trainers?'

They're talking in whispers, but their voices still ricochet off the ink black tunnel walls like a gaggle of excited goblins. The constant slosh, slosh of water around their thighs, coupled with the gradual slope down, leaves them in not one shred of a doubt that they are heading down into the belly of the beast - the city's intestines, and they're working their way down deeper and deeper at every step.

'You know how much those trainers cost me?'

'Please, you told me like over a hundred times. What is it with you and that girl, anyway?'

'Girl? I thought we were talking about trainers.'

Silence. But like a scab that needs picking, Marco can't leave Portia for long.

'Nothing. There's nothing between me and *that* girl.' His

words hang in the darkness, as final and disappointing as the end credits on a favourite film, because actually that's about the size of it; how can there be *anything* now? And Marco's glad for the oily blackness of the tunnel: Tee can't see the expression on his face. There are only the thin beams of light from their head torches, bouncing off walls and catching slivers of silhouette from their slippery-seal suits. That's all the light, all the sense of shape, that they have. It's too dark for expression.

Portia was right; the water might not be deep, but it is cold as hell. Marco can feel it welling up outside his suit, ready to sap him into hypothermia the first chance it gets given. The dry suits are proving essential.

'Oh, come on, man. You think I was born yesterday…' Tee has no intention of letting the subject drop. 'Every time that girl comes close…'

'Shh …' Marco holds up his hand, stops dead in the water. Too-late, Tee ploughs into the back of him like a pantomime horse's back end.

'No need to get…'

'Shh…'

'What?'

'Listen.'

They must have been walking for twenty minutes in the blackness, and there had been nothing; no sounds apart from the ones they're dragging along with them. Stopped and standing in the silence, it seems like all that nothingness is screaming out fit to burst. But Marco is sure he heard something. They wait, straining their ears into the silence till they feel like their eardrums are going to turn inside out.

'Nothing. I can't hear nothing. Don't spook me, man. Let's just get…' Tee moves forward, but Marco pulls him back.

'Shh. Listen?'

They stand still as if they've been Basilisked. At first,

there's still nothing, just that empty blackness mocking them. Then Marco catches it again. Just the hint of a sound.

'You get that?'

Tee's headlight bobs up and down in a nod.

'Squeaking?'

'Some kind of filter?' Marco asks, his voice quiet as a hiss as he peels his eardrums about as far back as they will go. And now there's more; it's not just the one squeak but a high-pitched clamour.

'No. Not a filter, too intermittent. That's organic.'

Normally organic's good. It's the sort of thing people rave about, but here? Marco doesn't like the sound of it one bit. 'Organic as in?'

'Water, dark, throw in a bit of sewage, reckon we're talking rats.'

'But there are no ledges. Nothing for them to stand on.'

'Rats don't need ledges. They can tread water for up to three days.'

Marco can't help himself; a shiver passes over his body like a wet eel. 'So, we're talking rats, we're talking plague.'

'I thought that was the OGs,' Tee's sounding confused. 'It's the OGs that've got plague, not the rats.'

The squeaking is getting louder.

'If you're after my opinion, most likely the two go hand in hand.'

A scratching, an itching, a bubble splash, a cacophony of micro noises all meshed into one, and it's getting louder. Marco glances into the dark, empty passageway behind him. 'There must be another tunnel we could take?'

'And another rat colony. We're kind of on their turf. Aim the beam as far out as you can.'

Marco does as he's told, unclipping the torch from his helmet and extending his arm into the cold, oily black air just about as far as it will go. It takes a while for their eyes to adjust. It doesn't look like rats, not at first. At first, it just kind of looks like the water's bubbling, like it's hot, or maybe running over rocks in a stream. But it doesn't take them long to make out that the bubbles are in fact small, hairy bodies powering towards Marco and Tee at a speed of knots. They shrink back a step into the darkness.

'Hungry little buggers, I reckon. Looks like it's feeding time at the zoo.'

'What!' Marco stares in horror at the rat army steadily approaching, laying like a raft over the top of the water.

'We got to go under.'

'They can't dive?' Marco asks hopefully.

'They can dive, but maybe they won't be expecting us to.'

'You're not exactly filling me with hope here.'

'Fresh out of that. Best advice? Swim fast.'

And with that, Tee flicks off his light and slips under the water, sure as a seal.

Marco pulls the headband off his torch and finds the small gluey patch on the back of the unit. Reaching up, he presses the back of the light against the tunnel roof. It holds. They could manage with one torch, and maybe, maybe, the light was what the rats were finding so attractive. Within seconds Marco filled his lungs with a full quota of dirty, dank air and is following Tee under the surface.

Seen from below, the rat-raft is a curious horror. There's very little light, just Marco's abandoned head-torch shining out from behind them, making the rats appear like a gigantic, many-legged fleece rolling over their heads. Marco and Tee swim slow, trying not to disturb the water. Trying not to attract attention. Feeling their way blind down the tunnel, Marco never losing contact with Tee's body. He hopes to God they're going in the right direction. He really doesn't fancy their chances on a U-turn.

They don't come up for a full three minutes; they want to be sure. When they do eventually surface, they find themselves by the junction. The squeaking is getting quieter, ebbing slowly away. They did it! For the moment, they're safe.

According to Portia, they have to follow the tunnel to the right; left will only take them back to the city. Thankfully, the water is shallower here, maybe only a metre or so. And there's a small walkway built up at one side.

Tee leaps up on to the ledge, pulling Marco up after him, then switches on his light, shining the beam directly into Marco's eyes.

'Hey!'

'You feeling tired?'

'Course I'm…'

'Want to go to sleep?'

'No, wait, what?' Marco bats the torch away. 'I have not got hypothermia. Why aren't we checking you?'

'I know the signs. That water's cold.'

'Like I don't know.'

The torch swings around yet again into Marco's face.

'Hey. Enough!'

Tee lets out a sigh.

'Shhh, listen,' Marco instructs.

Nothing. Just the cold slap of water.

'Reckon we lost the buggers.'

'For now.' Tee jumps to his feet and Marco wonders, not for the first time, at his friend's ability to bounce back. 'This is more like it.' Tee stamps his foot down hard on the walkway. The sound echoing off in all directions.

'Tee! We got to keep quiet. If Portia's right, there's a security post a mile down that way. Sound in a tunnel, it kind of carries.'

'Duh!'

'Yeah, well. You want to talk, we do it…'

'Telepathy.' Tee laughs.

Marco lets a sigh escape. Sometimes Tee is infuriating. Strike that – always.

'We do it like we do underwater. Jeez, man, you imagine how pissed off we'll be if they catch us at the next junction and put us back on their repat list?'

'You're not on the list.'

Marco drags himself to his feet and checks his suit. 'Like that's gonna matter if I'm found down here with you.'

'Public enemy numero uno. You know, I kind of like that. It's got a ring to…

'Quiet.' Marco hisses. 'Ready?'

Tee zips his mouth, comedy-style and nods. They walk on in silence, glad to have their feet planted on firm ground, even if it is only a sliver of the stuff.

Way before they get to the security checkpoint, they see the lights spilling out towards them. Luckily, the security voltage is a damn sight more powerful than Tee's head-torch.

'Off,' Marco hisses. And Tee, for once, does as he's told.

They hide in the shadows, listening. Voices. Marco holds up two fingers. Tee shakes his head, there's someone else. He holds up three fingers. Marco strains into the darkness. Tee's right. Marco can't make out the words, but the third voice is higher in tone. A woman maybe? The interactions are short, bored sounding. It's a security detail, but they're not expecting trouble. That's all good because that's the one thing Marco is also hoping to avoid.

They round a slight bend, more a dent in the tunnel rather than an actual turn. Immediately, the security post comes into full view. It's nothing special. A few chairs, a metal door with a heavy lock, the kind you get on submarines: turn the wheel and it'll open. The door must be watertight. Marco guesses there's a high chance of flooding here, and that door must lead straight up to Texicom's headquarters. Marco feels that sense of unease that he's started to feel every time Texicom puts in an appearance. These are government guards, guarding a corporation? Where does the line sit exactly? Marco's not sure he knows anymore.

They can't see much. The lights from the station are bright and shining directly at the two friends. So, the security guys are backlit. It's like watching some macabre puppet show.

Tee points to the water beside the walkway. Marco nods. The water will work the same for the security guards as it did for the rats. They're going to need to slip under the radar. But there's a tangle of passageways by the checkpoint, all shapes, all sizes. Marco remembers how Portia had told them that the flood ducts met here. They need to find the wastewater one. But it's near-on impossible from this distance to tell which duct is which. Tee must be thinking the exact same thing because suddenly, he gives a sniff, then a second sniff. Marco's about to belt him when he realises – of course – they're going to have to sniff their way out. The dirty duct will smell, well, yes – dirty. They need to get closer.

They drop down into the water and swim, keeping all limbs under, no breaking the surface. Breaking the surface is going to make noise. Noise is going to attract attention. The lights from the security point means Tee and Marco can just about see underwater, enough to get some basic sign language going. They inch closer. As they reach another curve, they surface. Security is now about fifty yards away. But the curve allows Marco and Tee to remain hidden in the shadows. There are only two guards left. One must have headed off for breakfast. Marco feels his stomach rumble enviously. There's an energy bar in the bag, but this isn't the time. No way is this the time.

The ducts all intersect above and below the security point. If they want to get in the right duct, at some point they're going to have to stand bolt upright in the water, ascertain which is the smelliest ride out, then jump in and swim like hell. But the plan has more than a few holes. In fact, the plan is so riddled with holes it's supernova style.

This is hopeless. This is all hopeless. Marco is tired, wet and hungry. There's no way they can get past security. It's just as Marco's about to give up, to suggest they should continue on in the duct they're in, see what happens, that Tee's eyes light up. He's spotted something. He points towards one of the other ducts, a dark tunnel that feeds to the left of the security post. Marco looks anxiously towards it, then realises it's bubbling. It's their old friends, the rats. The ones from earlier? Or perhaps another colony? Doesn't matter. The point is that there's a whole tunnel worth of high-impact distraction sailing merrily down a large duct towards security, and Marco recognises the arrival instantly, as exactly what it is – a slice of chaos.

Tee opens his backpack and rummages, pulling out one of the life-rafts. Marco's not sure. He shoots Tee his biggest and best skeptical look. The rafts are compact and hard, and yes, they would fly through the air pretty easily, and on impact, they could make one hell of a commotion. But don't they need the life-raft? As if reading Marco's mind, Tee holds up two fingers; they have two but... Marco's face must show that he's not convinced it's a good idea to lose a raft.

But... Tee shrugs and Marco doesn't need to hear it in words to know that really, they don't have a whole heap of options.

Tee dries his hands. He takes the raft out of his bag and unwraps the cellophane. Carefully, oh so carefully, because if it gets wet, if it springs into action, the whole damn turkey shoot goes belly-up.

One. Two. Three. Tee bobs up in the water. The water sloshing around him is probably barely audible to security. But in Marco's ears, it sounds loud as an orchestra warming up for the kill. It's risky, but Tee needs the height. He's standing now. Barely hidden by the curve in the duct with its small spill of shadow, Tee pulls back his arm and throws.

Marco stops breathing. He has no idea why, but everything stops as the small package goes hurtling, sailing, gliding through the air towards the tunnel. No one sees. In their small corner of the duct, no one breathes. A splash. Nothing. Maybe it's not going to…Then there it is: an almighty pop and a hiss and a whoosh and a squeak of plastic as the raft finds its form. And sandwiched between the noise of the raft, there's a desperate squeaking and squealing and joy-to-be-heard harmony of rats.

This is their cue. The security guards are running off towards the tunnel with the rats. There's a small window of escape, and they have to push through. Marco and Tee swim like hell, still moving underwater; they can't risk the noise.

In less than a minute, they're pulling themselves up on the security platform.

'My God. My God.' They can hear the guard's disgusted voices from the rat tunnel. Boot-thud-kicking, small, hairy bodies which are plop-plopping back into the water.

Marco hopes their luck holds that the duct with the rats and the security men is not the duct that smells. There's no way they're heading down that one. Tee and Marco dash from tunnel to tunnel, sniffing insanely. Nothing smells good. Not one of them smells sweet. But then, suddenly, just as Marco is giving up, just as he is thinking it must be the rat tunnel, that they've blown it, that Lady Luck's left them out to dry, he inhales. And the stink is so bad, so purely disgusting, he knows they've found it. Never in his life has Marco been so glad to smell something so utterly repulsive.

'Tee,' he hisses, and Tee's beside him.

'I'm going to get help.' The disembodied voice of a security guard can be heard. Footsteps, footsteps echoed back down the rat tunnel towards them. They don't have much time. A gun goes off, shooting somewhere into the rats from the sound of the nails-on-chalk-blackboard squeals.

'You keep shooting at the buggers and I'll…'

The guard rounds the corner just as Tee and Marco lower themselves into the duct.

'Wait!' The bright LED beam shines straight into their eyes. They can't see the guard's face, just the silhouette of the gun going up, taking aim. At this range, he'll get them. They're dead: rat food. But the guy's hesitating. Why? Why no warning? Nothing.

'For Christ's sake, get on with it,' Tee mutters.

Marco's shaking with fear and cold and thinking the exact same thought.

A rat runs out of the tunnel, knocking the angle of the light. It drops and Marco suddenly sees the guard – it's Stan. Stan is standing there holding the gun. Stan must realise the same thing at the same moment. He stares in horror at Tee and Marco. He bites his lip and time goes slowly, slowly, way too slowly. The kind of slow that they just do not have time for. Suddenly Stan lowers the gun flat to his side, and holds up one arm, one finger, pointing straight at Tee. A raised eyebrow saying *you owe me this one… but next time?*

'I'll get help,' Stan calls back over his shoulder to the other guard. Then he turns away, grasping the heavy turn-bolt on the door, as Tee and Marco lower themselves into the duct and shoot off with some pretty bad company. It's diluted, but still. Marco knows not to get the stuff in his mouth. Cholera. That's how you get cholera. Seems like at every turn in this journey, there's some new kind of nasty. But, despite all the bad news, the shit-stream is bobbing merrily along. It must have some kind of motor system powering it because they barely need to swim. All they need to do is keep their mouths shut and out of the mess.

It seems like a lifetime but is probably only a few minutes

before they shoot out of a pipe and fall twenty feet into a massive tank.

'You okay?' Tee shouts above the water roar when they surface.

'Fine. You?'

'Not exactly a picture for the social media page,' Tee says, wiping something indescribable from his eye. 'Smells better here, though.'

And Tee's right. Either they're getting used to it or the waste is thinning out big time.

Marco remembers Portia's briefing. She'd implied there would be a tunnel out.

'We need to look for some kind of suction point,' Marco says, scanning the walls. 'If there's a tunnel out of here, there's got to be suction.'

'You take one side; I'll take the other. Do a whole circuit. You're right, it must be here somewhere.'

They split up, inching around the vast vat.

'You found anything?' Marco calls out.

'No. Would help if we had some more light.'

'You saw the guard?'

'Jeez, we were lucky.'

'Tell me about it.'

'And all that training, all the underwater diving, it's like this is what we're meant for.'

'Wallowing in shit?'

'No, escaping. Action.'

'Weird really. I mean why do they train us so hard? It's not like we're ever going to really become amphibious.'

'Speak for yourself. Mate, I'm almost there.'

'Yeah, but why is it so important to the government? You ever thought about that?'

'Man, you know me, I love it. Why are you always asking…

Then nothing.

'Tee?' Marco looks back into the gloom, which is even darker now that Tee's headlight has vanished. 'Tee?'

There's no sign of him. He must have been sucked out! Groping blindly, Marco retraces Tee's steps, going back in the self-same direction Tee had been covering. Sure enough, suddenly he feels a short, sharp tug on his leg. There's barely enough time to clamp his mouth shut before off he goes.

It was like the joke, the one where this guy finds himself in hell being shown around by the devil. The devil says you can choose the room you want to end up in. First room, people are being flayed. Second room, people are being stretched out on a rack. Third room, people are sitting in a circle having a cup of tea with a pile of excrement in the corner.

The unwitting soul says, 'I'll take room three. It doesn't look so bad.'

Soon as the doors shut behind him, the whistle blows and the demon announces – 'Tea break over, headstands in the muck.'

The next stage in the process might seem like an improvement – less smelly. But the room is in perpetual motion, a spherical ball rolling around and around. Marco can see Tee balancing on top of the large wave.

'It's getting higher,' Tee shouts. 'The wave started off small.'

Marco doesn't like to say that none of this surprises him.

'I think those are doors over there.' Tee indicates a blue metal shutter. 'My guess is - that opens, we get spewed out, the really heavy stuff sticks to the bottom.'

'Into the sea? We get spewed out into the sea?'

'That's the plan.' Tee says, closing his mouth just in time as a wave sloshes back towards him.

Something sharp hits Marco's arm, and he realises there are bits of rubbish in here too, large pieces of wood and metal, all flinging themselves around the sphere.

'That's if we don't get battered to death first.'

As the wave grows, the two friends stop talking. It's proving difficult to tread water and stay on top of the constantly twisting mountain. It's way more difficult than any of the simulations they've done in the tanks. Just as the wave reaches such a high point that Marco feels sure it will roll back over and crush them to death, the door drops out of the bottom of the tank, and they start to fall, and fall and fall.

But it's not like they're on their own. No, that would be all too easy. Things are falling with them: heavy things. Marco hopes they won't fall on them. He's beginning to feel tired. He's not sure how much longer he can keep any of this up. Suddenly he feels something new, the cold, welcome, fresh slap of day on his face. They are out. They are free! Then he plunges, feet first, into salty, cold water.

He's only just surfaced when he feels a sharp tug pulling him back down. Tee has a hold of Marco's leg and is yanking him under. Marco slides back into the water till they're face to face. Tee points up to the wall of the levee, which looks even bigger from down here. Like an iceberg, it's not just all up top. It has an elephant, grey foot planted securely on the seabed. Tee's pointing back towards it, then cupping his hands like glasses around his eyes. Security guards. They still have to be careful.

They get their goggles out of their bags and head towards the blue wire perimeter fence. Surely all they have to do now is get through. Marco grabs the wire cutters out of his bag and cuts. The wire is more plastic than metal. The mesh is about an inch wide. It takes a few attempts to figure out the easiest way to slice through the wire, and then to get a hole large enough for them to squeeze a body through. But before Marco goes through the fence, he knows he needs a bit more air. He indicates for Tee to go first. Tee nods, pulls back, and then eases himself through the gap. He gets through easy enough. Marco's going to have to go back up one last time. He bobs to the surface, inhales one sharp, salty lungful, then returns to the fence. The hole is tight. Marco's bigger than Tee, but the hole should have widened after Tee's exit. It's all going to plan. They are out. They have one life raft: they are going to make it. Marco wedges his head through the hole and kicks out, pushing through the fence but, as he does, he feels a sharp dig in his upper right arm. He looks down. The fence is repairing itself. It's meshing itself back together, right through his arm!

You don't want to scream underwater. It's not just that no one is going to hear. The main problem is, you scream and all that precious O2 you've been saving up in your lungs, out it goes. You don't have to be an ocean scientist to know that's bad.

Marco keeps pulling, but the fence has 'grown' back, sealing itself into his arm. Panic grips his mind. What horror is this? He's never heard of this stuff before. How is this even possible? But whatever it is, it's keeping him fixed and firm. He jolts his backpack forward again, rummaging for those wire cutters, but the pain is so sharp. The more he moves, the more the mesh pulls him in. He has to cut through the damn stuff. He has to get out. He's expelling air too quick. He's not going to make it. He opens the bag and then… It all happens in slo-mo: the wire-cutters drop from his bag and sink to the seabed, floating down on Marco's side of the fence. Tee won't be able to get at the cutters. Marco's only hope for escape dissolves.

Tee switches into trainer mode; he's been coached to function in emergencies. He presses his mouth against the fence. At first, Marco doesn't know what the hell is going on, then he realises: buddy-breathing – passing oxygen from one set of lungs to another. A last grab at hope. They just have to fix those mouths together. And so, they continue, till the sun leaches out of the sky, and the ocean goes dark and the cold is so bad, Marco's fingers are frozen into blocks. And finally, Marco knows he cannot do this any longer, doesn't want to do it any longer. He pushes himself as far away from the fence as he can, and watches as a stream of angry bubbles shoots out of Tee's mouth. Bubbles of frustration, anger, fear at being alone. Now it's Tee's turn to scream silently into the void, as Marco blacks out. And in the end, it's a relief. It's all one big fat relief.

CHAPTER 26
AURELIUS

'THEY CALL IT POISON IVY. It should be illegal, but Texicom seems to think it has its uses.'

The words are floating somewhere above Marco's head. He's warm. His fingers no longer feel like frozen blocks. He can even feel his toes. He opens his eyes, tries to, but they're gummy. Everything is blurred and framed in a thin slice of lash and lid. A veil of red hair is waterfalling down over his body.

'It should be banned.'

'I think we might have to amputate the arm.' A woman's voice.

'You a doctor?'

Yes! He would recognise that sweet voice anywhere. It's Portia.

''Course I'm not a doctor. But I've amputated plenty of limbs before.'

'The arm stays.'

And Marco is glad he has Portia on his side.

'I mean, it's not exactly sterile down here.'

'Like they say, beggars and choosers.'

'I thought you wanted him?' Portia, again, on the defensive.

'Not like this. We got plenty of sick people with no ID's.'

'He's still got his ID. He wasn't being repatriated. Anyway, you said it was about that Clause…'

'Herbit award?'

Another woman, another voice, this time thick with Slavic tones. He recognises it immediately. But he must be mistaken. Katya? Katya Landersly. That settles it - he must be dead.

'And actually,' Katya's ghost continues, determined to strut her stuff. 'I am a doctor. Not of medicine. But like Mia, I've done my fair share of amputations. We've all had to adapt our skillset.'

There's something about this whole situation which is just not staking up. What are all these random people doing here? Mia Polanski? Landersly's dead wife? Maybe that's how the brain works when you die; it just throws up people you barely know, ones you have questions about. Only, if he is dead, why do they need to amputate his arm? Marco knows one thing for sure; he needs to get on the right end of the conversation.

'Hey. No one's taking my arm.'

'Marco!' The blur that is Portia squeezes him in a hug. She smells like Turkish delight, rosewater and sugar and feels fabulously real. He doesn't want her to ever pull away.

'When those painkillers wear off, you might be begging us to get rid of that arm.'

'I'm not dead?'

Portia's laughing with delight. 'No, Marco! I put a tracker on you. Knew you were in trouble. The dot was just static. So, I said I wanted to practice in tank ten.'

'You got out through tank ten?'

'Sure.'

Hmm. That sounded a hell of a lot simpler than the route Marco and Tee had taken.

'You wouldn't have had the clearance.'

She knows what's going on in his mind.

'I had to pull way more strings than you've got connected. I said Finbow was sick.'

'Texicom's CEO?' This is going way over Marco's head.

'No,' Portia laughs, 'The octopus.'

'Then I put Vikendar's Indoctrofix into the poison ivy. I nabbed it out of her locker when she wasn't looking. That stuff has so many uses, and boy can it expand. It broke the ivy for just long enough to get you out.'

Despite the pain killers, Marco's arm still burns like hell. He glances down at it; an angry gash, seeping pus and leaking small tentacles of broken, blue ivy.

'It's embedded in there.' Portia sighs apologetically, turning her attention back to Katya. 'Is it toxic?'

Katya shrugs. 'Everything about this place is toxic.'

'Katya, I thought you were dead?' Marco pulls himself up to a sitting position but realises suddenly, something is holding him back. Wait, what? Is he chained to the bed?

'You two know each other?' Portia seems surprised.

Marco glances at the chains bound tightly around his limbs. Were they immobilising him so that they could chop his arm off? He glances around the room. It's like a rusting submarine down here, all verdigris metal, water sloshing on the floor. It smells of wet iron and lost souls. The air reverberates with pockets of lost sound, and it's so badly lit the four walls are just looming shadows rather than support structures. Portia's right, this place is hardly sterile.

'Marco?' Portia's asking. 'You know this… lady?'

He suddenly notices Portia is looking awkward. She rescued him, but he's not convinced she knows these people or even where they are. This is a whole new world for both of them.

'Landersley, Marco's supervisor. I'm his wife.' Katya explains.

'Dead wife. She's supposed to be dead.'

Katya shrugs, as though this is irrelevant. But of course, now it is all beginning to make sense. He remembered the lift in the Museum of Human History. You could control lifts easy as pie if you had one of the greatest IT minds in the city on your team.

'But Landersly?' He's finding this all hard to fix in the right order. 'The man was heartbroken.'

Katya sighs. 'It's kind of a long story.'

'I'll bet,' Portia mutters.

'So, he's come around?' This time it's a man's voice, deep and resonant, the voice of a leader. Marco turns to see the larger-than-life OG, the one he had seen in the square.

'So, we meet at last. I'm Aurelius.'

'Is that your real name?' Portia's asking and Aurelius seems a bit taken aback. 'Mr Roman Empire.' There's more than a note of derision in her voice.

'Real enough.'

'Yeah, well, you can call me Boudicca. I mean if everyone is going for an upgrade on the name front.'

Aurelius smiles, amused. 'She's feisty, your little Boudicca.'

'Oh, please.' Portia spurts.

And Marco waits for another sharp barb. That *"your"* would have been hard for Portia to stomach, and he's willing to bet the 'little' didn't digest easily either. But instead, Portia lets it drop. He's guessing she's hungrier for info than for a run-in on semantics.

'I bought him here because I thought he'd be safe.'

'He's safe enough.' Aurelius nods, slowly to himself, as if mulling the situation over.

'Marco, we've been interested in your work: floating fields, terraforming.'

'It was a pipe dream. Stupid.'

'No,' Katya comes back so quick, it almost makes Marco jump.

But he just sighs, he's been pulling this through his mind ever since his run-in with Kendal. 'The rubber frameworks don't stack up. It's all…'

'And who suggested the rubber framework?' There's an intense, fixed look on Katya's face.

'Well, it was my project.'

'But my husband was your supervisor.'

Then it suddenly dawns on Marco; he hadn't suggested the rubber. That had been…

'Landersly, my husband. He suggested the frameworks, deliberately; led you down a dead-end.'

But this just isn't making sense. 'Why would Landersly do that?'

Katya snorts. 'Work it out, Marco. Now, he's appropriated your work. Six months ago, you were working on single-layer molybedenum disulfide.'

Marco is feeling confused. 'Yes, but … there was no future in it. I was looking at Graphene nanopores, but the $MoS2$ had more stable long-term results. Then I frameworked in rubber and…'

'Made yourself a laughingstock?' Katya's voice was cold and collected.

'No, yes, it was …' suddenly it's all becoming clear. 'Landersly said to use rubber.'

'The interesting part isn't the framework, it's the desalination material. He stole your research, Marco. He stole it, and now he's developing it under his own name.'

Marco shakes his head. He'd heard the scorn in Kendal's voice, had replayed it ever since it slipped out of her mouth. 'My research was stupid, unrealistic because of…'

'Because of his advice to encase it. The material worked.'

Marco can't quite believe what he's hearing. Could this be right? But Katya's barely pausing for breath. 'To be honest, if you hadn't wound up down here, you would have found yourself at the bottom of a stairwell with your neck broken.'

'Landersly?' Marco's finding this hard to believe.

Katya nods. 'You only narrowly avoided repatriation on the last count. You don't think people with influence aren't going to use it? I married Landersly for his mind, not his morals.'

Marco remembers that odd conversation in Landersley's lab, the sharp earbud things. Storage hadn't he said it was…

'Anyway,' Katya continues sadly, 'let's just say sometimes he pushed it too far.'

'Does he know you're alive?'

Katya lets out a brief, bitter laugh. 'No. That would be a bad idea.'

'But the research, your research, Marco, it's important,' Aurelias takes over. 'Land is power.'

Marco sighs. 'Look, this is all really flattering. But I'm not sure it's ready.' He winces. His arm hurts. He can't really hold all of this in his head at the moment.

'It's ready enough.' Aurelias smiles. 'With you onboard, we can pull it around.'

'But the council?'

'The council and Texicom will have to be dropped.'

'What do you mean, *dropped*?' Portia's journalistic nose has sniffed out what may well be an all too handy euphemism.

Aurelius shrugs. 'We have an *event* planned. We'll need to get rid of them.'

This is still way-too "cottonwool" for Portia. 'You mean slaughter them?' Portia must have hit the nail on the head because Aurelius pauses for just a moment too long.

'I wouldn't have used that word.'

'No, I'll bet,' Portia sneers.

But Aurelius isn't stopping; he's got all his justifications neatly lined up and ready to go. 'We're the good guys, Marco.

We believe in equality. They have abused their power. They must be put on trial.'

'What, like a fair trial, or kangaroo court style?'

Marco's getting the gist of it now.

'Look,' Portia sighs. 'The council think they're doing the best for the citizens, for the planet.'

'Said like a true GK.' Mia bites back.

But Portia's not giving up. 'With transparency, with more referendums, with freedom of speech and more individual responsibility, we can make this council work.'

'Too late,' Aurelius snaps. 'Time has run out.'

'What do you mean?' Marco's not liking the sound of this.

'Marco, take a look,' Portia hisses, a deep frown cutting across her face. 'Look around you.'

And then he realises – the shadowy walls are not blank. The room is lined wall to wall with guns, blades, bombs – homemade explosives and mechanisms professionally packaged and perfected, complete with barcodes. They are sitting in an arsenal. There's enough firepower in this small room to burn the city to the ground.

'We will fight them.' Aurelius says, nodding his head slowly in a calm, dogmatic manner. 'To the death, if need be.'

'Said like a true dictator.' But Portia's words are cut short. Aurelius' hand comes down hard and swift across her face.

'Hey!' Marco shouts, trying to leap up, but the chains pull him back. Not just for medicinal purposes then, he thinks angrily to himself as Portia slumps to the floor.

'That's enough.' Katya mutters. 'She's a child.'

'Old enough,' Mia sneers.

'You won't get away with this.' Portia mutters, but Marco can see it's said through tears of pride. There's a sharp, red mark, angry and stinging on her cheek, not to mention the fact that her pride has been well and truly dented.

'Oh, but I will. And you will help me. After we've cleared the ground, Marco will help us rebuild, and Portia, you will…

You will enable us to *persuade* Marco to help. Of course, you don't need to do that willingly. Willing or otherwise, you will discover that either way, Marco will work with us if we have you as an incentive. Get her chained up,' Aurelius barks, and two shabby OGs shuffle forward, chains in hands. One has the mark of the plague eating into his face. His left ear is dissolving seamlessly into his left cheek, and both have begun to slide, pulling the mouth down with them.

Portia can't help herself; she shrinks back.

Aurelius lets out a short, bitter laugh. 'This, my dear, is the face of the future. It doesn't kill you. Ugly? Maybe. But at least our ugliness will be on the surface. And you know what they say – what doesn't kill you only makes you stronger.'

The OGs string Portia's arms together, before fixing them into the same locks that are holding Marco so securely. As Marco stares into the sliding face of the plague-ridden OG, he can't help himself, instinctively he holds his breath.

The locks fast, the OG's stand back, leaving Aurelius more than enough room to gloat.

'Shame to split you two up,' Aurelius sneers, 'When you've obviously got this… *thing* going on.'

It was all one big nightmare, which just got worse at every turn and, to rivet the icing firmly to the excrement-cake, the painkillers were wearing off. The searing ache in Marco's arm is throbbing so badly he wants to vomit. All this while he's failing big-time to protect Portia. He feels useless. A total waste of space. If it hadn't been for him … she wouldn't even be here.

The doors pull closed behind Aurelius and his entourage, and Marco thanks whatever God has been left over after the disaster for small mercies. Portia must have been holding her breath too because, for a moment, no one says a thing. Marco stares around the room in horror at all the weapons. So, this is it. This could easily be the end. The OGs would rise up and kill anyone who kept the wheels of the city turning. And suddenly, Marco thinks of Stan, of Stan's wife, a woman Marco has never met. A woman who is vulnerable, who has a bad hip, who needs an operation. And Marco thinks of all the Stans, all the council operatives caught up in the massacre. Did Gran count as oppressed? Or did the fact that she cleaned the council offices have her fixed firmly in the oppressor's camp? Had she been unwittingly absorbed into the problem? Oiling its wheels and dusting its game plan. But surely nothing could justify the bloodbath that was being planned.

Portia sniffs, bringing Marco back to reality. 'Does it hurt?'

Portia shakes her head. 'An extreme case of wounded pride, mostly. I'll live, well, from the slap anyway.'

'I'm sorry.' The words seem totally inadequate. 'I can't believe I got you into this.'

'Hey, it's not your fault.' She looks at him with such gentleness, such sadness, such… 'It was me walked <u>you</u> in, practically through the front door.'

'You didn't know.'

'I was desperate.' Portia sighs. She's being eaten alive by guilt. Marco knows just how that feels. He can't get Benson out of his head. All the things he's done wrong, Marco's not the one to go throwing stones.

'I'm so sorry. I Didn't have a clue where to turn. Sometimes when you've got an oppressor, you just think the other people, the people being held down, well, they must be okay.'

'Bad journalism.'

Portia shoots him an ironic look. 'Bad life plan. Dad would turn in his grave. How's your arm?'

'To be honest,' he looks down at the red, pus-filled scar. 'I reckon amputation would be a godsend.'

'By a computer expert, a protestor, or a man pretending to be a Roman emperor?'

'If we go on much longer, I'll be begging you to do it.'

'Hmm, wheedle it off with a fountain pen.'

'Whatever you got.' He sighs, glancing around him at the

armoury; what the hell have they got themselves into? 'This is turning out to be quite a day.'

'Understatement of the year.'

'Portia, did you see Tee when you saved me?'

Portia shakes her head. 'It was just you. You think Tee got out?'

'He was ahead of me. He had a raft. He was buddy-breathing for me.'

'I didn't see anyone. I didn't really hang around. I had to get you back. Finbow left.'

'Wait, you mean the octopus?'

Portia nods. 'Funny, it felt like he'd had enough. Maybe he knew something. The waters will run red,' she said prophetically.

'I've seen all shades recently. But know what, now I think of it, red sounds like the worst. You know we have to escape, right?'

'Not a doubt in my mind. But this chain is kind of making things difficult. It's like an inch thick.'

It was hopeless.

Suddenly, the door swings open. A small, frail black kid is standing there holding a tray.

'Food,' the lad says, but he doesn't step over the threshold, just stands there, tray in hand, like he's kind of weighing something up.

'We're tied. You'll have to bring it closer,' Portia sighs.

'He hurt you?' The boy looks even more nervous.

'My guess is this is just for starters.' Marco's voice comes out bitter and tired. 'Not looking forward to the main course.'

The boy continues to stand just the other side of the door.

'He's got his own ideas,' the boy says.

'A lot of really bad ones, from the sound of it,' Marco sneers.

With that, the boy appears to make a decision. He crosses into the room and slides the door firmly shut behind him.

The drifting, dense fug of warm food only makes Marco feel worse. His body starts to convulse.

'You okay?' The boy sounds scared. 'Is he okay?' he asks Portia.

'Not really, his arm. And I think the food, it's turning his stomach.'

'I'm sorry,' the boy says, but makes no movement to leave the tray.

'Yeah. Me too… Wait?' A curious expression passes over Portia's face. 'Benjamin?'

The boy looks awkward.

'Are you Benjamin?'

The boy takes in a deep breath, then nods.

'I'll just leave this somewhere.'

He places the tray on the floor beside Portia, then takes a step back, glancing around the room, suddenly realising where he is. 'Wow.'

'You could say that,' Marco snorts. 'Looks like it's all in good working order and ready to go.'

'I had no idea,' Benjamin says nervously. 'I knew the OGs were planning something, but…'

'A massacre,' Marco mutters.

Benjamin's shaking his head. 'This is not good.'

'No. Benjamin…' Portia's using the boy's name, using it like a magic charm, 'We need to get out.'

Who was Benjamin? Marco couldn't work it out. He didn't look like a GK. He wasn't someone from the academy. How did Portia know him?

'He's going to kill you, isn't he?' Benjamin glances sadly at the ground.

'Not all at once. The long drawn-out type of death, just till he gets what he wants.'

'We didn't know what he was doing, mum and me. Aurelius, he's got the medicine, the insulin, but…'

Suddenly, Marco remembers. Of course, this is Benjamin, the thirteen-year-old that Portia had saved from repatriation.

'But?' Portia's asking.

'Well, there was a shortage of insulin in the city. Me and mum figured that's why I was being shipped out.'

Portia's eyes narrow, like she's trying to get her bearings. 'So, how does this…?'

Benjamin sighs. 'There was a shortage because… because the OGs had stolen it all. The stuff they have here; the same production IDs. They created the problem.'

'Jeez! But why?'

'Cause trouble? Not sure.' Then Benjamin's face cracks out wide into a smile. 'So, I've been kind of … well, mum and me, we've been stealing it back. We've got it stockpiled.'

Benjamin glances nervously behind him, but the door is locked, the tunnels outside are quiet.

'I'm getting out tonight,' he whispers.

'Out of the city?'

He shakes his head. 'No, there's a way. Just before I arrived there was some kind of tunnel; it led to a jetty with a boat and everything. But someone used the tunnel and took the boat. Think it was someone who was being repatriated?

Molly. It had to be.

'Aurelius, he was mad. I mean really, really mad. He blew it up.'

'The tunnel?'

'Yeah.' Benjamin nods.

Marco wonders, hopes, has to believe she got out in time.

'But to be honest,' Benjamin's saying, 'where would you go anyway? I need to stick close to the insulin. So, I'm just gonna hide up top. Mum's got it sorted.'

'Benjamin,' Portia's using his name again, trying desperately to maintain the connection, 'can you get us back to the city?'

'There are loads of tunnels going up. They can't man them

all. But ... well...' Benjamin looks unsure. He nudges the thick chains, holding Marco and Portia tight. 'Well, these are a big problem.'

'If you don't try, you don't get. Please,' Portia pleads. 'Take us with you.'

Benjamin sighs, shifting from foot to foot.

'I can't get the key. Aurelius, he's got it. He has all the keys.'

'Any bit of metal that will fit in the lock, it might work.'

Benjamin hesitates, like he's weighing the whole thing up.

Portia had been helpful. He has the insulin now. Marco knows all this will be going through Benjamin's head. But time is running out. They need to get out.

'Please.'

He looks half-irritated with himself, but nods. 'Okay.'

Without losing a moment, Benjamin searches the shelves. It's like an old army surplus store. Metal isn't exactly a rare commodity. He picks up a gun.

'No,' Portia says, quick off the mark. 'Chances are we'll get killed by exploding debris. Besides, it will make too much noise. Has to be manual. Anything straight-ish. The right size for the lock, ideally with a hook on it.'

His fingers clutch on an old Swiss army knife.

'That'll do,' Portia says, her voice full of hope. 'Put the small blade into the lock.'

Benjamin follows Portia's instructions.

'You'll feel tension, then turn hard.' Portia's talking like she's some kind of expert safecracker.

She catches Marco's puzzled look.

'My dad,' she explains. 'He got abducted once. Just keep...'

The lock clicks free, and the chain falls to the floor.

Portia rubs her wrists; red-marked and ringed, but no longer tied. She leaps towards Benjamin and pulls him into a hug.

'Hmm, hmm.' Marco clears his throat. If there's any human contact going, he's keen to get in on the action. Next minute, she's in his arms.

'My God, I thought we were dead.'

And she kisses him. She actually kisses him, and he wishes so hard that the screaming in his arm would just stop, just for a moment, so that he could savour it all. She smells so good, so warm, so alive. But no. She pulls away. There'll be other times, surely, hopefully. There will be plenty of other times.

'Sorry,' Marco says to Benjamin, who's looking embarrassed. Although sorry is about the last thing Marco feels right now. 'We've been through a lot.'

'We need to move.' Benjamin's already heading towards the door. 'My mother works at the council. She's just admin but if Aurelias has his way, he's going to get rid of everyone.'

Marco stumbles to his feet, feeling a wave of nausea wash over his body. Benjamin's arm reaches out quick and sure to steady him.

Be nice to the people on the way up. Wasn't that what Tee had said? Twice now, they had been saved by that self-same principle. Seems like, for someone who was not exactly the brightest button in the box, Tee had a shedload of good advice.

CHAPTER 27
THE WATCHMAKER

THEY LEFT Benjamin on the terraces, heading off to find his mum. He'd said how he was going to hide, hide anywhere, somewhere. Wait till the *event*. The OGs grand finale - whatever that might be, whenever it might surface - had died down. Him and his mum would just sit it out. He said Portia and Marco should do the same. No one was going to win on this one, but deep down, they knew that sitting on the sidelines was not an option.

Gran was already at Sanderling's when they arrived. 'What took you so long?'

Marco doesn't even bother replying. He's exhausted after the escape, and the nausea is now a constant.

'And just a note and a repaired toaster? Not even a proper goodbye.'

'Gran! I'm back.'

She must catch the *not here, not now,* tone to his and switches her focus.

'So, this is her,' Gran's sizing Portia up like she's measuring the poor girl for a coffin.

But Portia's unfazed.

'Portia Reynolds,' she says, holding Gran in a steady, full-frontal eyeball to eyeball lock.

'Reynolds?' Sanderling gives Portia a curious look. 'Abe Reynolds…?'

'He was my dad.' Portia says, and somehow all that bravado crumbles.

Sanderling just nods. 'He was a good man.'

And for a moment there's silence, like there are so many words being left unsaid they might never pick back up on the business-as-usual every-day again.

'Relies!' Gran scoffs, bringing everyone down to earth. 'You got your handkerchief ready to wave him off?'

Portia looked puzzled.

'Gran, she saved my life!'

'Barely,' Gran snorts. It's true Marco is in bad shape; he can hardly stand, and his breath is coming in short, sharp wheezy bursts.

Sanderling casts his eye over the wound. 'Your nan's right about that part, at least.'

They're sitting in Sanderling's workshop. It feels warm and secure after the dark, dank caverns occupied by the OG. But as soon as Sanderling's fingers touch the ivy, Marco lets out a scream.

'Can you get it out?' Portia's voice is cracked with concern.

'We don't have a lot of time,' Sanderling says, avoiding a direct answer.

'The OG are planning an uprising,' Marco blurts.

'No doubt,' Sanderling mumbles, without taking his gaze from the wound. 'But this arm will kill you way before cocoa time this evening, and years before the OGs get their act together. The arm needs to come off.'

Marco feels like he'd been hearing this same thing all day,

but hearing it coming out of Sanderling's mouth, Marco feels nothing but a sense of relief.

Gran and Portia get sent home, and as night falls over the terraces, Sanderling preps his workstation. This time, there are no boxes packed tight with tiny cogs and wheels. Instead, there are sterilised instruments lined up, neat and ordered on a white porcelain tray. Will is on hand to help. Despite the unorthodox surgical set up, Marco can't help being impressed by the efficiency of this impromptu operating theatre.

'You ever done this before, I mean on a live body?'

'Hmm.' Sanderling gives a quick nod of his head, not raising his eyes from the tray, counting each instrument.

'It's an extreme world we find ourselves in, Marco. Needs must, and time demands … etc., etc.,'

Extreme is the understatement of the century, but Marco's in so much pain he can't be bothered to answer. Besides, Will is offering Marco a steaming-hot glass of tea-brown liquid, stuffed with fresh mint leaves and lavender.

'To help me sleep?'

Sanderling looks amused. 'For your breath. You're dehydrated, amongst just about everything else. We'll have to strap you down, I'm afraid, and give you something much stronger than tea. I'm sorry, Marco, but I can't afford any kind of movement.'

But Marco feels so sick, he doesn't care. With not one word of protest, he slips his good limbs into the straps. He just wants it to be over, and to be honest, any kind of *over* will work.

'I think I'm going to vomit.'

'Septicemia starting to set in. We need to act quickly. I may have to remove the entire arm.'

Marco shakes his head. He doesn't care. He just wants to lie down and sleep. He wants to forget today, forget everything.

Sanderling takes a hypodermic needle from the tray.

'That the stronger than tea stuff?'

'Morphine. Should do the trick. Now when you do come around, I don't want you to get up, move, or try to get out of here. Not till Will or I tell you it's okay. Understood?'

Marco nods. He has no intention of going anywhere. The pain is excruciating. He just wants the damn thing off.

CHAPTER 28
WAKING UP

WHEN MARCO WAKES, he knows something is badly wrong. He's in a shell, some kind of case like a coffin. For a moment, he has no idea where he is, then slowly he remembers. He remembers his arm. The pain. He remembers being laid flat out on Sanderling's workbench. Then it dawns on him he's inside the case: a protective cover that Sanderling used to fix over his automatons while they were work-in-progress. Marco knows there's a trigger to open the thing. It's somewhere at the bottom, near his right foot. He feels around, presses his toe down. The lid slides up.

'Sanderling?'

But there's no answer, and nothing feels right. The gramophone record, the old-fashioned one, needle and all, is rotating round and around playing nothing, just emitting a static buzz. His head hurts. No, strike that, his head feels like it's got an axe slicing down the centre. He glances around him, his breath coming short.

'Sanderling!'

Something is badly wrong. The workshop that is always so immaculate is a mess. Plants straggle out of the hydroponic tubes; some have fallen to the floor. A spout of water seeps from a pipe on to a stack of papers, making the ink run and stain. None of this is exactly Sanderling's style. Marco tries to sit up but fails. Glancing down, he realises that he's still strapped. Three of his limbs are held fast by wide belts attached to Sanderling's workbench. Only one arm is free: his right arm. It's just laying at the end of his shoulder, lifeless.

'Will? Will?' No answer. What the hell is going on?

He tries to move his right arm. If he can move his right arm, he can undo all the other straps, but it's not responding.

'Will!' No answer.

Then he remembers. It all comes flooding back. The failed escape. Losing Tee. Locked up by the OGs. The blue ivy. His arm. Portia. The bloodbath. He has to get out of here. He has to do something. But his arm is so not playing ball. He looks down at the lifeless limb. Sanderling was amputating his arm. Maybe he didn't have to? It looks okay. No scar. No ivy. But crucially - no movement.

'Will!' No answer.

'Christ!' Suddenly, his arm shoots up uncontrollably. It gives him the shock of his life. It's hovering above his head, just resting there. Did he move it? He didn't think he went to move it. Just as he's puzzling over how in the hell it got to being where it is, the arm flops back down, hitting the bench with a hard funk, denting a large gouge into the wooden trim. That should have hurt. He should have felt something.

He stares at the arm once again.

'Move.' It twitches, but not in any meaningful way.

'Up' It shoots up. 'Down.' It sticks out to the side. Not quite what he intended.

It's not his arm. He can see that now. It looks similar, same muscle tone, same shape, same shortish, clean-filed nails. Couldn't Sanderling have built him up a bit? Extra large biceps would have been good. But then, Marco supposed the new arm had to match the other one. He had spent way too long at his desk, lifting a pen rather than a weights system. It was too late in the day for an upgrade.

He stares at the clocks and suddenly realises that's what's wrong. The clocks are all silent. All the hands have stopped in their tracks. Marco reckons it's maybe forty-five minutes, maybe an hour, since he started wrestling with his damn arm. Forty-five minutes while the rest of the world is going to the dogs, and what's with all the chaos in Sanderling's office? All that deep, dark silence? Mustering all his concentration, Marco imagines the arm moving across his body, untying his other hand. It's slow work, but slowly, gradually, the hand moves as instructed.

'Sanderling, you are a genius,' Marco mutters, but the whole process would be a hell of a lot quicker with two. 'Sanderling?' He calls again. Nothing.

After another thirty minutes or so, Marco manages to untie the straps. With his old arm, it would have taken him under five. The arm-thing might be new, but Marco's not sure it could be described as an *upgrade*.

'Sanderling?' Still no answer.

Marco pulls himself up off the bench. He's feeling light-headed and has to steady himself for a moment.

He stares at himself in the full-length mirror on the back of the door. You can see where the arm's attached. Looks like Sanderling did have to get rid of the whole thing. There's a dull red line curving right around his shoulder.

'Will?'

Dull red? He looks closer. The operation isn't recent. If it were recent, the skin would be screaming angry red. But no, the scar has dulled with time. Almost healed. What the hell's been going on while he's been *sleeping-beauty* out of it.

'Sanderling?'

He looks again at the hydroponic system. The clogged pipes, the leaking water, the dropped plants, the ruined notes.

Pulling his shirt over his head, Marco heads out to the

shop. It's empty. Not just of Sanderling and Will. It looks like someone's been looting. The display cases are broken. The watches, most of them, have gone. Thank God whoever went through here, tornado-style, didn't find Marco inside the workbench.

'Sanderling? Will?' But even though he's calling out the names, Marco knows there will be no answer.

'Tex. News.' Marco instructs the wall unit.

Has the uprising happened? Has the bloodbath taken place without him? Could they have organised it that quickly? How quickly is *that*?

The screen buzzes into action.

'The criteria have to be widened.' There's an image of the council office. Kendal, dressed in her habitual grey suit, her features Indoctrofixed into a mask, but despite all the cosmetic assistance, Marco can tell she's looking strained. She shifts awkwardly in her chair, and she's drumming those fingers like a percussionist on a talent show. Images of the repat centre appear, large as life, over Sanderling's walls.

'We simply don't have the space. We thank all citizens for their continued support,' Kendal says, as the lines and lines of people queuing outside the centre are broadcast all over the city. 'Repatriation should normalise within the next two weeks,' Kendal continues, but her words fade into the background as Marco sees …. Standing in the crowd, face almost hidden behind a mass of bodies, is Sanderling.

'Until then…' Kendal's voice appears to falter. She says something off-line. Marco's not sure what. But it doesn't matter, because the image is ingrained into Marco's brain; Sanderling standing, hat on head, case in hand, his familiar, wool overcoat pulled over that thin, straight body. Sanderling is being repatriated.

CHAPTER 29
CAUGHT IN THE NET

WILL IS NOWHERE to be found as Marco speeds out of the shop, but that's no longer important. There's not a doubt in Marco's mind that he needs to get to Sanderling. There's been a mistake.

He doesn't have his trainers. He doesn't even have any shoes but, as he soon discovers, being desperate is a sure-fire way to improve performance on the running front, better than all the fancy high-tech micro-weave fabrics on this side of the waves.

When Marco arrives in the plaza, it's way-more packed than he's ever seen it; we are talking sardine central. The air hangs thick with eau-de-human, which is most definitely the wrong side of pleasant. But Marco knows he has to get to the front. He pushes through, easing his body side on through the crowd. Switching his shoulders when necessary, as though they're a blade slicing through the masses. Not even bothering with pleasantries; not even one *thank you* or *excuse me*. He doesn't have the time or energy. His arm is a constant irritation. It hangs at his side, a dead weight. It's going to take some getting used to. But then at least, he supposes, it's not throbbing anymore, and the nausea has gone.

When he gets to the front, the barrier is down and blocking his way. He can't go any further, but that's okay because Sanderling is on the other side. He's about ten yards away, pushed up against the back of the building, standing ten-deep in a line which is being policed by an all-white, all-mean security detail. Sanderling is just out of reach.

'Sanderling!'

The old guy doesn't even glance up.

'Hey, Sanderling!'

This time he looks, but then turns his head away again real quick, a look of irritation flicking across the old guy's features, like Marco is a gnat, a pesky irritation.

Had Sanderling even seen him? Marco wonders. No, he can't have. This is no good. Marco has to do more.

'Excuse me. Hey! Sir?' Marco calls out to the guard standing directly opposite. 'There's a problem.'

'Always is, son,' the guard says in a bored fashion – he's heard it all before.

'No, that man.' Marco points. 'That's Sanderling Beamish. He made the automatons in the Museum of Human History.'

'They're holographs.'

'No. Before. They were automatons before.' Marco sounds desperate. He's not wearing his tie. He looks a mess. He knows he's not always the best 'colour' for getting this kind of work done; bureaucracy is a white man's game, and Marco is presently looking way-more like a kid from the terraces than someone who should be listened to. 'Look, I'm from the academy.'

The guard gives Marco the once-over, his eyes coming to rest on Marco's two bare, dusty feet.

This is going badly. Why hasn't Marco got shoes on? Why hasn't he got his tie? Marco has to make the guy listen.

'Honestly. That man,' Marco points over the barrier, through the line, towards Sanderling. 'He is valuable. He's an asset.'

'Academy. You?' Another guard's arrived at the barrier, keen for a bit of sport. 'Because kids from the academy, sonny, they don't look like you.'

'I'm fourth generation.'

'Here we go.' The first guard looks heavenward.

'I tell you, I'm in the academy.'

'He's right.' The jeering stops. Marco looks around, thankful that someone's speaking up for him. If he can just get Sanderling out of this mess … but Marco's relief is short-lived. Ms Vikdendar appears from behind the barrier, the usual frozen look on her face. Marco wonders if she knows that her Indoctrofix saved his life. He's guessing she would be none too pleased about that.

'He is academy, but he's in disgrace,' Vikdendar says simply. 'Repatriate him as well.'

The guards look unsure. The first guard stutters, referring to a list on his hand monitor, about to do a whole *jobsworth* speech. But Vikdendar cuts him off with a cool, sharp slap of that ice-maiden tongue.

'Do it, you idiots, before I have you all deported.'

Maybe she got wind of the locker raid?

'Well, that went well.' Sanderling mumbles as Marco and Sanderling are shuffled into the repat centre and issued with blue armbands.

'Yeah, sorry. Not the outcome I expected. Thanks for the arm.'

'No problem. Looks like it was a waste of parts, though.'

'Hey!'

'You weren't supposed to be here. Do you ever do what you're supposed to?'

Marco doesn't answer because on the whole he would have said he did, that he was law-abiding and that he kept his head down. And to be honest, now he could see why. They are standing in a hospital-style waiting room. It smells of bleach so strong, Marco can't help but feel uncomfortable; it's as if someone's trying just that little bit too hard to mask something they'd rather not have on their radar. Nurses travel up and down long lines of punters - those ear-marked for repatriation. The nurses wear blank expressions; each one is way too processed and packaged for smiles or any glimmer of humanity. They're armed with trays holding hypodermic needles and cotton wool swabs. And giving out injections, easy as if they were handing out flyers for a club-night.

'Typhoid,' the nurse explains to the guy in front.

The man doesn't offer his arm.

'I'm European, there's no…'

A curious, hard look fixes over the nurse's face, and without the nurse even glancing in their direction, two heavy-built male nurses? Security guards? Take a step forward. The *European* sees it all. He sighs briefly to himself before reluctantly rolling up his left sleeve.

'Rabies,' The nurse says, with smug satisfaction as she jabs at the man's arm. Then pushes a cotton wool ball up against the entry point, indicating with a nod of her head for the European to hold it. 'Vaccine has got just about all you need wherever you're going.'

'Give them your right arm,' Sanderling whispers.

'But that's my…'

'Right.' Sanderling hisses.

So, Marco rolls his right sleeve up.

'It's normally the left,' the nurse scowls.

'I'm left-handed,' he lies.

The nurse looks uncertain, but then, with a quick shake of her head, dismisses the problem as clearly not hers, and jabs the needle into what, to all extensive purposes, should be Marco's flesh. For a moment, Marco expects to hear the crunch of the needle as it hits a bar of solid metal, but no. The needle sinks effortlessly into Marco's new skin.

'Wow, that was easy.'

The nurse gives him a cold, hard look. 'We aim to please.'

And Marco wonders who exactly it is that the pleasure is really intended for.

As soon as the nurse clears earshot, Marco examines the entry point. The false skin had broken in front of the needle, but now less than a minute later, it's almost completely sealed back over again.

'That's good stuff.' Marco says, looking at the meshed skin, and wishing he could place it under a microscope.

'Similar to the blue ivy, only with a more humanitarian purpose. I'm a craftsman. What do you expect? Here...' Sanderling slips his ring from his finger, the Guild ring with its curious insignia – a circle with a hammer, a map and what looks like a pen twisted inside.

'But...'

'Yours. Put it on. Don't lose it.'

'You know there's something I didn't tell you.'

'Just the one thing?' Sanderling smiles ironically.

'The OGs, they're planning some kind of uprising.'

Sanderling smiles ironically. 'Actually, you did tell me. You were pretty out of it. You probably don't remember. But uprising? They'll never get their act together. Always infighting. Which is just as well. Not sure I'm keen on all of their ideas.'

A nurse's voice rings out over the tannoy system. 'Blue group.'

Marco glances down at the armband sitting on his shirt: blue. It must be their turn.

Their long line shuffles forward, centipede-style, into what appears to be a narrow, elongated waiting room. Rows and rows of chairs are set out in a row down the length of the room.

'How long was I out?' Marco asks.

'Five days. Gran and Portia visited.'

'There was no uprising?'

'Nope. Well, maybe between Gran and young Portia, but eventually I think your young Portia won. I like her. Knew her dad. Long, long time ago.'

'But the OG's...?'

'Like I told you. Business as usual.' Sanderling moves forward towards the chairs. 'Shakespeare okay?'

Sanderling doesn't know! Sanderling has no idea that Will's disappeared, that the workshop has been looted, that the watches have been stolen, that each and every glass case has been smashed.

'Fine,' Marco says, using Molly-style advice on deception front: keeping it short and sweet.

'Sit,' a large, male orderly instructs, and they do as they're told.

'What will they do with us?' Marco whispers when he's certain the orderly isn't looking.

But instead of answering, Sanderling takes Marco's left hand between his and gently pats it.

'You know, I have to say that since I rescued you, you have been a right pain in the arse. If I asked you to do something, you would always give me fifty questions. But then, I guess that's just how people learn. And to be honest, lately, it's been worse - you've stopped asking. Sometimes there are questions that need to be asked.' Sanderling fills his lungs and lets out a deep sigh. 'Since the world sank, life's been pretty bad. But you're my hope, Marco, my new world. People like you, people like Portia, and Molly, you're our world now. You can carry that thought with you always, my boy.'

Marco isn't sure what to say to all this. He's never been comfortable with emotions. Despite all that they've been through, it's not something that Marco and Sanderling do,

'I'm sorry,' he says, simply. Because he's fully aware that in life there is always something to apologise for. 'Know what? I should have come around more when I started the academy. I should have …' But then he realises Sanderling's not listening. No one in the room is listening. Every man, woman and child has slumped down silently in their seat. The nurse had been right, that injection had just about everything in it, and a little bit extra for good measure.

For a moment, Marco just stares around him in panicked silence. Then he realises – he needs to play dead too. He drops his head to his chest and closes his eyes. The arm has saved him. He guesses he might rust up a bit from the inside, but it looks like a quick coma is off the cards.

He keeps as still as he can for what feels like an eternity, till the excitement of the day, the trauma of the operation, the confusion of losing Tee, every single unanswered question he has about Molly, till all of that catches up with him, and he doesn't need to feign sleep any more. He genuinely is out of it.

When he wakes, he takes a moment to get his bearings. There's a new noise now and a kind of motion under his feet, as if the building they're in is moving. He shoots Sanderling a look, but the old guy is still out for the count. At the sound of footsteps, Marco drops his head once more to his chest. An orderly is moving around the room. Marco can hear the gentle pad of the man's trainers as he goes from body to body, checking pulses, till the shiny shoes stop directly in front of Marco. The orderly picks up Marco's right hand, feels nothing, lets it drop back onto the chair. It clunks. There's an awkward pause. The orderly's shoes shuffle slightly, like he's not entirely sure what just happened. He lets out a brief sigh. Was the arm too heavy? Too fast? The orderly picks up the offending arm once more, gives it the once-over, feels for that elusive pulse. Nothing. He places the arm down firmly on the armrest and fastens a bolt over it. And suddenly Marco's brain fills with dread; if the orderly was looking for a pulse, does that mean he's checking to see if they're all alive? But Marco has no pulse in that arm. Then, is the orderly checking to see that they're all dead?

After another half hour or so in which, Marco guesses, all the detainees have been checked and secured, Marco's seat gives a short, sharp jerk and he allows himself the luxury of opening his eyes, just a slit. He's moving. They're all moving. What? The whole line of chairs is snaking off out of the room. It's a conveyor belt. They're all fixed to some goddamn factory-line conveyor belt. As Marco passes out of the 'waiting room' he sees the Texicom logo emblazoned on the wall and Finbow's smug smiling face beaming down. So, this is repatriation, corporate style.

How long he's been travelling on the belt, Marco isn't sure. For the most part, he keeps his eyes tight shut. Occasionally he hears voices, once even music, but the belt never stops. It hesitates, it judders, it strains as it navigates inclines and turns, but it doesn't stop. After the initial fragments of noise, quiet descends. A quiet set against the constant low, mechanical whir of the belt. Marco opens his eyes just a little, peeping out to see a spaghetti junction of conveyor belts lined with chairs climbing all over the warehouse. Each chair containing the body of someone who is no longer deemed useful.

Marco's track climbs higher and higher. Up it goes, snaking through the building. There are no more guards. The drop between Marco's chair and ground level is over fifteen feet and steadily rising. The lack of guards leads Marco to guess that this part of the process must be deemed *secure*. No trouble is anticipated. After the climb hits thirty feet, the chairs turn a bend and are met with another line of chairs, this time empty and heading in the opposite direction. Are these the same chairs? Are they new chairs? Are they... Suddenly Marco feels a cold wind edge across his face. Whatever's happening, whatever this process is, it's almost done. Marco takes one last look at Sanderling. Then gasps, as a door in front of them opens, the chair is thrust out, and Marco finds himself falling and falling and falling.

The water is blue, a bright blue reflecting the sky. But the bright colour gives no comfort. Marco is sinking. The weights that had attached him to the chair have come with him on his journey through the air and down into the deep. On hitting the water, he realises that the weights are the type activated by H2o. They had been designed to hold their captive to the bottom of the briny for as long as it takes. Empty eye sockets, bones picked clean, flesh long-gone: that kind of 'as long as it takes.'

Marco plummets through the clear, blue water towards a mountain of bodies, young, old, twisted and straight, all sizes, shapes and colours. At least the fish will enjoy the feast. Small mercies, Marco thinks to himself as his legs gently thud down onto the pile, and the bodies below him shift momentarily, accommodating his weight. He doesn't look down. He doesn't want to see what / who he's resting on. Instead, Marco glances up and catches sight of Sanderling's body floating down through the water, his bright blue eyes shining lifelessly out into the sea.

So, this was it. This was what civilisation had become. Did the government know? Marco found it unlikely. This was a corporate decision – get rid of waste as quickly, efficiently, and cost-effectively as possible. Should the government have been more on the ball? That was a different question.

Marco stares up at the undulating blue sky above. He has to get out. He knows Sanderling wouldn't thank him for sitting at the bottom of the ocean, turning minute by minute into fish food. It's then that Marco notices the pulsing. A beating light shining out over the bodies, coming from … He looks down. The pulsing light appears to be coming from the ring on Marco's finger, Sanderling's ring. Crafty bugger. The thing was giving off some kind of signal. Someone somewhere was tracking him. He has to get these weights off and get top-side.

He struggles against the locked-fast metal, trying to ease his wrists through – too tight. Trying to break the bands open – too strong. Now, he thinks bitterly to himself, as he tugs and pulls with his left hand, *now* would be a great time for that bionic arm of his to start working. He tries shouting at the arm from inside his brain. No joy. He strokes it, moves it with his legs. Nothing. He's been underwater for what must be a good three minutes. He's in no doubt that he will all too quickly be up and over his top LC count. He shuts his eyes, blocks out all the blank faces watching him and pleads with his arm to move. It jerks into action. His fist balls, the 'muscle' appears to shoot up, then down his arm like a wave. The right manacle breaks in two as the *muscle* pulses through. Marco pushes his left arm under his right and wills, prays, and thinks about pulling that second manacle open. The right-hand responds, and in one short, sharp, easy move, the second weight is off. Tumbling down the pile of bodies and out of sight.

There's not a moment to lose. Free, Marco swims towards the spot where Sanderling had fallen. In the short time that they've been under, the old guy has been covered over by a thin layer of bodies. But Marco can still see the familiar sleeve of an old green overcoat and, poking out of it, one white, grey, wrinkled hand, complete with a small band of virgin skin where Sanderling's ring used to sit. Marco pushes at the other bodies, using his legs, his arms, everything and anything he has at his disposal, to clear Sanderling from the wreckage. He pulls and pushes till the old guy is loose, staring up at him with those cold, glassy eyes. For a moment, Marco's lost. He stops dead, having a *what's next* moment, lost in the horror of those dead eyes as if he is being pulled in.

No. Marco shakes his head sharply. He has to focus. What would Tee do? Triage. He parks his emotions; switching into contingency mode, Marco runs over all of Sanderling's pulse points, just in case. Nothing. Not a murmur, not a beat, not a flutter. Sanderling has gone.

Marco suddenly feels completely grown-up. The advanced guard of adults is dropping out of existence. Marco has never felt so alone. Gently, he kisses Sanderling on the forehead. In his mind, because there's no speaking words at the bottom of the sea, Marco makes a small prayer of thanks, not to a God, but to the man who put the backbone of Marco's life in place. Then he let Sanderling's body drop back towards the pile.

Ten years ago, Sanderling had pulled a lifeless Marco from the waves. Now here they are again, but this time there would be only one of them returning to the surface. The anger he feels is all-consuming; a pulsating red wave of pure hatred rushing through his body. This wasn't over. Marco would find out who ordered this genocide, and he would make them accountable. Someone would pay. He kicks his legs and starts the ascent to the sky. The manacles might be off, but he knows he's still in danger. His heart is heavy enough to drown him. He has to swim up, for Sanderling, if not for himself. Marco knows that he has a responsibility. He is now a witness, a survivor and, as such, he has a duty to keep fighting.

CHAPTER 30
ALL AT SEA

ONE THING that has always struck Marco as bonkers mad - swim under water and everything looks calm, like the world's been switched to slow-mo but, soon as you hit the top – a whole different story. Fast forward world: no time to catch up. Today is no different. The water surface-side is looking Atlas Mountain style and acting way-more-than-willing to throw the odd saltwater slap down Marco's throat. Should he be daft enough to try and catch a lungful of air. He glances around him. The weather is now looking nasty. A sea mist is rolling in, gobbling up the miles and miles of nothing that must lay just out of sight in every direction.

There's no sign of the building, the ship, the … whatever it was that dropped the chair-folk oh-so-neatly into the water. It must have been a ship, surely? Buildings don't just disappear. Then a thought strikes Marco sharply as the edge of a lightning bolt: was this the ship Landersley designed? Was that why Landersly's marriage got cleavered good and proper into two bitter halves? Maybe, but whatever the processing contraption was it had moved on, pulling the mist in place like a curtain call, leaving the sea feigning innocence.

Marco thinks about Tee, who is most probably still out there on his lonesome, squeaking around in his inflatable rubber dingy, looking up at the self-same sky. East, that's where he was heading. Chandler's Peak. But which way is east? He's just going to have to wait and watch the sunset. Rises in the east goes down in the west. But then it would be dark, and then he would be lost. They might as well be in different universes.

If Marco swims, there is not a doubt in his head that he will end up moving in some wide, great circle. His new arm (when working) is so powerful that the left side of his body doesn't stand a chance of keeping him on the straight and narrow. Marco treads water and tries hard not to think about those rats. Three days, wasn't that right? Tee had said rats could tread water for three solid days. Personally, Marco doesn't know if he has the heart. Not after all that's happened. What is he living for? Portia? Yeah, well … like that's all going to turn out just fine and dandy. Justice? Surely, that was it. That's what he had to live for now. Justice for Sanderling's death, or was it vengeance? Vengeance always had an uglier taint to it. But to be honest, his mood is ugly. He looks at the ring merrily pulsing away to itself. Could it really be signalling coordinates? That small ray of hope that had hit him as so certain under the water now seems daft, the absolute pinnacle of stupidity. The thing probably doesn't like getting wet. The batteries are no doubt about to corrode, dissolve into an acidic mess over his fingers. No one is coming. Realistically, who in the world would care about him? This one little Marco speck in the middle of the ocean?

But time passes, and the ring doesn't spill acid; it just continues to pulse. Resigned, Marco flips over on to his back and stares up into the mist. He's just going to have to wait, wait and hope.

.   .   .

A few hours later, surprise, surprise, he is still waiting. Less hope, more dogged determination. He watches the mist clear, the sea calm, and the sun start to sink down over the horizon. Mackerel-scraps of cloud light the last traces of the day with a brilliant russet fire. Would he be here in the morning? He'd never been the best swimmer. He would love to believe that possibly, maybe, this could be a long night. But in fact, he is all too aware that this night could be surprisingly short.

'Everybody knows that the dice is loaded…'

That tune, bobbing up in his head; one of his dad's.

He must be exhausted. He can almost hear the words. Leonard Cohen's downbeat voice singing along in that low grumble of his. Telling how the game of life was fixed. The good guys would always lose. The bad guys walk away unscathed. Life was rigged.

Wait! He <u>can</u> hear it.

'Everybody knows that the good guys lost…'

He actually can actually hear it! He must be going mad. No, he wasn't going mad. It really was happening. Someone was playing Leonard Cohen in the middle of the ocean?

He flips over onto his front to see a boat chugging towards him. A small fishing boat, musical notes painted over the side, is blaring out Leonard Cohen full decibel. And a woman, a girl, a what? Wait … a Molly! A Molly is standing on deck waving those large hands over her head, calling over and over again.

'Macko, Macko. Macko.'

There is nothing so reassuring as dry clothes after you've been saved from a watery grave. Even if the clothes are on the jumble-sale-jones big side. Marco empties his wet pockets. He was travelling light. The only thing in there – the small tin watch. He smiles to himself, shakes the water out and puts the old watch into his new, dry trousers.

'God, never thought I'd say this, but it's good to see you, Dork-face.' Molly is leaning in the cabin doorframe, a look of utter relief pasted over her face.

'With the insults, now? Even after?'

'It's the personality type. Yours. It just kind of demands abuse.' She laughs, but her smile is being scaffolded up with bravado, within seconds it crumbles into a million emotions. Tears pin-pricking those proud-as-a-lioness eyes, and Marco draws her into a big bear-hug.

'You can call me dork anytime.' He holds her hand between his, touching the fingers he thought he'd lost. 'You see, I know how people with limited vocabs have to revert to...'

She laughs, pulling back and punching him hard on the shoulder. It clunks.

'Ow! What?' She rubs her knuckles.

'Long story. Look.' he glances up at the sky. It's getting late.

'Moll. Can you drive this thing?'

So as the sun snuffs out the dregs of one hell of an eventful day, the boat turns on its tail and sets sail for Chandler's Peak. It's worth a try. The whole way there, Marco keeps his eyes peeled, straining into the fading light till his retinas feel like they'll come unstuck. He's desperate to get some kind of hint of his lost friend. But the empty sea carpets the globe and laughs back at him. It's been a week since they tried to get out. The sea could easily have swallowed Tee bones-and-all without a shred of rubber seal-suit left to tell the tale.

They park as close to Chandler's Peak as they dare. The

waters are tricky: unpredictable depths. As darkness hits, the boat shines its brilliant-white beam into the night, throwing back one hell of a lot of empty slap-slap silence.

For a solid thirty minutes, Marco calls Tee's name into that great, watery darkness. He calls way past the moment when they switch the beam off. He calls till his throat feels sore, till he forgets all other words but the name of his friend. A sound that keeps ringing like tinnitus in his ears. Until Molly comes up behind him and wraps him in a large, coarse blanket that smells of wooden cupboards and soap.

'We'll try again tomorrow,' she says. 'It'll be easier in the morning. The sea looks vast tonight; it's all mixed up with sky. Tomorrow, they'll separate. We'll stand a better chance.'

He's not so sure. He doesn't want to leave his post.

'We'll leave the music on. If he's around, he'll hear.'

But still, Marco looks out into the cold, oily black.

'Marco? Come on.' Molly rubs his shoulders through the blanket as if she's trying to remind him that he's still alive. 'There's a fire going. I want to hear everything.'

Wrapped in their blankets, Marco and Molly curl up on the creaking wooden deck, warming themselves beside an open brazier. The sound of music filters out over wrinkle-ironed, black waves. A radio ship, that's what it is. Not a threat: no voice-overs, no messages, no polemics. Not one advert. Nothing to attract attention. Only songs - Marco's dad's complete, one hundred percent live-and-kicking playlist. The same songs that Marco caught the edge of so many times in Gran's kitchen – her *sounds to cook by* – his dad's songs.

Molly explains: 'Sanderling had his own private pirate radio station. He'd come into problems with Texicom. They wanted to advertise, but he refused. Didn't believe in selling people stuff they didn't need.'

'Sounds like Sanderling. And this is before the flood?'

'Yeah,' Molly pulls the blanket over her legs, rearranging her body so her skin faces away from the cold night air. 'Way before the flood. Only, when the whole disaster thing happened, the ship got destroyed. Sanderling lost all his music. Everything got wiped out because he was old-school: wasn't keen on digital. It was all tapes and vinyl. So, the ship goes under, the music goes down with it. He got another ship, this one.' She taps the deck, and the wood sings out under her knuckles. 'But he couldn't replace the vinyl. Then along came you.'

Marco looks puzzled.

'Well, to be precise, your dad's playlist, and Sanderling was up and running again.'

Marco can't help but laugh, the old guy – always making the best out of a wreckage. Breaking everything and anything down into useful parts.

It felt good hearing Dad's old sounds. Marco had always known he didn't have them all – not enough storage on his hand-held. Then he kind of forgot about it. Turns out Sanderling had retrieved the entire catalogue, digitised and cleaned up. There were a lot of tunes Marco hadn't heard for years, not since before the flood. It was as though the music had always been there for him, like a guardian angel, waiting in the wings until the time was right.

'Remember this one!' he shouts, grabbing Molly's hand and singing along to *I am the Walrus*. 'The Beatles,' a band from way before his time. The bizarre lyrics fly off into the night, with macabre thoughts of *crabalocker fishwives*, and *custard dripping from a dead dog's eye*. Molly laughs, then suddenly stops stock-still. They've been through so much. She's holding his hands. Looking into his eyes. Sad-smiling, like there's pain all wrapped up in the joy, and it is near-on impossible to get it all untangled.

'I didn't think I'd ever see you again,' she says, her voice cracked like pepper out of a mill.

But Marco knows he can't afford emotion. He can't let his guard down, not now. There's too much to do. He's got friends still AWOL, and a score to settle with the city. Self-pity's a surefire way to run out of steam on the action front. 'Touch and go there for a bit,' he says, his voice holding just a touch too much Brave Heart, considering what the past twenty-four hours had in store for him. He swings her arm gently in his. Then notices the bare patch on her wrist. Of course, her tin watch, it's gone.

She follows his gaze. 'Yeah, sorry. I kind of got into a spot of trouble.'

'I heard it! I heard you running.'

'No!' Molly laughs.

'And gunshots?'

'Yeah, that all got a bit…' she searches for the word. 'Tense.' Then laughs at the understatement. 'I had to get out through OG central. Wow, that plague does nasty stuff to a person. You see any of that?'

He nods. He remembers the guy's melting face and shivers. He's guessing they're all right. Surely, they would be showing symptoms by now?

'Takes a week to come out.' She says. She must have seen his mind slip into paranoia mode. 'Which means we're both good.'

He lets out a small sigh of relief. That would have been the last thing they needed.

'Sanderling got me past the OGs.' Molly's saying. 'He knew they had a boat. I mean, let's face it, I've never been the best swimmer.'

Marco doesn't bother to correct her. They both know it's true.

'Once in the water was more than enough.' She shivers,

the memory of that first wave still sloshing around somewhere in her brain.

Marco takes his own tin watch from his pocket. It's dried out now. He flips it on. White noise fills the air.

'Mine got kind of crushed,' she says quietly, like she's mourning an old friend.

He remembers how Molly's broadcast cut off.

'I'll make you a new one.'

'He trained you well.' She says smirking, but suddenly, her bottom lip trembles and another tear pricks her eyes. 'Jeez, I'm a mess.'

'What happened to the warrior queen?'

'She's in here somewhere, just...' She sighs, gets a grip, wipes her eyes. 'What I'm trying to say is that I am so sorry ... about Sanderling.' She turns her face away. Neither of them like self-pity. Gran always said it was a hole you couldn't crawl out of.

'Yeah, well,' he says, his voice sounding hard and controlled, 'know what? I'm not sorry. I'm mad, mad as hell.'

His fixed eyes reflect the flames from the fire like they've gotten into his soul. He is mad. He is livid and seething, and there's only one single thing holding him altogether at the moment: justice.

'If it wasn't for Sanderling...' Molly looks around her sadly at the boat. 'And even that old watch ... So that was the reason you knew I was on the run?'

'To be honest, it was kind of cryptic. Next time text.'

She laughs, taking the watch from his fingers.

'You know, he always used to say he was the last watchmaker. You remember that?'

Marco nods. He did remember – the pride in Sanderling's voice. The pleasure in being a craftsman.

'I guess he was wrong all along.'

'Sorry?' Marco's lost.

'You. The last watchmaker? It's you.'

The breath catches in his throat. And he can't help himself, he wants to dissolve into a pool of tears. He had thought that he'd lost her, this wonderful, sassy, larger than life young woman that he had spent most of his life growing up next to. Marco turns away from the fire, hoping Molly won't notice the tears pricking his eyes. If she does, she's choosing not to make a big deal about it. Instead, she's staring at that old tin watch like it's got all the answers.

'More heavy-duty transmitters next time. That would help with the communication thing. Oh, and then 'course, Gran uses her pigeons.'

'Sorry, what?'

'They're carrier pigeons. They carry messages. It's what people did before texting.'

'Not quite accurate. Hot chocolate, anyone?' Elena Cobey has appeared, or at least the automaton of Elena Cobey, her copper glinting in the firelight. Turns out, Elena is the sole crew for the ship, and since the job of steering is over for the night, she's switched into chef mode. In her bronze, glittering hands, she's carrying a tray of hot drinks. 'There were a few steps in-between pigeons and texts, not that I like to be picky but the pigeons do work surprisingly well. And luckily, Texicom appears to have forgotten about their *traditional* use.'

The cup slips from Marco's right hand, sending hot choco-late sliding straight down his front. 'Damn. Sorry, it's new.'

Molly touches his arm, looking confused.

'It got injured when we were trying to escape. Sanderling gave me a new one, but…'

The arm suddenly shoots up, causing Molly to dissolve in shrieks of laughter.

'Think it's got its own brain in there, too.'

'It takes practice. You get used to it.' Elena says. 'I, of course, have the full quota.'

She twists her body on top of her hips, one full 360 degrees, to demonstrate.

'That gives me indigestion just watching!' Molly laughs.

'I've got some antacid.'

'No, Elena!' Molly smiles. 'It's just an expression.'

'Hmm. I would appreciate it if you would limit the scope of your dialogue. Literal meanings are best. I'm not programmed for sarcasm, puns, irony, or colloquial expressions.'

Even though Elena's not capable of frowning, Marco gets the feeling that this is exactly what she would be doing given half a chance. He decides to change the subject.

'So, Elena, you've been here since they took you out of the museum?' He asks, letting the warm chocolate spill, but this time across his tongue. He hasn't tasted chocolate for years. Sanderling made some kind of herbal substitute, but it just did not taste the same. 'Wow, this is good.'

'I, of course, can't drink it. Lack of internal organs. But to answer your question ...' Elena continues. 'When they replaced me with a holograph, truth be told, it was a relief. I was finding it tedious, no one ever letting me tell my whole story.'

'Just like they didn't let you warn them about the meteorites.' Molly said ironically.

'Exactly. Believe me, I take not one ounce of satisfaction from correctly predicting that two meteorites would graze the earth, and knock it marginally, almost imperceptibly, off its trajectory. I should have been hailed as a hero but, sadly for myself and the rest of the planet, fate did not have that treat in store for me. Because? No one listened.'

Marco wonders if Elena has somehow slipped into monologue mode, but the chocolate is good, and the fire warm, and Elena continues oblivious, keen to get the whole thing off her copper-plated chest.

'According to the White Paper, commissioned after the

event, there are three main hypotheses: a) I used a power point presentation, with poorly chosen fonts and colour palette. b) I was a quiet woman who, although known for her studiousness, was regarded as unremarkable. c) I gave my speech just before the conference lunch break and thoughts were on the beef wellington, which had the reputation of being really rather good.'

'Beef wellington?' Marco asks, curious.

'Steak, pate and puff-pastry, all wrapped together in a parcel. You don't get it anymore. Wheat shortage, livestock shortage, culinary enthusiasm shortage. But I'm not sure it matters,' Elena says simply.

'The wellington? Or the disastrous lack of action?' Marco asks, and Elena chooses not to reply.

'The lessons of history,' Marco sighs prophetically. 'We only get to understand them after the horse has bolted.'

'Apart from Texicom,' Molly raises one eyebrow skeptically. 'They seem to have done okay out of it all.'

'I guess Texicom was big on the scene way before the disaster.'

Molly gazes into the firelight. 'They weren't as big as they are now, but Sanderling said they were...' She searches her brain for the word. 'Invasive.' She nods, satisfied: that was it, that was what he'd said. 'They started off on government contracts, hospitals, transport, infrastructure. Sanderling said the early 21st Century was a bit of a mess. The government were in debt. Texicom took over the utilities.'

'What, like electricity?'

Molly snorts. 'Understatement of the year. Like everything: water, power, sanitation. Oh, and the newspapers. All apart from one.'

Abe Reynolds, Marco thinks, but doesn't mention the name. Portia is a dull ache at the bottom of his soul. Talking of her father might well bring her up and dust her off into fully fledged heartache. 'I knew Texicom re-directed the rivers before…'

'And the levee, the bottom level, that was up long before the meteorites.'

He hadn't known this. And a cold shiver runs down his spine. 'Hang on a minute, are you saying they knew it was going to happen?' Marco had heard Sanderling hint at something along the same lines before, but it was all too far-fetch. 'I mean the meteorites came from outer space. Texicom couldn't have…'

'They knew about global warming. They knew the icecaps were melting. It was probably just…'

But Marco can tell there's something else bothering Molly. 'Moll?'

'Okay, so this is weird.'

Marco thinks of all he's been through in the past week and feels he can probably manage *weird*. 'Spit it out.'

Molly draws in a breath as if needing to give her words that extra bit of support. 'Sanderling said there was no trace of Finbow before Texicom?'

'Texicom's CEO?'

Molly nods. 'He just appeared with the company. I mean, there was sort of camouflage stuff: job descriptions, social media posts, but Sanderling claims it was all surface.'

Marco's not understanding this. He must look blank because Molly draws in another deep breath and continues. 'He didn't exist before twenty-one ten.'

'What!'

Molly shrugs. 'I'm only repeating what I…'

'But he's got to be sixty if he's a day.'

'Yup. Sanderling thought that maybe he was KGB.'

Now she's really lost him.

She looks heavenward, like this is all basic stuff.

'Russia, that great big landmass pre-disaster: Stalin, Marx,

Gulags. Tolstoy. Ballerinas and defection during the cold war. We did it in…'

'… Pre-Civil Collapse. History.'

But he's still not getting it. What has Finbow got to do with Tolstoy?

'The KGB were the secret service. And relations between Europe and Russia pre-disaster, well they were pretty strained.'

'So, Sanderling thought Finbow could be a Russian agent?'

Molly shrugs in a you-follow-it-through, see-what-you-get, way.

'And he started Texicom and the academy. But why the academy?'

'Yeah, well, it's a brain drain. Take all the brightest and the best.'

Marco's shaking his head, none of this is working for him. 'But what about all the training? The LC counts?'

Molly shots him a long look. 'You're not going to like this.'

But that's fine by Marco because he's not liking anything he's heard so far. Surely it can't be right, someone deliberately profiting from a global disaster.

'You ever hear of Seals?'

Now it's Marco's turn to laugh. 'Duh! They have them at the academy. Blubbery looking things.'

'No. Not that kind of Seal, Dork-face.'

She smiles, and he smiles back. He never knew how sweet an insult could sound. Can you miss being insulted? Well, he has. But she's in explanation mode now, motoring on. 'The Seals were a special division of the navy: special operations. A lot of the training, the action was water-based.'

'But why?'

'Marco!' she laughs. 'Do I really have to spell it all out for you? All that tank training. You were being trained for manoeuvres. Well, maybe not you, because your LC count was pretty...'

'Actually, it was up to five minutes.'

She raises her eyes like this doesn't make a blind bit of difference.

'Manoeuvres on what?

'Yeah,' she says, her voice heavy with sarcasm. 'Like I know everything. Who do you think I am, the bloody Oracle at Delphi?' But then her tone softens, 'All I do know, and putting two and two together and all that, is 'if' that's what was happening, 'if' you were being trained as an army, there must be something left out there worth taking.'

And of course, she's got a point. They stare out into the vast emptiness, conspiracy theories gnawing at their brains like a cloud of gnats. But deep down they know – it's all hopeless. Even if there was some kind of cover-up, some kind of conspiracy, how in hell could they do anything about it? The cold, wet air cuts into their faces, bringing the present back into view.

'So, where do we go from here?' Molly asks, breaking the silence. 'I mean, we can't just stay bobbing around.'

'We wait for Tee.' But even as he says it, Marco knows it's hopeless. One way or another, Tee is long gone.'

'If he was here,' Molly's voice sounds small and lost in the night, 'he would have found us by now.'

And Marco knows she's right. But just because he's not here, doesn't mean he's dead, and if he's not dead, he can't have got far. 'Are there other communities?'

'Some, but bobbing is kind of my business,' Elena replies briskly. 'I pick up the wounded.'

'Like us?' Marco asks, feeling oh-so thankful. 'Are there many?'

'Last six months, just the two of you. People don't tend to have the homing device.'

Marco glances at the ring on his finger.

'And Texicom appears to be getting a little more *thorough* on their disposal methods. I have to be careful, move the boat about a bit. We don't want to draw attention to ourselves.'

So that was what Sanderling meant when he said that it wasn't the right time for Tee's escape. Tee would have been going out around a week ago. Elena and the boat weren't in the location. In his mind, Marco can picture that line of chairs, all those bodies, the hard cold sea. 'We need to let people know what's happening.' His voice sounds hard-bitten. Like a protestor's crawled into his throat. 'We have to let them know that repatriation is really genocide.'

Elena nods. 'We've had our suspicions, but we simply haven't been able to prove anything. We thought the people we saved were … let's say, the fall-out. The odd person who got lost in transit.'

'Turns out they all get lost in transit; that's kind of the point.' Marco's words cut bitterly into the cold air. 'I guess we've got a few days. They won't be doing another mass-repatriation right away.'

'We can get word to Gran,' Molly says eagerly, 'using the pigeons.'

But Marco's not so sure. 'A little old lady in the terraces? No one's going to believe her. Besides, we need to tell every-one. Pigeon power, it's a bit… niche?'

Molly lets out a long, low sigh. 'Okay. Get the message to Gran, then Gran gets the message to Neil. Has Neil still got access to the satellites?'

'Not many of them are working.'

'We only need one, the one for the mainframe.' Suddenly Molly's face falls: she's thought it through. 'No, this won't work. Neil would never stand up on camera and…'

'Portia,' Marco blurts. 'Portia Reynolds. People know her.

People trust her. She's a journalist, kind of. Abe Reynolds' daughter.'

Molly looks blank.

'The guy who had the last free paper. She's already got *media presence*.'

'And she'd do it?'

Marco nods. When Portia hears about the genocide, it's going to be difficult to stop her shouting it all over the city, satellite or no.

CHAPTER 31
MUTINY

THEY WAKE AT DAWN. Standing on the deck, a light wind flutters through their clothes, cutting into the edges of their bodies like the sharp bite of a cookie cutter. Molly has handwritten a message.

'That way, she's certain it's me.'

But it's difficult; the letters have to be tiny and so legible a computer could read them.

GRAN. REPATRIATION IS REALLY GENOCIDE. GET WORD TO PORTIA. NEIL TO HELP. PORTIA BROADCAST CITY-WIDE.

Then Molly shows Marco how to fold the message till it's so small it almost disappears.

Marco wonders about Neil. Will he go for it? Is he brave enough? Or will he crawl back into that shell?

'And this really works?' Marco asks as he watches Molly ease the message into the silver band circling the pigeon's foot.

Molly laughs. 'Yeah, me and Gran, we've been chatting most days. Just got to hope Texicom don't get bored of turkey and design a new pigeon-pie slurp carton.'

'Can I send a note to Portia?' He can't help himself; he has to know if she's okay.

Molly smiles knowingly. 'Ah, so this Ms Portia Reynolds, there's more here?'

'No, well…'

She's staring him down with those dark brown eyes, her Midwich Cuckoo stare that she learnt from Gran, and Marco knows there's no hiding anything. Besides, he's fed up with trying.

'She's amazing, Moll. Amazing.'

'Yeah, yeah.' Molly shrugs. 'And no.'

Marco looks puzzled.

'No, you can't send messages scattergun all over the city. These are <u>homing</u> pigeons. They fly <u>home</u> – Gran.'

They send out two for luck. Molly has a point about the slurp cartons. Leaving Texicom out of the equation, Marco is all too aware that there are plenty of hungry mouths in the terraces. Hopefully, two pigeons will cover all bases.

After the release, they go back to bed, Molly lying on the top bunk, Marco turning over and over again in the cramped bottom crib. Would this work? If Portia did get the message out to the city, then her life would be in danger. She might be able to escape through the levee, but security would be up, and the ivy was tricky.

Tank ten! Tank ten was the only answer. She'd know that, surely? These would be her exact same thoughts. It wasn't too far to go. She knew the route; she'd done it before. She could buddy-breathe with Neil or grab him a tank. It would work. Marco had to get the radio ship lined-up, ready and waiting near tank ten.

• • •

'So, these are the only plans of the city you've got?' Marco asks when the sun has finally pulled itself into action. They're staring at a thrown-together map of the city, bits added, bits taken away. He wishes he still had his plans.

'It's not easy getting communication out. There's only so much a pigeon can carry,' Molly says defensively.

Elena, unaware of the implied criticism in Marco's tone, continues to explain. 'Mainly we re-edit the designs based on eyewitness accounts: the people we pull out of the sea.'

Marco wishes he had the plans he'd taken from the repat centre. But he's just going to have to work with what he has.

'So, you think this is the tank room?'

Marco points to a small rectangular building at the edge of the academy complex.

'I think so,' Molly shrugs. 'It's got those windows. You can only just see them over the levee. But they're the windows you told me about – segments, like Grand Central Station.'

'Must be it then.' Marco is sure the tank room is the only place in the city with those windows.

They leave the wall-set monitor on continually in the background, blaring out news from the city till they think their brains will curdle. But they can't afford to miss anything. When Portia's announcement goes live, they want to hear it. They've been listening for hours, and there's nothing about genocide on any of the channels. It's all everyday stuff. No urgent broadcasts. No air of panic. The city is surviving as it always does. Well, Marco is damn sure he's going to throw a spanner in the works on that one. If Portia doesn't get the message out, he intends to go back in and post it all over town himself.

'I'm thinking we should pull around to the east side of the

city, as close to the tank room as we can get without drawing attention to ourselves. Then we just wait. When Portia gets out, we'll be ready.'

'And Gran?' Molly asks, but they both know there's no way Gran is going to make it out.

'Gran's going to have to hold the fort,' he says, not entirely happy with the situation, but it's what she's good at. 'She'll be okay. No one is going to suspect her of anything.'

Molly huffs. She's not buying it. 'So, we just run off into the sunset?'

'No.' He has no intention of going directly for the happy-ever-after. He wants justice. 'We re-group. When the city's safe, we go back in with Portia. Portia's the one making herself a target here. She's the one in trouble.'

'You always need someone on the inside,' Elena says, cool as a cucumber. 'Old women are best. They have that air of invisibility. If someone has to be left, Gran's your safest bet.'

They pull the boat around and head to a location close enough to the tanks to grab Portia when she gets out, but far enough from the city so they won't be noticed. And all the time, all the way during the journey, the news blares out over the wall-set. The trifling concerns of a city that has no idea of the horrors built into its foundations; the pile of bodies, the empty eye sockets, the chairs looping around and around on their insane merry-go-round of death.

Marco stands staring out over the water, watching as the city draws closer. They're still a few miles off their location, when suddenly the continual drip, drip, drone of the news channel stops.

'Macko, quick.' Molly's shouting from the cabin. Something's happening. He runs, hell for leather, back inside. Anxiously, they stand in front of the screen, hoping to God that their small, skinny plan comes up trumps.

The words URGENT TRANSMISSION appears on the wall. It's working. Something is happening.

'Yes!' Molly shouts.

And there she is, Portia. Marco's heart leaps into his mouth. Seeing her at any cost is so much better than that dull ache of absence.

'People of the city, the repatriation programme is a form of genocide.'

She's not mincing her words. She must realise that the government will try to shut her down the instant she opens that pretty, well-informed mouth of hers.

'Your loved ones are being killed.'

And suddenly Marco thinks of Mr Benson, thinks of how he walked the man right up to the gates. How Benson had thanked Marco. How… But the broadcast continues.

'We must rise up against corporate governance. There are piles of bodies being dropped into the sea just a stone's throw from the city. This government is abdicating its responsibilities in…'

The picture cuts out, replaced by an image of Kendal.

'Citizens, please be calm. Our systems have been hacked by a militant group spreading propaganda. There is no genocide. I oversee the repatriation project myself. I can assure you…'

There's a voice off-camera, barely audible.

'I thought Texicom did that now?'

'No. We are…'

The off-camera voice again, louder this time. 'Texicom and its CEO, they designed the repatriation infrastructure?'

'Yes, but…'

And Kendal's face is beginning to blanch.

'We need to get closer to tank ten,' Marco doesn't need to hear anything else, which is just as well, because the news item cuts out abruptly, replaced by dancing. People dancing! Typical.

'You think she'll go there now?' Molly's looking concerned.

'It's the only way out.'

Suddenly, his pocket buzzes. He reaches inside. It's the watch.

'Marco?' Portia? Her voice sounds breathless, like she's running.

'How did you...?'

'Neil told me about these Dr Krypto doll things. I'm running, holding the damn thing in my hand. It looks odd.'

'Doesn't matter. You've got to get out.' Marco finds himself shouting at the watch. His breath so short it's like he's doing the running, not her.

'Marco, you're safe!' Her voice is packed full of relief.

'Yeah. But you're not.'

'Kendal won't hurt me.'

He thinks Portia might be relying on a bit too much good-will. Marco imagines that Kendal will actually, probably, in all reality, want to murder Portia.

'You need to get out.'

'I know. Usual exit.' She wasn't giving anything away.

'Yup. We're the other side.'

'I've got Neil with me.'

'Hi.' A second voice tweets.

Portia again, 'He'll need a tank, but... We're almost... Shit.'

'Portia?' Marco snaps back. This distance, when he can hear her but not touch her, is a new kind of torture.

'We can't get out that way.' It's Neil. From the tone of his voice, Marco knows it's panic time.

'We have to.'

'They'll kill us.'

'It's the only...' The signal goes dead.

'Portia?' Nothing. 'Portia?' Marco shouts her name so loud, it's like he doesn't even need the phone anymore, like the sheer volume of his voice is going to carry itself across the waves towards her.

When the noise of his own voice fades from his ears, he sees Molly standing there, gently shaking her head.

The wall-set with its 'official' news feed buzzes into action.

'We ask you for calm.' It's Finbow, the CEO of Texicom, looking unflustered in his smart suit. 'We are investigating allegations against the government. We are…'

The screen blurs, there's just white noise and Finbow's voice. 'Lost picture. Do you still have sound?'

But the question is never answered.

The pixels dilate and reform into a face Marco would know anywhere: Aurelius. Those deep, assured, resonant tones are soon riding over all airwaves.

'I am Aurelius. Leader of the OGs. We have taken the city. We understand the repatriation scheme is indeed genocide. We have lived under the yoke of tyrants for too long. The balance will be redressed. No more this imposed, unjustified hierarchy. Today marks the first day of a new world. Anyone involved with the government and with Texicom should report to the repatriation centre. Rewards will be given to those citizens who join the cause, who help round up the oppressors. Citizens, friends, comrades, we will triumph.'

Gunshots. A pleading from someone off camera. An official? A cameraman? Someone just caught in the crossfire? A spray of red covers the screen before the image fades to black.

For two days they wait, two days drifting aimlessly but never far. Always at a distance that they could spot her if she swam. Marco has the binoculars stuck on the end of his nose even when the sun goes down. He's looking for a telltale splash.

Listening out into the darkness for a scream or a cry, anything. The wall-set has been quiet since Aurelius' broadcast. There have been no pigeons, not one. Whatever is happening in the city is staying in the city. The handsets have all gone dead.

Marco doesn't want to think too deeply about life under OG rule. He knows that, for Aurelius, Portia is part of the problem, part of a corrupt system that needs to be purged.

'We need to go,' Molly says after one of Sanderling's old alarm clocks wakes Marco yet again. It's set for thirty-minute intervals. If he falls asleep, it will only ever be for thirty minutes. He will not miss her. But day three of waiting is coming up over the horizon, and Molly and Elena are getting twitchy.

'If the OGs have taken over, it's only a matter of time before they get one of the guard's speed boats and drop over to see what we're up to.'

'She'll get out. I know she will.'

'But if she doesn't, what good is it, us going back in? We need to find someone on the outside who can help.'

Irritated by his lack of sleep, and frustrated at having to bob here doing nothing, Marco stands and starts pulling off his clothes. There's a dry suit on the deck beside him, just waiting for Portia's call. He'll put it on, get himself back in the water, get back to the city, and get her out. He can do this. 'I'm going in.'

But Molly shakes her head, grabbing the suit away.

'There is no way back in. You honestly think you would get back in through tank ten? Like they'll open it?'

'Through the levee. I can do it that way.'

But Molly is still holding tight to that suit.

'No. You only just made it out alive the last time, and that's because you were heading in the right direction, going with the flow of the water. You'd need to be a bloody salmon going back up that stream, and even then… Marco, it's not workable. You wouldn't survive, and a fat lot of good that would do. We need to regroup.'

But Marco shakes his head.

'It's not just us anymore, Marco. It's everybody. Okay, so Portia's probably got caught, and okay so Gran, she's trapped in there, but it's not just them either. It's everyone. Look, Tee's out here as well, somewhere.'

'If he's even alive.'

'Yeah, well, we need to work on the premise that he is, and if he is, we are wasting time.'

Marco stares at the city. The levee circling it like a shield. It was giving nothing away. This was a waste of time. And Molly was right; eventually, the OGs would pay them a visit. Three people, including Elena, it was not much of a rescue team. Maybe other people would be willing to help? Elena said there were other communities. And if they could find Tee, with Tee's LC count, perhaps they could get back in.

'We need to find Tee.'

'*Get the right person moving in the right direction, and everything will just fall into place,*' Elena says.

Sanderling's words. Ironically, Marco guesses, in some small part, they've both been 'programmed' by the same guy.

'But Elena, you missed out the crucial bit. *All the cogs in a watch need is for someone with the big picture to realise what the end game is.* You know the end game?'

And, curiously, Elena chooses just this moment to re-boot.

Marco glances at Molly. She's not looking so brave anymore. The vast ocean seems to have shrink-wrapped her. She's looking lost.

All his life, Marco had kept his head down, trying to use science to help mould a better future for humanity. Now he's out here on the coalface. He's going to have to carve out a better future with his bare hands. Luckily, one of them is a damn sight stronger than it used to be.

'You remember Pandora?'

'Greek myths!' Molly snorts, 'Now?'

'All the beasties get let loosed on the world, and the only thing that's left is...'

'Hope,' Molly says.

'I reckon it's time to pull it out of the box,' Marco smiles. 'Because, like you always said, the test for humanity?'

Molly laughs. 'It's an ongoing practical.'

They are the future now, part of something bigger than themselves. They might be few in number, but they represent hope. The Resistance. The good guys.

A NOTE FROM THE PUBLISHER

Thank you for reading this book. If you enjoyed it please do consider leaving a review on Amazon.

We hate typos. If you find any, please do let the team know and we can get it amended. publishedwithpassion@aol.com

ACKNOWLEDGMENTS

With thanks to Eileen Ryan, Claire Hawes, Betabeck, Axy and all those who helped in getting this novel on to the shelf.